EDITH SCHEFFER

Hunting Love

I want to thank Sylvia June, for giving me the time I needed to just be me. For your friendship, love, guidance, and support, I have been truly blessed. I love and appreciate you, Syl. 6. Always.

1

———

*I*t's not like this is the direction I planned for my life to take. I didn't sit down when I was six, Barbie in hand, and have her act out killing Ken. Far from it. My Barbie was a nurse, I thought, as I pushed a plume of smoke from my lungs. None of this was planned. Then again, neither were the circumstances that drove me to the edge that, admittedly, I willingly jumped over. But…what are ya gonna do?

It all started in a bar in Florida. No wait, I should go a little further back…

I had been happily married for six years when my husband died in a tragic car wreck. Shaken and frightened, I drove to the scene. I still hadn't been told if he was living or deceased. I clung onto hope, and tried to take the curves as safely as my jumbled, frightened mind would allow. I remember praying and saying over and over, "He's a good man. Please don't take him from me."

Pulling up to the scene, seeing all the emergency vehicles, my heart dropped into my stomach. I wasn't sure my legs would carry me, as I was ushered under the yellow tape. I stood on the edge of the closed off road, where a car had missed the curve. A car with my husband's plate number. I wanted to run down into the shallow ravine, go to him. Tears streamed down my face while I waited for some word. Still chanting the same prayer, "He's a good man. Please don't take him from me," I begged for a miracle. The only sound I could hear was my own heartbeat.

Suddenly I heard the EMTs making their way back up to the road from the ravine below. I held my breath, hoping to catch some word of hope. Some reason to still exist in this world. But what was offered instead, almost stopped my beating heart. Brazenly, the EMTs discussed my husband's last moments on Earth.

"At least he went happy," one of the EMTs surmised.

"Yeah, but the woman with her mouth wrapped around his junk? You probably couldn't say the same of her," laughed the other paramedic.

I felt as though I had been hit in the stomach. All the wind had been knocked out of me, while I wondered if they had called the right person. Surely this wasn't my husband they were referring to. We were happily married.

"I'm surprised she didn't bite it clean off on impact," the blonde EMT said to his partner.

Was I invisible? Did they not know that this onlooker, who had been invited behind the yellow police tape by a detective, may be someone who once mattered to the deceased? Or, even someone who loved the deceased? Logically, you would think they would question; is she family? Was I, I questioned? Or was I just another jilted wife of an unfaithful husband who was now dead?

The detective, a black gentleman, very tall, wearing an off-the-rack-suit that stretched across his bull-like shoulders, turned his sorrow filled brown eyes to me as he approached. Overhearing the conversation that was being had within my earshot, made him glare a silent warning to the EMTs. Coming to extend his apologies, I nodded my appreciation to him for making the dialog stop. Unlike some people who lose a loved one, it wasn't just my husband's death that left me shocked and bereaved.

Turning my eyes to the detective, I asked, "Who was in the car with him?"

I couldn't tell where his apprehension lay. Was it because I wasn't supposed to know there was another body? Or was it the fact that the body in question had her lips around my husband's manhood when he lost control of the vehicle, sailed down the ravine, and careened into a tree?

The detective let out a long sigh, "Does the name Francine Bowler mean anything to you?" he asked.

I had to fight to keep from grinning. This was too predictable; a little too on the nose. A man screwing his secretary was the biggest cliché ever. Well, right next to the wife that thinks she's happily married and somehow beat the odds of having an unfaithful husband.

"His secretary," I answered blankly.

"Would you happen to know her…um, next of kin?"

I let out a long sigh, "That would be her husband." I turned to look the detective in the eye. There it was…pity. God I hated that look.

It dawned on me; I was now completely alone in the world. No parents, siblings, aunts, or uncles. No children, thanks to my inhospitable womb. And just like that, my tears stopped. And I…stopped praying.

Francine's husband came to the funeral. He cried big salty tears and talked of what a great man my husband was. It was obvious he had no idea what they were involved in right before their lives were snuffed out. Having been out of town when the life-altering disaster occurred, he had been spared this revelation about the woman he loved. Some part of me wondered why I should have to wallow in this shit alone. But when I looked into his eyes, I knew there was no way I would ever want to make him feel about Francine, the way I now felt about Derrick.

Over the next two weeks, as the life insurance company did their best to find any loophole they could to not payout his policy, I kept a straight face. There was never a moment, not one, that I missed my husband or felt the grief of loss. There was nothing. It was as if something in me shattered that day. Reality as I knew it, had no meaning anymore. Everything I had once *KNOWN* to be true, had been ripped from me. And for that, I would never mourn him.

Now came the hard part for me; going through his home office. Would this melt my cold as ice heart? As I sat at his over-sized leather bound chair, I took in a deep breath. My father's words kept ringing in my ears, "Only look for what you are prepared to find." His hand was tightly wrapped around a healthy sized glass of whiskey. He told me this after finding the body of a missing child. He had promised the young girl's parents that he would find her, and so he did. And what he did find that morning…broke his soul. I was only fourteen at the time, but I had lived by his words of wisdom ever since.

I opened the top drawer that I would never have dreamed of opening while Derrick was still alive. It was his personal space, that until now, I had never been given any reason to invade.

I looked down: a checkbook, letter opener, stapler, roll of stamps, paperclips, and a file of important papers stared back at me. Pulling out the file and placing it on the desk, I tried to steady myself. Opening the manila file, I was face to face with the last Valentine's Day card I had given him. A small smile pulled at my cheeks. A spark, *something*, I thought to myself. Opening the card took that smile away instantly. There, stashed in the card that gushed about my love for him, were pictures of him and his secretary in various stages of undress; in various positions. Dates on the Polaroids went back three years.

Seeing her like this, dressed like that, sent me back to an old memory. One I wish I could have forgotten. I was forced to remember when I had dressed up for him. Trying to stoke a different kind of fire, I wrapped myself in a leather bustier, crotchless panties, completing the ensemble with thigh-high-hose, garter belt and five-inch heels. I wanted him to release his inner *animal* with me. I wanted to be taken, commanded. I wanted to drive him wild.

When he walked in and saw me lying there, spread eagle, touching myself, he wasn't aroused. Instead he yelled at me, before walking out the door; "You are my wife, not my whore!" I was so embarrassed at the time. But now I understood; I couldn't be both to him. He didn't work that way, couldn't combine the two. He couldn't treat his wife like his whore, but that didn't keep him from wanting, and indulging in one.

When the Insurance payout did come, made out to Audra Stanton, I deposited the million dollar check. I guess crashing while getting a blow job, was still considered an accident, so they paid the double indemnity on the claim. My first act after the check cleared, was to change my name back to Murphy. Never again would I carry the name Stanton. I wanted nothing from him, or our previous life.

I walked around our house, looking through room after room. I wasn't totally convinced that I could feel nothing.

Maybe something would spark a beloved memory, cherished moment. As I went through the house, there was only this cold, dead feeling. I had regret, but it was because I hadn't known about the affair sooner. In fact, even though it scared me a little, my regret came from not being able to punish him myself. I felt cheated…in more ways than one. I decided on therapy as a means to break me away from this deep-seated, all-consuming anger.

Sitting on a little floral couch, in a room too cheery for my liking, I explained the whole thing to Dr. Marie Cher, licensed therapist. I explained all that had left me numb to everything except for rage; a deep anger that I couldn't release. I woke feeling its ugly presence moving around me, like a ghost. And when sleep did find me, this feeling, tucked itself in, next to me.

My therapist, a delicate looking woman, thin, modestly dressed in an ankle length floral dress, fingered nervously through my file. Her big blue eyes, bore the look of being overwhelmed. She sat herself down in the oversized floral chair across from me. Clashing floral prints, assaulted my vison. Timidly, in a voice that I assumed was part of their training, she said, "You need to let all of this go. You need to find closure!" She was mouse-like in her demeanor, almost skittish. I couldn't help but wonder if I was her first client. She seemed very unsure of herself, and a little frightened when I admitted that I had only dark thoughts of my belated husband. Even once beautiful memories had been blackened.

I sat staring off into nothingness, wondering. She said what I needed in order to heal, but never said how to attain this break from my current mindset When I said as much to her, she offered the opinion that I should write all my feelings down, the rage, anger, hate, deception, and read the letter at his graveside.

I nodded to her, but the wheels were spinning as I stared into her big blues, "Have you ever been cheated on…by someone you trusted. Someone who made sure that they were your whole world?"

"Well…this isn't about me?" she shook her demure little head.

I stared some more until she began to fidget in her floral covered wingback chair. She crossed, and uncrossed her legs. She shifted her weight repeatedly, while I sat mute. Finally she answered the question.

"In collage…I was engaged," she admitted.

I never dropped my gaze.

"We were together for almost two years. He was pre-med,"

I could tell by the way she was starting to stare-off, she was reliving a moment that was still captured somewhere inside, despite learning all the ways to rid herself of unwanted thoughts and feelings.

"I was supposed to go with the girls on an overnight to Santa Barbara," she said. "But the friend who was driving us, well, her car broke down not even twenty miles out of town."

I offered her a gentle nod.

"I decided I would just take this opportunity to sneak into his dorm room. It was a bold move for me. I was always a little on the reserved side."

I saw this in her; it was part of her nature.

"Well, when I snuck in, I heard him call out a name."

I stayed silent….waiting.

"It wasn't my name. When I clicked on the lights, he was lying there…with his…ya know…in his hand. I was so shocked, I didn't move, couldn't move. Then this girl bounced in behind me…also naked. She took one look at my face, and ran back out door."

I nodded, "What did he say to you?" I questioned.

Her stare turned to ice, as the memory visited her again. "Are you going to finish me off, or what?"

Ah, I knew that look. I had seen it in the mirror. "And you…?" I asked.

She gave me a heavy sigh, her shoulders slumped, "I just ran…out of the room…out of the dorm. I was humiliated," her eyes closed.

Ah yes, humiliation, the cherry on top of the fuck-you, sundae. "Then what did you do? Did you write about how devastatingly fucked-up that whole situation was? Did you drink a glass of wine while you burned the seething letter that he would never see?" I gave her a slight grin.

"No," she shook her head.

"So…what did you do?" I leaned back and crossed my legs.

As I watched, this sweet woman's jaw jutted out, "I keyed the fuck out of his Camaro." A smile so sinister, one I would have never thought her capable of, stretched across her face.

I smiled back and nodded again.

All the sudden, it looked as though the realization of who she was now, dawned on her. "Oh my God, I just admitted to a felony!" she gasped.

I shrugged, "Most likely a misdemeanor."

"Oh no…it was definitely of felony quality. I also broke every window in his car and dented the whole damn thing with a baseball bat," she covered the laugh with her hands.

So it turned out that maybe she wasn't fit to tell me how I should deal with my rage. She and I spent the next twenty minutes working on her need to push feelings down inside of her. When I left, I wished her the best, and cancelled my next appointment.

Now fast forward a year…

I moved out of the Los Angeles area almost twelve months ago. Florida seemed an unlikely place for someone like me to end up. I hated both heat, and humidity; hated the night life. But for my new found…hobby, Florida had plenty of what I needed; Men who cheat on their wives. Not that you don't find this in every zip code, but Florida was known for rich men; rich enough to think of morality as something only poor people needed to embrace.

I rented a one bedroom bungalow just blocks from the sand. Even though I could have purchased anything my little heart desired (thanks to the insurance payout, profit sharing, the sale of our home, which butted up to Bel Air, and a healthy nest egg). But I didn't need much. I wanted to stay below the radar that flaunting wealth can bring.

The 1920's bungalow was modest on the outside. I bedroom, one bath. Nothing special. A thin walkway made its way through the middle of my lawn, up to the five stairs that led one to my small covered front porch. Two planters, one on each side, boasted lilies, under the two front windows. The house was small, symmetrical, and unassuming. It was nothing like my previous home, with its sprawling footage and unused rooms. I was more than happy downsizing. But I still needed some of the comforts of home. And that meant my home had to be exactly that, comfortable. I decorated with the antique flair of oversized wood furniture, and hues of my favorite colors. Neutrals, throughout what would be considered the common areas, if it had been common for me to have visitors. But my room, my sanctuary, was painted my favorite shade of true red. I melted into my home, my safe place.

Scanning the morning paper as I leisurely sipped my Columbian roast, I wondered where I should hunt tonight. The front page made some recap of the cold cases from the past year. Of the over a hundred bodies found, six were mine. Found in various places, killed by various methods, they had little to tie them all together. In fact, there was only one thing they all had in common. One thing the paper hadn't mentioned. Each of these men, had been married. I knew the police were already aware of this fact. But if this was the only tie between the victims, it really wasn't much to go on. Having no absolute M.O., was the key. I hadn't felt bad for any of the men I had killed. They were all cheaters. I was slowly ridding the world of a *type,* which had no place in polite society. And in my mind, society should be polite, at the very least.

A new club opened about three months ago, a Salsa club. By now it wasn't being bombarded like it had been the first two weeks of opening their doors. It was a large club, multiplying my anonymity. This was one of the keys to a successful kill; you needed a place big enough to disappear unnoticed. This was the first rule on the female serial killer's check list.

Second, you never want to go full drop-dead gorgeous. You wanted to be hot enough to entice someone to their death, but not so memorable to everyone else. Usually wearing something that showed a lot of cleavage was a good idea, as it was most men's kryptonite. They would remember boob size, shape and even what restrained them, yet were fuzzy on things like height, weight, hair color, eye color, tattoos, age…all the things that lead to someone being identified. Or, all the things that were easily changed with some creativity, and a great pair of heels.

Next, lots of costumes; I never tanned my alabaster white flesh, but would use a self-tanner or spray tan when going for a big change in appearance. I found one that worked well with my skin and could be lightened quite quickly with a lemon bath. I used subtly colored contacts, no need for the ones that popped. My natural eye color being green, every color worked for me. I had a slew of wigs that were real human hair. Expensive, yes, but they could easily pass for natural. Heels in all sizes created the illusion of being up to five inches taller. I was already boasting a pleasantly firm C-cup, but would sometimes use a padded push-up bra to change my physical attributes. All in all, I knew how to be noticed without being memorable.

Makeup had been overrated in my earlier life. But now I found that contour could change the shape of my features. I could make my jaw line appear more pronounced, sharper, softer, or I could make my nose more tapered, even bulbous, with some well place shading.

The name of my hunting ground tonight was Club Carpe. It was by the waterfront, and I was itching to use my new gun. I hadn't been shooting in several years, but my father having been an officer and later in life, a detective, took me often before he passed away. Dad believed all women should know how to defend themselves, and he made sure I did.

Derrick, my now deceased husband, had claimed to be a pacifist. He didn't want firearms in the house. Now, I thought that was brilliant of him, considering what he had been up to, and the fact that he knew I was a crack shot.

I had stumbled across a Glock 40 Cal a few weeks prior down at the waterfront. Under a patch of poorly cared for shrubs, the muzzle of the gun peeked out catching my eye. I was sure it had been quickly ditched there in hopes it wouldn't be found. Undoubtedly used in a robbery, or possibly something worse, I had a new murder toy. With no serial number, it would be wiped clean, and ditched as soon as the job was done. And when I did, it would eventually be placed somewhere that no one would ever find it.

My other kills had been varied in method, like I said, no M.O., was necessary. I killed one man with a flathead screwdriver to the heart as he lay sleeping in a posh hotel room. Another I had drugged, and watched as he tried to gasp through his own vomit for ten long minutes of suffering (that one had been ruled a suicide). My favorite thus far had called out to me to come and take a bath with him. I guess he was hoping for a different kind of water treatment; I didn't get in, but a small CD player did. He thrashed and smashed about, as every muscle went ridged with electric shock. This one was ruled accidental.

But none would ever be more memorable than my first kill. I was worried; would I be able to do it; take a life? Would I throw up, leaving precious DNA behind? Would he kill me first? Was there some part of me that hoped he would?

I was surprised by how calm I was; my breathing and heart rate normal as he pulled off a little back road looking for a more secluded spot. I had the knife in my handbag, just waiting.

He was a larger man, with a beer gut that was more keg than case. I would have guessed him around forty-five, freshly shaven but already donning a dark shadow, salt-n-pepper pomp hairdo with a *mob* feel to his attire. His jowls wiggled when he spoke to me, putting me in mind of a St. Bernard.

Unzipping his fly, he said, "I like to see the back of a woman's head."

I glanced at the hand he had gripped tightly around his

cock, "Are you married?" I asked, nodding toward the ring on his finger.

"Right now, I'm not," he smiled and wrapped a big meat hook around the back of my head. Pushing my face down toward his uncircumcised little soldier, I carelessly dropped my hand into my bag and palmed the handle of the six inch blade.

Kissing all around his ridged member, he said, "Look, just start suckin,' or get the fuck out of the car!"

"Just put your head back and relax," I smiled. I was going to need him to lift his triple chins from out of my way. When his head fell back, I saw his body relax, awaiting my warm, wet mouth. Quickly, I pulled the blade, ramming the steel in a downward motion into that soft spot in the front his neck, just above where the collar bones converge. Twisting the knife quickly, and with all my might, I felt the blade grind against a bone in his cervical spine.

The surprise on his face said it all. For as deeply as the instrument of his impending demise was embedded, I wasn't taking any chances. I leaned away quickly just in case I hadn't done the damage I was almost certain I had. I watched him choke on the blood that had begun pooling into his broken airway.

He turned his frightened eyes to me and for a moment I knew true panic as one hand twitched a little. Throwing open the door and sliding out quickly, I watched him suffocate. Letting out a contented sigh, I watched his last panicked searches for air as they left his body. I hoped the last moments of his life were filled with the remorse he should have had before treating his marriage, his vows, as an afterthought.

Amazingly, I hadn't gotten any blood on me, so I quickly wiped down the door handle, and ripped the knife from his neck. This was no easy feat, as the slippery tip had lodged between, or possibly even imbedded in, his spine. His frightened, glazed over eyes, giving me what I craved. I was almost ready to abandon the blade and get my ass out of there when it broke free and slide out from its blood lubricated gash.

Into a nearby body of deep murky water, the knife was cast. I walked about a mile south skirting the nearly abandoned road and disappeared into the night.

The next two days I watched the news. They found the body, but said little more. On the third day it was released that he was in fact low-level Mafia, and it was suspected that his murder was a hit from a rival family. The only thing I would have done differently: I would have put his sad little soldier away. But it didn't seem to matter this time. I would, however, pay more attention to details in the future. But, I told myself, *there is a learning curve for every job done well.* So on to the next victim, I thought, as I stared into my dressing room mirror.

My dark hair, often referred to as black, was kept short in a layered bob. It was just easier to put it into a wig this way. Tonight I would don a long wavy blonde wig. I decided that my green eyes, would be blue. The all American girl worked well in Florida. Letting my bronzing body tint dry, I picked out a colorful cotton halter dress that clung well to my curves and a pair of stiletto, open-toed pumps. As much as I loved big designers, and owned a closet full of their frocks and shoes, this was another rule; Wear nothing memorable. No Prada, Versace, or Jimmy Choo heels, were allowed while hunting. Plus, this held another intention; I never ruined something I loved with blood spray.

Before I left the house I filled a bathtub with water and two dozen cut and squeezed lemons. I also slipped on a cheap wedding band I had purchased for the hunt. My previous rock (a symbol of the vows I had planned to keep till the grave), I sold to a reputable jeweler for a nice return on the 2.5 carat flawless diamond. It held no emotional value. People who cheat on their spouses oftentimes feel more comfortable cheating with another married person. It lessens the fear of having their infidelity brought to light if they're both trying not to get caught.

I took a cab to a little unknown destination two blocks from Club Carpe. This was another trick, and a great way to build an alibi. I would be dropped off by a cab at one club, go inside and order a drink. Before long, I would slip out the back, and head to another destination. This way the cab driver, bouncer, and the bartender all knew I had been there, but had lost track of me in the crowds that infest these places on Friday and Saturday nights.

Down to Club Carpe I went. This was my favorite kind of club. Not only was it packed with more memorable people than little ol' me, it was on the first floor of a hotel. This meant a better chance of no long drives out to the boonies, no valets remembering you leaving with the victim, and not having to walk home from God knows where. This was less likely in the city, but one never knows where they'll end up. If you could ask my kills, I'm sure they'd agree.

I paid the ten dollars to get in with a two drink minimum. Inside the club they had different areas illuminated by different colored lights. The bar which took up almost a whole side of the building was bathed in a red glow. It seemed appropriate that I would be sitting in the sinner's section, even if in my mind I was just playing the role of justice.

Taking a stool, I quickly noticed the women at the bar were

drinking red wine. So that's what I ordered when the handsome bartender asked what my poison would be tonight.

This is another 101 from the serial killer's handbook: *Don't order anything that makes you stand out.* You can't be anonymous if you make the bartender run the blender for one of your frothy, fruity drinks with an umbrella. Also, no matter how much you want an expensive whiskey on the rocks, going unnoticed requires you fit in with the crowd. Fortunately, I enjoyed wine.

The back bar had a long and wide mirror so I could see everything and everyone behind me. As couples grinded against each other to Latin music, I wondered who tonight's victim would be. Or my gun's victim, I grinned. I knew better than to shoot without muffling the sound. (Not that *silencers* worked the way they did in the movies, but the sound could be more easily mistaken.) A throw pillow, a couch cushion, even a wrapped hand towel could do the trick in a pinch. Plus these common household items also held a secondary purpose; they minimized *blow back* blood spray.

As the grinding continued, I spied a gorgeous man at the end of the bar. I watched him through the mirror as he put the moves on a beautiful Latin woman wearing a wedding ring so big, I could see it reflecting the light from the other end of the bar.

He had dark hair that the sun had lightened, tanned skin, but not born that way. I assumed his hue was from long days spent in the Florida sunshine. He, too, wore a ring, but judging from their body language, they weren't married to each other. He was over six foot tall, easily, and even in a suit, his well sculpted body was almost as visible as his devilish grin.

He was reluctant to touch her, yet got as near to doing so, as he could. And even though she may have been complimented by his advances, she kept him at bay. At one point I saw her smile, and show him the huge rock on her ring finger. He leaned in to whisper something in her ear. I watched her smile broadly before shaking her head, no. He pled his case, putting his palm to his heart, unleashing his crisp white smile. But again, she shook her head and sent him on his way.

I grinned. A woman who could resist him was either happily married, or she was being watched by a jealous husband or private investigator. Either way, good for her, I thought.

I watched the man slowly walking down the bar in my direction. His movements were fluid; like he was more than comfortable in his body. He was carefully eyeing his next possible tryst. He stopped in front of a woman sitting four stools down from me, but then our eyes locked.

One side of his face pulled up into a grin as he moved closer. If I had to describe the smile he wore; devilish would be the only word that came to mind.

"I couldn't help but notice you," he said approaching me.

I almost laughed out loud. I had to decide quickly if he would be more receptive to sarcasm, or if his ego was easily bruised. "Well, it was only a matter of time before everyone else shot you down," I smiled.

His grin broadened, as he gave a slow nod of his head. "May I?" he asked, pointing to the stool next to me.

I gave him a curt nod.

"So, what are you doing here, tonight?" he asked.

I was perplexed, was this like: *What's a nice girl like you, doing in a place like this?*

"Same as you," I raised my wine glass.

"You're alone, then?" he painted on a confused look that was anything but.

"I am. Why?" I played coy.

His eyes fell to my ring finger, "It's just not like a married woman to be in a bar alone," he answered.

This, I also believed to be true, but that came from my raising. I was taught that a married woman alone in a bar wasn't there for anything innocent. She was looking to do married things with someone she wasn't married to. I gave the same half smile he had turned on me, "Like I said, same as you," I nodded toward his own wedding ring.

Cocking his head at my comment, "May I buy you a drink?"

I pretended to ponder the thought before finishing the last of my wine, "Why not."

As he motioned for the bartender down at the other end of the bar, he said to me, "I'm Rudolpho."

I had to fight the urge to laugh out loud. That was the worst made-up name I had ever heard. Plus, like I said, this man had not a drop of Latin blood in him. More likely he was a Rudy or Randy, anything, but not a Rudolpho.

I extended my hand, "Lila," I said.

"Two more please," he told the bartender.

After my next glass arrived, Rudolpho asked me, "So Lila why aren't you home…in bed…with your husband?" his eyes shooting again to my ring.

Staring down at the gold band, I said, "Because my husband isn't home…in bed."

"Out of town?" he shifted his body toward mine.

"Something like that." As much as I loved the banter, him speaking of my husband made it harder for me to keep a straight face. Normally, men like him couldn't care less where my husband was, or why I was alone in a bar.

"How about you, where is your lovely bride, tonight?" my eyes flickered with mischief.

"Ohhh," his head shook, "it's a long, sad story," he moved closer into my personal space. "My wife…" he sighed, "…she's not interested in me anymore."

I shifted my body toward him, "Could that be because you pick up women in bars?" I asked, bringing my hand to his knee.

Looking down at my hand, he then leaned closer to whisper in my ear, "Do you know where I'd like that hand to be?"

"I bet I could guess," I whispered back.

"Do you have a room here, Lila?"

I shook my head.

"Maybe…your place?" he suggested.

I gave him a sidelong glance, "That seems like a likely scenario to you?"

"I could get a room," his brow raised, waiting for the offer to be answered.

Moving my hand up his thigh, resting ever so close to his manhood, I slowly nodded, never taking my lusty stare from his.

Lifting my hand from his thigh, he brought it to his lips for a quick kiss before walking off toward the hotel lobby.

I sat drinking my wine, indulging in the moments before the kill. There was always that rush of anticipation. This *needing*, it caused a pulsating through my whole body. It was exhilarating, like all my senses were coming alive.

Ten minutes went by while I finished my wine. Soon, Rudolpho was approaching. Leaning in close to my ear, he said, "Give me ten minutes," as he discretely pushed a room key into my palm.

On the elevator ride up to the sixth floor, I popped a breath mint, checked my makeup and hair on the mirrored walls. I was ready. I unzipped my hand bag, and there sat the 40 Cal, loaded and waiting. I smiled at it, "Soon."

Opening the door, it was your standard mid-grade room. The glow of candlelight, and the two glasses of wine sitting on the bedside table, seemed unnecessary. I had to laugh. So the ten minutes he needed was to get the room oozing with seduction? What a waste, I thought. But ambiance would be a nice change for me. I had enjoyed the flickering of the lights as *Bathtub Man* convulsed.

"I'm in the restroom, I'll be right out," he called.

Walking over to the bed, I removed my 40 Cal from my handbag and went to slide it under the pillow. A clinking sound of metal hitting metal caused concern. Lifting the pillow, I looked down at the knife.

"Hell of a housekeeping crew they have here," I joked quietly. I looked at the blade; 6 inches of black steel, curved at the tip with two hook-like barbs. The handle grip had been wrapped with electrical tape. I looked toward the bathroom and slit my eyes. For a moment, I thought of slipping away to safety, just walking out the door. He was bigger than me, stronger; he would easily overpower me. But…what would it feel like, to kill someone, who intended to kill me? I admit the thought titillated me; like the most twisted game of cat and mouse. And, I did have the advantage of having my gun, and a reputation for being a quick draw.

"What say we move you, shall we?" I told the knife, as I pushed it as far in between the mattress and box spring as it would go.

Putting my gun under the other pillow, I began undressing.

Standing in my red push-up bra and panty set, garter belt and thigh high stockings, I adjusted my girls, and waited for him to emerge.

Stepping out of the restroom, he wore nothing but a pair of body hugging black brief shorts. I had to admit, he wasn't like my other kills. The vision of him made my eyes automatically soften. Sandy brown hair and piercing dark blue eyes were complimented by that devilish grin. His chiseled chest, eight-pack stomach, and strong thighs, were quite the view. For a moment, the thought of killing him was almost a shame; this magnificent creature. But, I reminded myself, he was exactly the kind of man I hated; exactly the kind of man who deserved to be the recipient of me and my gun's fast and furious temper. And no part of me had forgotten the knife under the pillow.

As he approached, he stopped just short, looking me up and down, surveying his playground.

"You are a delicious treat for the eyes," he bit his bottom lip as he scanned every inch of my curves.

Damn, he was hokey, I thought, but I tried to stay in the moment. Closing the short distance between us I said, "You're not so bad yourself." I reached out my hand, running my fingertips down his chiseled chest to the fine hairline that ran down, and disappeared into his briefs.

He leaned in, I thought he was going for my lips, and I had a moment of panic. I didn't kiss kills if it could be avoided. But at the last second, his head turned, as he moved to my neck. Just below my ear, he placed a warm kiss. Then another met my skin just above the collar bone. I couldn't help but wonder; did this spot work for everyone, or just me? This spot had always made me melt. Arguments were once forgotten, if not won, by kissing this spot. My eyes fell closed, remembering how much I loved and missed being kissed there.

My body responded naturally; every hair rose, nipples hardened, and chills ran to all my best places. My hands searched out his hips, to feel his body real beneath them. As on task as I wished to remain, a barely audible moan vibrated in my throat as I pondered the unthinkable: how horrible would it be for me to enjoy him before the kill? A physical explosion followed by a mental release…a twofer. It had been a long, long time, I thought.

Guiding my hips backward, he sat me down on the edge of the bed. As he stared down at me, I started to worry a little about what I may have gotten myself into. This was not a vantage of control for me. I assumed that this would be when he would present his manhood. None of the men I had encountered had really wanted more than a set of lips around their cock. But I knew he wanted more; my life. Slowly he kneeled on the floor in front of me.

On his knees, he leaned forward to kiss my lips. I hadn't been kissed…in how long? I could barely remember. At first I was scared. I pulled back a little, staring into his eyes. To me, kissing had always been the most intimate of acts. A grin played across his face, as he leaned in again. If this is what I needed to do to get him into position, was what I was telling myself. At first his lips just gently brushed mine, punctuated by a soft pucker. Without being fully conscious of it, I let out another little moan. More soft kisses were placed around my lips. I felt myself automatically pucker when he put his lips directly against mine. Something was happening to me; I started to want something more than this. I began wanting a real kiss, the kind where you melted into the other person. Sensing that my reluctance was fading, he put a hand behind my neck and slowly pulled me into his kiss. And his kiss, ah, it was amazing: soft, so sensual, and sweetened by wine.

Him taking control this way, was nothing more than him luring me into his web; how he directed the show, and how enticingly he dragged his prey along. A small part of me was trying to forget that this man's plan was to make me his victim. The knife I had found left little doubt of that in my mind. This thought caused me to grin as his lips slid down my neck to my chest, knowing all the while that when he went for his knife (carefully placed, as it was) he would find nothing but his own fears. He would be too busy, too preoccupied by his own agenda, to even realize I was reaching for something.

He put his hand over my heart and with a little grin and gentle pressure, he leaned me back on the bed; my legs hanging down, off the side. I had to smile; *NOW* I was in the best position to grab my gun. If I wished it, he would never even see the end coming. And to think, a pillow-silencer was within reach as well. This was all working out well, I thought, as I enjoyed the wet kisses that now worked their way down my torso, to the curve of my hips. I felt a shock of a long lost sensation run through me. As his tongue licked, long, and slow following the bone; my hips arched instinctively. They knew what they wanted, even if I had forgotten their needing.

Curling his fingers under the sides of my G-string, I wondered: Was I really going to let this happen? He was taking me too far away from my comfort zone, where I held all the power. The thought was momentary as he pulled my panties off my heeled feet. It's been so long, my body tried to reason with my brain.

Pushing one hand under the pillow, like I was stretching in

ecstasy, I felt my gun. The grip was hard, real. I was still in control, I told myself. I smiled knowing that within the next minute or two, I would be sated. I was about to pull my weapon, my partner in crime, when he gripped both of my knees. Before I fully understood what was happening, he moved them apart, and dove in, headfirst. The well placed kiss made my breath catch in my chest, my back arched with sudden shock and delight.

Oh, my God it has been too long. My jaw dropped open as a quivering moan escaped my lips. Oh my God, what was happening? What was I letting happen? True, this had always been a favorite of mine. To see his head between my thighs, the wet heat of his tongue, his full lips puckering as he sucked my tender little spot. An ache began to take hold of me. *I should stop this*, screamed a voice in my head; END HIM! I wanted to…I had every intention of…but this man was a master, I thought. He was licking my common sense out of me with every lap, flick of his tongue. Unlike my husband who had searched and searched and searched for that spot that made me suck in my breath, this man knew exactly where he needed to be…where I wanted him.

My gun free hand pushed its way into his hair, my fingers curling as my hips began to push upward, giving him more access.

Was I really going to let this happen? With a knife under the mattress and my gun under the pillow? Could I really…that's as far as the thought traveled before the pleasure, and pressure, began to build to a point of no return. My free hand tightened in his hair, while my toes tried hard to curl in my pointed heels. Holding him right where I needed him, I began to pant.

He was right there…right there! Silently I prayed, *Oh, God, please don't move; please DON'T MOVE!* The tickle from his magical tongue brought me to a place where logic, all logical thought, is pushed far away. Only pleasure, remains. As I felt my legs begin to shake, my hips rocking upward, faster, and faster. Suddenly, my voice rang out, "Oh my God, Oh my God," I whimpered through bated breaths. Exploding, I released completely. My body shook uncontrollably, my eyes squeezed tightly as a mind blowing orgasm was liberated from somewhere deep inside. Somewhere, something that I had forgotten had ever existed within me, gushed with pure creamy ecstasy.

Head spinning and just trying to catch my breath, suddenly I was brought back to the reality of the situation. When I felt his hand slide toward the pillow to his right, I was ready.

Even as light-headed and disoriented as I felt, I was still ready to pull my gun any second now. But then I felt his hand move away from his knife's previous hiding place. Grabbing underneath both of my hips, cupping my ass cheeks tightly in his strong hands. He pulled my body closer to him; to his waiting mouth. Again he started on me, his tongue lapping at my wetness; licking me clean.

At first I twitched and writhed at the sensitivity his returning mouth caused. Some part of me thought his second round of oral was a waste of both of our time. My brain screamed to be heard, KILL HIM NOW! But then, the tickling that usually left me annoyed, and scurrying my ass away, drifted into the abyss. Again somehow, all my desire, the building, returned. But his time, it was almost tender, gentle, as he teased the whole area with kisses and licks. He was going to bring me there, again, but slowly this time.

He could hear my rising anticipation as I held him there, right there.

Why I looked, why I couldn't just enjoy the sensation, I didn't know, until I did. His eyes met mine. The hunger within them, was taking me even further than the act itself. He wanted me to come…as much as I did. I could see it in the burn of his dark blue eyes. The need they showed, without an ounce of shame, would bring me to the edge again.

It was a whole different kind of release being offered this time. It was almost intimate. He let out a muffled moan that vibrated my sweet little spot. As I began to gush again, he released another moan let me know he was more than invested in what he was doing to me.

Some horrible part of me couldn't help but think what a lucky wife the cheating bastard had. That one thought, drew me back. It renewed my desire to rid her of him. I curled my hand around the grip of my gun. How I didn't pull the trigger as my whole body convulsed, was my definition of gun control.

When he finished round two, I knew I had to act. I grabbed my gun from under the pillow and raised my other hand to join it. With my shaking legs still hanging over the side of the bed he had just pleasured me on, I pulled back the slide. Chambering the round that would end this lying, cheating bastard, I smiled.

Scooting away quickly, he stood. His eyes rounded.

Leaning up with the gun in hand, we stared at each other a moment. "I moved your knife," I said plainly.

I wasn't surprised to see the not easily hidden, rather impressive erection, quickly subsiding. A gun pointed at a man's face should do this very thing. The vision made me grin. I must admit, this was my favorite part, what I liked to see; that fear gripping them.

Normally, I would have already pulled the trigger. But my *normal* had been lost the moment my panties slid off. Some part of me wanted answers before I put a bullet in his head. His plan was to make me the victim. In that respect, we were the same beast. I had to admit, I was intrigued by the thought.

"Take a seat," I pointed to the striped armchair by the window.

Standing, I held my aim on him. At first, I wasn't sure where to begin my questioning. "So, I take it I wouldn't have been your first?" I finally said.

He gave me that one sided grin and slowly began to shake his head.

"As you may have guessed by now, you aren't my first, either," I grinned back. "So, you are a killer…who what?" I shrugged. "Finds a woman in a bar…has a little fun with her… then *ends* her?"

Some part of me was judging him for partaking in the victim before administering his code of justice. Maybe it wasn't about justice at all. Maybe he had no code. Maybe he was one of those sickos, who just killed for fun. Those people had real problems, I assessed.

"Not exactly," he said, leaning back and looking way more relaxed than a man should with a 40 Cal aimed at him.

"What's not exactly? I know I'm not your first. By my count, at least six women have been killed this way…in a hotel room, with a knife…"

He cut me off, "But…no signs of sexual activity."

He forced my mind to go back over the article. My eyes slit as I studied his face. According to the articles, there hadn't been a homicide fitting this description in over a year. And…no, no sexual activity had been found.

"Are you trying to say you're not him?" I was amused by the thought of him trying to convince me.

"Oh no…I'm him," he whispered his confession with a sinister grin, and a slow nod.

I stared, more than just a little confused: He had deviated from his M.O. with me; why? Maybe his M.O. was evolving.

Cocking my head, I continued to study him. "Why me then? Why was I the one you were willing to leave your D.N.A. in?" I asked. "I'm assuming you know what D.N.A. is, and how it's used," the condescension oozed from my lips. "It would have taken more than a bleach bath to erase what you just did to me." My mind was pulled back to the feeling of his tongue deep inside me.

With this question, he gave a shake of his head, "I'm not sure."

My eyes slit again, but I continued to stare. None of the six bodies found had been cleaned or flushed in any way. If these were his kills, there really hadn't been any sign of a sexual encounter. I couldn't imagine he was a copycat. Something in the way he moved, the confidence…it just wasn't likely. Even now, how calm he was, was telling.

"I felt you reach for your knife," I told him.

"Did I?" he raised his brow and smirked.

The truth was…he hadn't…not really.

"*WHY ME*?" I demanded.

"Why did I plan to kill you?" he cocked his head.

"No. Why did you mouth-fuck me first? Twice." I added.

"You're such a romantic," he chuckled and rubbed his fingertips against his chin, like he was storing this piece of information. He looked like he was wondering exactly what it was, as well. Was he just horny? I mean I get that. That's how I ended up with my eyes rolling back in my head, right? Surely judging him for this would make me a total hypocrite. Finally, he cocked his head, "There was just…something."

For me, this wasn't an acceptable answer, but then he continued.

"I saw something. When you drank your wine…the way your lips opened slowly…then puckered slightly…like you were gently sucking on the rim of the glass."

One of my brows rose.

"The way you held the glass…your hand was relaxed…but sure, confidant."

Did he think this line of shit was going to charm the gun from my hand? Was this his last ditch effort at leaving this room in any other way, than becoming stuffing for a body bag?

"The curve of your neck…I could see your pulse beating there," he pointed. "It was the only thing that gave away your increasing heartbeat as we spoke, your excitement."

His eyes still searched every part of me with the same yearning I had seen there from the moment he saw me standing in my bra and panties. I swallowed hard.

"Right there," he said quietly and pointed again." When you do that…I pictured you…swallowing me. Those delicious lips… wrapped around me." Now he swallowed hard, like his own mouth had begun to water for a very different reason.

A moment passed where we just matched stares.

"The scent of you," he continued, "it's smoky…but sweet." His eyes fell closed, trying to place the scent that had unlocked his psyche, as well as other parts of him.

I couldn't help but notice that his magnificent boat, was boasting a full sail, again.

"As I kissed down your body," he continued, "the scent, your scent," he let out an almost inaudible moan, "it drove me on. I had to taste you," he whispered.

His eyes were now burrowing into mine. I had to give him credit; this wasn't as cheesy as his bar banter.

"I was sure…I would love the taste of you," he sucked on his lower lip like he could still taste me there. "You were warm… almost sweet…but the kind of sweet you get from honey, not sugar…and you were so wet," his eyes closed tight, like he was trying to relive the memory.

I couldn't help it. Even completely sated, he made me want him back between my legs. If this was just a ploy to get the upper hand, it was masterful. One I wouldn't have thought him capable of, previously.

His dark blue eyes opened slowly, "Do all of the men you kill…entertain you first?" His line of vision traveled down my body to my honey pot.

I stared at him, wondering why I would even answer his question. I was the one holding the gun. But finally I said, "No."

"Have any of them?"

I took in a deep breath, "No," I exhaled.

"So I guess I could ask you…why me?" that devilish grin that had first caught my eye, was back.

Shaking my head slowly, I said, "My answer isn't going to be nearly as good as yours."

"No?" he gave back a little shake of his head.

One of my cheeks pulled up, causing a cockeyed grin, "I was horny. It's been a while."

He chuckled, "That's it? You were horny?" his eyes were still boring into mine, looking for my truth behind my words.

Slowly I nodded, "Afraid so."

"No other reason you can think of…or are willing to admit," he added.

I studied him: his eyes, his smile, "I guess there's also the fact that I've never been attracted to a kill."

"Until me!" he leaned back in the chair, locking his fingers behind his head.

I'd call him a little cocky, but the words *little* and *cock*, didn't belong in the same sentence when it came to him. I couldn't help but wonder what it would feel like to have him inside me. Was he a master at that, too? I had to take control again.

I had answered his question, now I had another for him: "How do you pick your kills?"

"Kind of a personal question, isn't it?"

"I had your head between my thighs just a few minutes ago."

"Yes…yes you did," he sucked his lower lip again.

"And I have a gun aimed at you."

"That you haven't used for some reason," he pointed out. There was a moment of silence before he said, "I have a thing about cheaters." I watched his face turn from hot to cold and hard in the beat of a heart. "Your wedding ring…" he searched out my hand and pointed, "…you were going to die for it."

A grin pulled up my cheeks. Was he kidding? I had to laugh out loud. I asked for clarification, "You kill married women… who cheat?"

He nodded slowly, never pulling his eyes from mine.

"Fuck! This is," I shook my head while I tried to find one word that summed it all up, "hilarious."

He didn't see the humor that had me shoving my tongue in my cheek and shaking my head.

"Why does this amuse you?" he asked.

"This whole fucked up situation," I sat down on the edge of the bed, my head still shaking in total disbelief.

It only took him a moment, "You're not married, are you?"

"Well, technically I would be…if he weren't dead."

Rolling this over in his head, "Did you kill him?" he asked plainly.

I shot him a look, "*That's* a little personal, isn't it?" I used his own words against him. "But no, I didn't kill my husband."

"So, you wear the ring because…you miss him?" his brow rose with question.

I shook my head, "Not even a little bit. I wear the ring," I looked down, "to attract married men…who cheat on their wives."

A moment passed while he studied my face, "You're not kidding, are you?"

"Nope! I guess I should be very grateful I wasn't unlucky number seven."

"Unlucky thirteen," he corrected.

I gave him a curt nod, "Kudos." I let out a long sigh, "So… now what the fuck do we do?"

His devilish grin returned.

"You're not serious?" my eyes widened.

"Why not? I know I could use the release," he reasoned.

"And we're supposed to…what," I asked, baffled by the absurdity of the thought, "just forget that we're both killers and armed? No offense, but I have trust issues."

He shrugged, "You did say that it's been a while?"

"You already took care of that," I reminded him.

The Devil danced behind his eyes, "You don't know how much more I could take care of you." He looked down at his partially swollen member, then back to me.

My teeth dug into my bottom lip, while I spied him rearing again toward full attention. I had always had an oral fixation, of sorts. My eyes warmed over at the thought of sliding my lips down his shaft.

"That look, right there…you can't tell me you don't want to."

I sighed, hating to admit that I really would love nothing more at the moment. "Fine, I want to. But like I said, trust issues."

"Do you think you could hold the gun on me…while I'm fucking you? Would that make you feel safer?" he joked.

I had to laugh, "No, I don't think I could. Plus, if I come…as hard as I did earlier, I might accidentally pull the trigger."

He laughed, "Come on, my knife is…somewhere," he looked around and shrugged. "Unload your gun so you know I'm not going to go for it, and use it against you."

"I still have the problem of you being able to overpower me. Me being the weaker sex, and all," I added sarcastically.

That devil's grin played across his face again, "Would you like to tie me up…or down?" he suggested.

"You just have a solution for every problem, don't you?"

His joking manner disappeared. His face took on a seriousness that couldn't be mistaken. "I just want to be inside you."

All I could do was stare as I mentally went over every reason why this was a bad idea. If I was smart, I would put a pillow over his face, end him and quietly sneak from the room. How stupid would I have to be to let him live, knowing what he knows about me? Chances were, he felt the same way about the situation. My father always said: there is no honor among thieves, murderers, or liars, and I've always believed this to be a simple truth. And we, he, and I, had proven ourselves to be two of the three, by my count.

"Wow, you really do have trust issues," he said, as he watched me wrestle with my inner demons.

When he stood, I raised the barrel of my gun, training it back on him. I had no problem ending him if he took even one step in my direction.

"I'm just trying to give you the full view," he put his arms out to his sides to show me that aside from his impressive manhood, he was unarmed.

Quite a mouthwatering specimen, he was; every muscle defined and tanned to a golden brown. And that smile; sexy as all hell, and heaven combined. But I still had to wonder which one he was offering me.

The only thing between my eyes and his now fully erect manhood was a thin layer of breathable cotton that was having trouble containing his God given gift. Smiling that crooked little grin, he slowly pulled his briefs down, letting them drop to his feet.

Yes, he was quite the specimen. Seeing my eyes warm over from the deliciousness of my new view, he wrapped one hand around his impressive rock hard erection and began slowly stroking himself, while staring at me. I felt my mouth begin to water.

I had to admit, I had always enjoyed watching a man touch himself. I found this act to be an immense turn on, and I was at least this. My mind was already replaying pictures of his hungry mouth between my legs.

Seeing that my interest was piquing, he said, "Look what you do to me."

I was still wrestling with the predicament I could be getting myself into, the danger. But the wording he used, *"What you do to me,"* had struck a nerve; plucked a cord deep inside. As we continued to stare at each other, I heard my inner voice scream, again and again, "Are we *really* going to fuckin' do this?" As if my body reacted without hearing my mind's argument at all, a *click* and *thud,* was all that could be heard as I released the clip, and let my gun drop to the floor.

2

———————

We held each other visually. Our eyes locked, but still we remained silent. We both knew what we wanted, needed. But I was unsure of how we were going to proceed; what to do next. We both knew what we had come to this room for, what we planned to do to each other. And this… wasn't that. Moving cautiously, I stepped toward him as I held his eyes with mine. Some part of me reasoned, *you aren't his M.O.!* But then again, double dipping his tongue deep inside me until my legs quivered hadn't been, either.

He looked amused by my trepidation. His eyes moved down to my bra, "Take it off," he whispered.

This stopped me dead in my tracks as I cocked my head to one side. The question visible on my face. Did he really think I was going to let him *order* me around?

"Please," he whispered.

This caused a small grin to pull up one of my cheeks. I slid the straps down each arm, one at a time, before letting it fall to the floor.

I liked the way he looked at me; his eyes hovering over his

favorite parts, taking me all in. It was sexy as hell, that my eyes were included in his hovering. He gave me the *come closer* finger curl. I began to walk toward him, slowly. I couldn't tell if it was passion that kept our eyes locked on each other, or suspicion. He still had that giant mouthwatering cock in hand.

Approaching, three feet separating us, I stared at the treat he had his palm wrapped around. Taking the last step, I was within his arm's reach, within the danger zone.

His hand still stroked, awakening the voyeur in me. Watching as he slide up the shaft, then rolling around the engorged tip before pulling his grip all the way back down to the base; left me wanting. I wanted to feel him, to taste him. Licking my lips, I dropped to my knees.

Looking up at him, I put my hand over his, to move with his as he stroked. He was teaching me what he liked, how he wanted me to touch him. The look on his face, his jaw falling slightly open as his breathing increased; excited me as much as it did him. "Please," I turned a wicked smile his way. He reached down and ran his fingertips from the top of my cheek bone to my lips. Tracing them, I let them part so he could slide his finger between them. The smile that pulled up his cheeks let me know…he knew exactly what I wanted. Now I was teaching him.

He let out a low moan when my open lips wrapped around the head. Squeezing them lightly, before puckering them tight. Around, and around, I worked the tip, swirling. Gifting my tongue with the softness of the skin there, I suddenly pulled back. Tracing my lips with his engorged tip, I was teasing myself every bit as much as him. I could feel myself moistening from the thought of what I was doing to him. How it drove him, was driving me as well. How he reacted to my working him, was telling. His hands thrust into my hair, fingers locking. Over and over, he rocked forward and back, in and out, slowly fucking my hungry mouth. I loved this, the act *of.* I never knew who was in charge at this moment. Was he in charge, as he held tight and pumped himself between my lips? Or was it me; the bringer of the pleasure he craved?

The thought was making me swell. Working harder now, my lips tightened around him. My need, it was taking over. I heard his breathing accelerate. His hands cradled the back of my head, as my mouth slid up and down. He was getting close, and every time he moaned, it made me moan. This wasn't just his pleasure. Gripping his thickness, my mouth followed my hand up and down his shaft.

"I knew you'd be good," my eyes lifted to his. I was sure he could see the hunger in them. He held my stare, "I knew the moment I laid eyes on you," he whispered. His vision moved to my fervid mouth. "Are you wet?" he asked, biting into his lower lip.

I moaned harder. Deeper, and deeper I went, growing more excited with the thought of taking him to where he had taken me. I needed to taste him.

It was building, I could hear it in his breath, feel it as the thrusts quickened. Suddenly he stopped me, pulling himself from my ravenous mouth. My eyes full of question, as he stepped back.

"I need to be inside you!" The look on his face was almost primal; the overwhelming desire to rut. A thought danced across my brain: *we're just animals, he, and I.*

Quickly pulling me up against him, a well delivered kiss, deep, wet, and warm, left me dizzied. I had to wonder, was there anything this man didn't do well? He had already reminded me how much I had missed kissing, the feeling of his tongue writhing with mine. He had already reminded me how much I missed a man's head nestled between my milky thighs; the pleasure a talented tongue can bring. I couldn't help but wonder just how much I had missed the feeling of a rock hard body against me, inside of me.

Lifting me off my feet, my legs automatically wrapped around his body, as our mouths found each other again. Crossing the tiny room, he laid down on the bed, with me held captive beneath him. I could feel his member, hard, sliding between my moist folds, to tickle my clit.

Down my body, with wet, warm kisses he went. Taking my nipple into his mouth, his tongue swirled, again, and again. The sensation made me swoon, chills running through me. Cupping my breast with a firm hand, he began kneading. Just being touched by hands other than my own, was a welcome change. But I was no flower, meant to be held as if my stem may snap at any time. I wanted to be handled! He was being gentle, like a lover would be. He was just feeling out what I liked. But I wanted more, and I wasn't afraid to ask. "Harder! Suck harder," I directed.

My request ignited something within him. A naughty smirk, spread across his face. I heard a growl before he began sucking.

The moan was pulled out of me from the long the lost sensation, returning. My body lit up beneath his. I arched as he sucked, writhing, as my nails dragged up his back. Licking and flicking then sucking, his hot breath was teasingly irresistible. It has been so long…

I panted, my pleasure almost unbearable, running to all my favorite spots. I hadn't remembered ever needing this way; the way my pussy began to ache, pulsing with a desire to be seized.

Moving further down my body, I began to protest. Pressing a fingertip to my lips, he said, "One more taste." His eyes sparkled as he clutched my ass in his strong hands. Raising my mound to his consummate mouth, I awaited my bliss.

"Spread for me," he whispered.

Letting my legs fall open, he dove deep.

There was no way I could move away from him. I couldn't even rock my hips, he held me so tightly in place. I let out a broken gasp as the air was sucked from my lungs. My eyes rolled back, once again gifted by the sensation of his talented tongue. It has been so long…

I needed to feel him inside me. I was now beyond aching from the anticipation of him. Well placed kisses continued to tease as he moved back up my body, worshiping every inch of me. Finally his lips found mine; hungry, savage, as the weight of his body held mine. My hands roamed down his strong back, his sides, to cup his hips. He was in position. I felt the head of his fucker, rubbing against me, using its tip to tease me. At that moment, I wanted him more than anything I could ever remember wanting. I was sure of it.

"Do you want me inside you?" he asked.

Breathless, dizzied from the overload to my revived senses, I nodded.

I was there, needing, when he gave one short push into me. The breath he exhaled, the sound he made, the look on his face as he stared deep into my eyes, it let me know…he was there, too.

My breathing: just short pants. Little whimpers escaped me as he worked in the tip. I had forgotten how fantastic the *working it in,* felt. It's been so long.

Inch by inch he pushed, a little deeper with every slowly

rocking thrust of his hips. My eyes closed, my mind focused solely on the sensation of him opening me like a hidden tomb. It's been so long.

I had forgotten how amazing it felt; how much I used to love this feeling. And now, I remembered how I craved this feeling, once. He pushed himself a little deeper, whenever she would allow.

"Fuck, you are so wet," he whispered in my ear, "so tight," he buried his head in my neck and moaned as he pushed again.

He didn't have to tell me. My sweet girl, definitely wanted him, but didn't have the space needed to easily accommodate him.

Still pressing to gain full entry, I thought he would never end, like my whole body was already filled by him. I had never experienced anything like him before. I felt her giving; little by little, her cream trying to oblige the sheer size of him. My eyes squeezed tight, with every slow push, with every inch by unbelievable inch. He pushed one more time; and finally the base of him met mine. I felt as though I could fully exhale.

"Fuck...you feel so..." I moaned, unable to finish my thought.

"Amazing," he asked, rocking slowly.

"Huge," I swallowed hard.

"I'll be gentle," he promised.

Just moments before, I wondered if he would be animal enough for me. And now I was just hoping he wouldn't break me in two. As he slowly made himself at home, my hips began to roll, finding rhythm with each other's bodies. Everything about him; his scent; musk and smoke, his rock hard ass cheeks working as my fingertips dug into them, just holding on for dear life, really. The weight of his sculpted body pressed against mine,

I could feel his power. I was being taken in the most delightful way. Somewhere between a grunt and a moan, the sounds he made, drove me wild. He stayed deep, keeping his body against mine. He knew where he needed to be…to bring me back to that place. I felt his hand move to one side of my neck. Some part of me was reminded of the situation I had put myself in: had I just fallen victim to the murderer I had known he was? And another part of me, just a fleeting thought, *I'd go so fucking happy*.

He lifted my jaw, so he could look into my eye, "I need to watch you come…come for me."

I had been right there, just right there on the edge, I thought. And hearing him speak these words? These words pulled me over the side. Eyes fixed, he watched as my jaw fell open and began to quiver, my breathing quickened. Lusty pants turned into rolling moans. My eyes squeezed closed at the last second from the waves crashing inside me.

"Yes," he whispered, "Yes, come baby, come for me!"

That *baby* part, hit me wrong. It almost made me lose my *fuck yeah*, completely. But as quickly as the warning sign flashed in my mind, it was forced away by my body's need for its own impending explosion. Such a selfish little cunt, she had become. Again, my legs began to vibrate, my toes tried to curl, my eyes squeezed closed. A moaning howl was released, as I burst into that magical place of total release.

He watched as my wild howls turned into whimpers of pure satiation. This was all it took for him; to watch me come. "Where do you want it?" he asked.

I smiled wide before my lips parted, making a giant O. I had waited patiently for my reward, and now I wanted it more than anything. He pulled his magnificence out of me, pulling himself up on his knees, as I sat bolt upright. As he stroked, my lips opened wide, causing a smile to stretch across his face.

Placing the tip on my tongue, he gave a thrust. My hungry lips, puckered around his deliciously pussy-drenched cock, as I sucked all of *me*, from him.

"I love the way your mouth fucks me," he murmured.

I watched as his eyes fell closed. His head rolled back, his jaw fell open with a soundless cry. If there was a picture that could depict the word erotic, the vision I had of him right now, this was the one.

"I'm gonna come," he warned.

I felt him start to pull himself away, and I panicked. Grabbing his ass so tight, he couldn't get away from my hungry mouth if he tried. He looked down into my eyes and grinned from ear to ear.

He came hard, making me moan through each lovely shot he gifted me. Not one sweet drop of him escaped me, as I swallowed burst, after delicious burst. His panting slowed, his body shook, as he watched me suck and lick him clean. The taste of us mixed together, was pure ecstasy.

It had been so long, I thought. But never; never had it been like this!

Cupping my shoulders, he pressed my body back into a laying position, and brought himself down on top of me. His head between my breasts, he tenderly nuzzled my nipple then said, "I could fuck you all night…and then all day."

This was when panic set in for me. He was cuddling, cupping…nuzzling. What the hell was happening? I was pinned underneath him. Placing exhausted kisses on my breasts, he put his ear to my chest, listening to my racing heartbeat.

I didn't know what to do with my hands, so they remained

at my sides. I went ridged. What the fuck was I supposed to do, now? I wasn't about to lay here in the twinkling flicker of *after-fuck-glow*, with him. The invasion of my personal space was fine when we had to invade each other's space in search of orgasm, but now? I felt more threatened by this, than I had when I realized his plan was to kill me.

"That was…" he searched for yet another word.

"Yeah," I said, and shifted myself up slightly, sliding my body out from underneath his. Wasting no time, I pulled on my panties. I could feel him watching me as I re-hooked my bra and searched out my dress.

"So…that's it?" he asked.

I bit into my lip, "Yep, that's it," I grabbed my purse, dropping my gun and clip inside, before heading for the door.

At the door, I finally looked at him, "Thanks Rudolpho."

Naked, looking better than a Playgirl spread, he leaned up on one elbow. "My name isn't Rudolpho," he admitted.

I smirked, "That's okay. My name isn't Lila," I walked out.

As I waited for the elevator, I saw him coming down the hallway. Shirtless, buttoning his pants, I quickly turned my attention away from his chiseled chest and the well-defined stomach. Just moments ago, I had been held as a happy captive below that unbelievably sexy, and God gifted body.

When he made it within earshot, he whispered, "Don't you think we should talk about this?"

I stuck my tongue in my cheek, "I can't imagine why we would."

"I think we probably have a lot…in common," he raised his brows to me.

I let out a sigh, "We have an orgasm and a somewhat twisted…hobby, in common," I corrected him. "It's not like I don't appreciate…the fucking…but I don't think we need to read anything more into it, than *THAT*."

His head cocked, "Boy, you really are a romantic," he said sarcastically, unleashing that smile that made me bite into my lower lip. "And if I have the numbers right, you are a couple ahead of me."

The elevator dinged, and quickly I stepped on board when the doors opened.

He turned his palms, up, "At least tell me your name."

I smiled as the doors closed, leaving him just as he was meant to be…a fucking-fantastic memory.

3

Well, this wasn't what I had in mind, I thought to myself. Although, to be honest, it was a much needed release, and a damn good one at that. I shook my head, amazed by the whole situation. What were the odds of two serial killers being in one room? We were both armed with a clear agenda, and means to an end. But somehow we instead end up with eyes rolled back, while calling God.

It had never been like this with my husband. No matter how hard I had tried to reel him in, to make him take his time, enjoy the moment, enjoy me, I was always left to feel like I was nothing more than a depository. But this? This felt like a mutual desire to bring the other to a place of great ecstasy. I could have asked for anything, and I know he would have submitted, offered himself fully. I also knew I would have willingly submitted to all his desires, as well. In him, I had found my sexual equal. And this made him a danger to me. I knew that this experience would be welcome fuel for many lonely nights. But this was the way I aimed to keep my life…solitary.

The valet called me a cab and I headed home to sit in a tub

of cold water and cut lemons, while sipping whiskey on the rocks. Tucking myself into bed, images played out behind my closed eyes. Something about his smile, his kiss, his ability, had me wanting more.

The next morning while reading the paper, it dawned on me that I should be reading a breaking story about how they found another body. My guess was he, too, Rudolpho, was thinking the same thing. I still grinned at the ridiculous name he used, while I sat shaking my head.

With no plans for today, I headed to the beach. Something about the crashing waves always made me calm. Walking down the coastline, I enjoyed the warmth of the sun, the sounds of the seagulls crying out to each other. I wasn't sure I would hunt again tonight, my mind wasn't in it. This was when people made messy mistakes. Murder is a work of great focus.

Instead I decided on a pulled pork sandwich and a beer from my favorite little hole in the wall.

Dango's was right on the boardwalk. It was an open air bar/eatery that was a well-kept secret of the locals. It wasn't often that you would spy college kids, and vacationers taking up the stools that surrounded the bar. I hadn't made any real friends to speak of, choosing to keep the lowest of profiles. But a few of the waitstaff knew my face and my first name. They also knew my standing order, so all I had to do to get my pulled pork sand-wich, was nod to the waitress.

After finishing my sandwich, and on my second beer, I thumbed through the newspaper. I was busy paying no attention at all when someone took the stool next to mine. My eyes fell closed when I heard him say, "I like your hair better this way."

I tried to act like there was some way, anyway, he could be

talking to anyone else. But I knew his voice. I well remembered him telling me to come for him.

"So what IS your name?" he asked.

I let out a sigh. "You tracked me down." I turned to see Rudolpho. He wore a dark pair of sunglasses that hid his amazing midnight blue eyes. But that smile of his, devilishly enchanting, was front and center. His white cotton button-up shirt was open at the top two buttons, giving a peek at his tanned chest. The rolled up long sleeves, gave him a relaxed look. Dressed down, he was even sexier than the well-dressed man I met at the bar the night before.

"Aren't you going to ask how?" he shifted in his stool to angle his body toward me.

I took a sip off my beer and gave my head a small shake, "If I had to guess, I would assume you followed me."

"You assume correctly," he ordered himself an IPA. When the bartender set it down and walked away, he asked, "Are you not happy to see me?"

"It's not what I had intended," I allowed.

"Hmm, I thought you had no intentions. Tell me then, what did you intend?" he put his hand on my knee.

I looked down at his ring-less hand, "I intended to eat the best pulled pork sandwich in Florida, have a few beers, lazily make my way back to my bungalow, and take a nap."

He nodded, "Good plan. And when you say nap?" He left the question hanging in the air, as his palm found my knee. Leaning in close to my ear, "I can't stop thinking about you," he whispered. "Have you been thinking about me?"

I took in a deep breath and let out a heavy sigh, "Not really," I shook my head.

"Why don't I believe you?" his hand crept higher, moving slowly up my thigh.

Truthfully, I had to fight my own brain to not think about him: what his hands felt like on my body, his warm tongue on my nipples, him erect in my mouth. These thoughts brought a pulsating to all the places that I assumed had received their last rites. Places I thought I had left for dead.

"Is that why you followed me? You want another go-round?" I asked.

He slid his sunglasses down his nose to reveal those eyes. The eyes I remembered staring into mine as he pushed himself deep inside of me.

"Yes please," he whispered, removing his sunglasses.

"Look, I don't think this, we," I pointed to him and then myself, "it's not a good idea."

"I disagree," his hand had meandered up, to just inches from my honey pot, and I was having trouble not imagining how good his touch would feel. "Tell me you didn't like it…when I licked you clean…just to make you all slippery wet, and deliciously dirty again." he whispered.

I swallowed hard, trying not to envision this act.

"There it is again," he pointed out. "Right there…that swallow…like your mouth is watering from the thought. Did you like it when I had your nipple in my mouth…sucking. Gentle at first…but you like it harder, don't you?. You prefer sucking to licking. Or at least that's what you asked for if memory serves. Remember? Harder!"

At this moment, I became very conscious, and even self-conscious, about my body's reaction to him.

"Did you like me in your mouth? I think you did. I can still feel the vibration of you moaning on my dick," his eyes searched for mine. "I've never had a woman moan so hard while I was coming in her mouth."

My breathing was doubling when he pulled his hand back down my thigh. For a moment, I thought he was backing off, and I was grateful. My body's desire for him was growing harder to deny; harder to hide. But then a moment later, his hand disappeared completely under my skirt. Up, it inched, lighting a fire inside me, as it crept.

"What are you gonna do? Bang me under the bar?"

"I'll drop to my knees right now and lick you dry, if you'll let me," he grinned with just a flicker of the devil that I knew existed in him. "Are you wet? I'll bet you are." Rubbing the hood of my clit over the top of my silk panties, he said, "Just a little lower. Does she want me to move lower?" his breath warm in my ear as he moved my panties to the side.

No one was paying any attention. No one seemed to notice the two people sitting at the far end of the bar. His finger moved to the spot that made me suck in my breath. It was slow at first, grazing my clit, just playing to see how far I'd let him go. The light brushing he offered, teasing her before sliding a little further down.

"Oh…you *ARE* wet!" he hissed, then licked his lips.

I was trying to keep some semblance of decorum, "This is my usual spot. They know me here. The last thing I want to do is draw attention to me, or to you."

He smiled but didn't stop, "Just lean back a little…so I can take one quick dive, and I'll stop. I promise."

Turning my eyes to his, we held each other's gaze. Mine; was stone. I didn't enjoy the position I felt backed into. And part of me was chastising my vagina for her response to him. Still I tried to control my breathing. Crossing one leg over the other, I leaned my body against the backrest of my chair. Moving his hand slowly to the underside of my thigh, I felt his finger creep under my panties, again.

"*Mmm*," he said into my ear. "I think she missed me. She wants me to kiss her."

My nipples were hard as steel from the memory of his head between my thighs, his tongue swirling, his lips sucking.

"She wants my tongue deep inside her…"

"You promised," I reminded him.

"So I did," he smiled. As he pushed his middle finger inside of me, pulling the tip forward. He hit my g-spot and held pressure there.

My breath came harder as I tried not to shudder from the intense pleasure I felt. I repeated, "You promised."

"I did," he repeated as he discretely removed his finger from under my panties then turned back to face the bar. "I can't help but think she likes me," he whispered.

"Well she hasn't always made good choices. That's why she's no longer in charge." I looked down to see his jeans fighting to hold down his massive erection of stone, "Looks like you're having troubles of your own."

"Yes, I am. He does like you. I can admit my truth…"

My eyes slit, wishing they could shoot actual daggers.

"…and he likes *her*…very much," he smiled. The finger that had been inside me was brought to his lips. Sucking at it, from the tip, all the way down, he said, "I woke up missing the way you taste."

"I can't help but think that's not conducive to helping you with your current problem," I looked down at his bulge, again. I swear I could see it pulsating.

"I just think we should be friends. *Really. Good. Friends*," he added.

I let out an exhausted sigh, "I'm not looking for a friend," I shook my head.

"We could join forces," he suggested.

"As what, the *Dynamic Duo of Death*," I asked.

He let out a chuckle, "Something like that."

I turned my body to face him, "Well, this has been fun, but it's time for me to go."

"You know…" he caught me by the arm as I tried to pass him, "I know enough about you to make life…difficult," he smirked.

Standing there, I weighed just how I wanted to react to this comment before I leaned in close to his ear, "Is that a threat?"

"Just a truth," he whispered.

"Ah," I nodded. "Then let me share a truth with you…I know about you, too. And just a guess, just putting this out there…I'm assuming you haven't been as careful at covering your tracks," I put a kiss on his cheek. "Think about that," I smiled and walked out of Dango's; a not so well kept secret haunt.

Walking into my bungalow, I was furious. How dare he try to blackmail me for sex? This was so far beneath me. At this moment, I was ready for a kill. But I had to examine myself and my thoughts. Was I going to hunt because it was time, I was ready? Or was I going to hunt to prove to myself that I was still in control? As angry as I was, I still couldn't calm down this needing he had set ablaze in me.

In my bedroom…legs hanging off the side of my bed in the same position he had *had* me…I allowed myself to release. Coming hard, my last mental vision was of him on his knees. He flashed through my mind.

Chastising my own thoughts, my own mind, I asked out loud, "You could have thought of anything, ANYONE, why him?" But I already knew the answer to this question. It was the same reason I always went back to that little shack on the beach, for a pulled pork sandwich. It was the best I had ever had.

You never shit where you eat. This was another little rule of mine. It was rare that I would *hunt* the same place twice. But never, ever, did I hunt a haunt.

Dressing in low-cut, emerald green dress that hit me mid-thigh, I debated which wig I would wear. The club I had picked boasted a more diverse crowd, so it really didn't matter how I baited the hook. Someone would bite.

I put on my blonde bob wig with the straight bangs. Winging my eyeliner up for a dramatic effect, I blackened my lashes and reddened my lips. I wanted them to look full, pouty; the kind of lips any man would want wrapped around his cock. It couldn't be denied that a great pair of dick-sucking-lips, would draw a man like a moth to a dick-sucking flame.

The club was only a few blocks away. This made it tricky. Close to home had some advantages; no cabby to remember driving me anywhere, and no trek home. But it also had disadvantages; neighbors seeing me leave or people on the street remembering the girl in a short dress with the D.S. lips.

The bungalow had been rented with this in mind. Out the backdoor, through the backyard, was a gate that led to an alley. If I left one way, I returned the other. This kept most of my neighbors from ever being *sure* if I was home or not. To be honest, most of my neighbors were elderly and asleep by nine. This was also to my benefit.

Any good hunter knows that 11pm is the magic hour. By this time, true partiers were just arriving. But married men would usually want to get *theirs* and be done by the stroke of midnight (with excuses of *working late* for their loving wives). I usually showed up at 10:30, picked my prey, and turned him into a victim by the time the clock struck 12:01 am. Most of these types of men wore suits: their ties loosened and shirts untucked from their waistbands. Some were blatant enough to wear their wedding bands, while other's just sported ringed tan lines. Either, or, their intentions weren't well hidden.

I started out my back gate into darkness. I could smell the trees and flowers in bloom. The sky sparkled with stars on this clear, yet still muggy, night. I was feeling revived though…in charge.

With my 40 Cal tucked into my hand bag, the club's logo was stamped on the back of my right hand. The music was a bit much for me. Some kind of techno bullshit. I was more a fan of music that used real instruments, and vocal ability.

Every wall was mirrored in this huge space that I assumed was once a warehouse. Blue overhead lighting with shooting laser beams of white, would have been an epileptic's nightmare. Oh the things I do to hunt, I told myself.

I found space at the bar and casually looked around to see what the other women at the bar were drinking. *What fresh hell was this*, I wondered as I saw the fruity drinks with umbrellas. Was I too old for this place? I shook my head at the thought. Maybe my pallet was just more refined? That thought felt more acceptable for me.

"What can I get you?" asked a handsome young man, barely old enough to be serving alcohol.

"I'll have a Bay Breeze," I smiled, not looking forward to its arrival. Taking my first sip, I tried not to cringe at its sugary sweetness.

Now whom would I put the moves on? I looked around as nonchalantly as possible. You don't want the wrong ones to think you're interested.

At the end of the bar, were a group of well suited business-men. Not a good choice; too many friends who would remember the woman he was talking to.

At the other end of the bar, was a man eye-fucking every-thing that passed by him. He didn't seem to have a preference; ass, legs, tits. Everything caught his attention. The desperation wafting off him was repulsive. I should kill him just to put him out of his misery. I cocked my head at the thought of a mercy killing.

It's a little known truth that most people can *feel* when someone is staring at them. I don't know what they call this. But I assume it's a hunter/prey instinct, which goes back billions of years to when we were one of the animals lower on the food chain. Whatever it was, it always worked for me. A man at the end of the bar made me his focal point.

I made my fleeting glance, one of deliciousness. I softened my gaze, let my lips fall open ever so slightly in a big, red D.S. pout. Angling my body toward him, I pushed my shoulders back to show off not only my great rack, but also to give him a phys-ical sign of being *open to him*. Now all I had to do was pretend I hadn't noticed him staring. When I raised my eyes to finally meet his, it was a look of deep yearning I received. He raised his beer to me with his ringed hand. Smiling, I knew I had the fly in my web.

"Hello," he said as he approached. "May I," he asked pointing to the stool next to me.

"Be my guest," I said.

He was younger than my normal prey, I'd guess late twenties

or a well-kept early thirties; blond hair, slightly receding at the temples, blue eyes that bore some kind of needing. I looked down at his ring.

Catching me looking, he asked, "Is that a problem?"

"Not for me," I gave him a slow shake of my head.

Banter, banter, banter, it was all part of the hunt. He started with the usual; What's your name? What do you do for a living? How do you like summers here in sunny, hot, muggy Florida? But as the clock ticked toward 11:30, his questions became a little more personal, almost risqué. We were getting close to a proposition. We were knee to knee now, as we faced each other. Periodically, he would shift his weight so that his knee rubbed mine. He was closing the distance between us, one little movement at a time.

Knowing I had him, I laughed at something he said and reached out to pat his upper thigh. He looked down as I let my hand work in a slow circular motion. His smile was all the validation I needed.

Leaning over, he whispered in my ear before standing, and walking toward the restrooms and backdoor.

I leisurely finished my horrible drink then headed down the long hallway to the exit.

Out in the back alley, we were alone. Darkened windows of closed businesses offered anonymity. He stood on the other side of the dumpster, waiting for me.

So it wasn't a place I would normally be found dead. But, I reminded myself, I wasn't the one who was going to be found dead, here.

As I made my way up to him, I asked, "Now what do we do?" I licked my lips.

"Will you suck it? She won't suck it," he asked hopefully, like this was the greatest gift he could ever receive.

I laid my purse down in front of me and began petting his crotch. But the hour was getting late, and his impatience was growing. He reached down with both hands, fighting his belt for access. Dropping his pants around his ankles, I dropped to my knees.

I tried not to show any visible sign of shock as the little guy was presented. I had no doubt his wife didn't put that little thing in her mouth. I had seen toys that were considered a choking hazard, that were bigger than this. On the plus side, if you wanted to feel like a deep-throat-queen, it would be an easily attainable feat.

I kissed around the area, much to his growing agitation.

"Come on!" he demanded, "Suck my cock!" He tried to shove the little thing toward my mouth. Within two seconds I had the gun in my hand. I was ready. I was going to blow his balls off. Where, apparently, God had over-gifted him. My mind began to ponder, and wander. It was possible that the tragically tiny penis, just made them look huge.

I had my lips almost to the lipstick-tube-sized tip of his teeny-peeny, when I heard a voice from behind me, growl, "Don't you *DARE* suck another man's dick."

The man standing in front of me holding his tiny member with two fingers, the way you would hold a baby gherkin, jumped back against the wall. Looking quite surprised, his eyes shot to the man standing a few feet behind me. His panic rising: was this my husband…boyfriend? But only after looking down and seeing the gun in my hand, did he realize the full gravity of the situation.

Tiny penis man yelled, "What the fuck are you doing, you crazy bitch?"

He tried to kick at me, or run (I wasn't sure which). But with his pants around his ankles, they prevented his attempt. His breathing was that of a trapped animal as he opened his mouth as if to scream.

In that same moment; in one very quick movement, Rudolpho pulled me off my knees, and out of the way. Dragging his blade deeply across the man's throat, not even a sound escaped him.

Sliding down the wall, Tiny-Penis-Man grabbed at the slash across his neck. Blood streamed from the wound, gushing with each fading beat of his heart.

"What the fuck was that?" I asked, pushing Rudolpho away from me.

"I just saved your life," he raised his brow to me.

I shook my head, "No, you didn't. You put me in jeopardy. I was in complete control of the situation! Then you come along, all Mac the Knife and shit, and complicate things. I had him!" I wanted to yell at him, scream at the top of my lungs. But drawing attention to a crime scene was not in my best interest. Huffing, I started walking away.

"Where are you going?" demanded Rudolpho. "We need to talk about this!"

"I don't think we do" I spun to face him. "But even if I did, I wouldn't do it here, while what was supposed to be *my kill,* is *oozing life.*"

Rudolpho caught up to me and grabbed me by the arm, "You don't understand…he was like us."

The look of confusion I sent his way couldn't be denied, "What?"

"His name is Carl, but he goes by Adam. He's a lady killer. Go look in his hand if you don't believe me!"

Huffing and visibly pissed, I stomped my heeled feet back to where Tiny-Penis Man's body lay. There in his hand, was a wound up coil of wire.

"I know you've heard of him," Rudolpho said. "He's *The Piano Man*."

I stared down at his corpse, mentally wrestling with what I knew about this man from the articles I had read. "I thought he only killed prostitutes." My eyes shot to Rudolpho for an explanation.

He shook his head slowly and gave me a palms-up, "I...I think you look nice."

I furrowed my brow and huffed at the thought that I could ever be mistaken for a street walker. Spinning on my heels and still breathing hard through my nose like a pissed off bull, I passed Rudolpho, and headed back down the alley.

Rudolpho caught up to me, "Look, I'm sorry if I interrupted your kill. I just knew who he was, and what he was going to try to do to you," he explained.

"Why were you following me to begin with? I told you, I don't want a partner, in any capacity!"

He stared at me, "You're welcome."

I turned and continued my stomping away, "You better get rid of that knife," I warned.

"Why? This just changed my M.O.," he said to my swinging backside.

I pulled off my clothes and threw myself down on my bed. I was frustrated as fuck. A kill would have gone a long way to quell this feeling. As pissed as I was that Rudolpho had followed me, I couldn't help but acknowledge how badly this interaction between me and *Tiny-Penis-Man,* a.k.a. *The Piano Man,* could have gone. Yes I had a gun, and no I wasn't about to start on his mini-meal, but what if I hadn't been the faster of the two of us.

I put my forearm across my brow to block out the light in my room. I had to face facts. Rudolpho saved my life tonight. God I hated facts interrupting my loathing. The worst part was how pent-up I felt. This *close to* a *kill* was the same for me as getting *close to an orgasm* and then…nothing. No happy ending. But unlike what I would have done with a missed orgasm, I wasn't going to kill myself for relief.

I had been happily dead inside for well over a year, finding my arousal in the kill. Now, because of him, I felt like my desires were warring. I went back and forth between wanting him inside me, and wanting to make him my next victim. Why had I let him? It's not like I couldn't get laid anytime I wanted. But the truth was, I hadn't wanted to, until I saw him standing there wearing nothing but black boxer briefs and a white smile. There was always the chance that he just served some physiological need that had presented itself, like coming into a heat cycle, I thought. I could admit that he had me against my better judgment. That alone would point to nothing more than a need to rut. I twirled the thought around in my head coming to one conclusion. It wasn't heat, or a rutting cycle, it was him. I wanted him…and that pissed me off even more.

When I woke I pushed brew on my single serve coffee maker and headed to the porch for the morning paper. Sitting at my kitchen table I read the headline: *The Piano Man Found Murdered.* It's not like I hadn't heard of him, but I assumed he would be older. My profile of him was way off: 50's, heavyset, unmarried, introverted, and I assumed raised by a controlling woman. But I hadn't known about the outlandishly small unit he was packing. Having this be the boast of your manhood, I imagined it could make any man bitter. Especially toward the women who couldn't help but look at it…and squint a little. If I stuck my pinky finger straight up, I had a better erection than he did.

The report went on to speak of his wife, who had been his childhood sweetheart. She seemed genuinely heartbroken and shocked according to the article. She gushed about what a good man he had been to her. "He even insisted we wait for marriage to have relations." When I read this, I choked on my coffee. It was in his best interest, I concluded. At least she wouldn't know what she was missing.

Carl, the paper confirmed the name Rudolpho had called him; had 18 kills under his belt, all prostitutes and all strangled with wire. Again, I wondered if I should reevaluate my hunting wardrobe. It was embarrassing to think that this man had mistaken me for a whore.

I hadn't had a 9 to 5 job since my husband graduated collage. And now I didn't work because I didn't have to. Of course I had worked two jobs just to keep a roof over our heads and food in our stomachs while he went to school. But when he graduated four years later, he thought my being a housewife was more than enough for him. Sweet words. But I now knew it was more likely because he was afraid that if I had ever had human contact outside of the home, I'd do exactly what he had been doing. It was like that for most people. They thought others were just like them. It's a mistake of grand proportion, but guilty people always seem to see themselves, their thoughts, their sins, their flaws, in others.

Not having a job always left me wondering: What am I going to do today? The house was clean, and the laundry and grocery shopping were done. This thought was forced out of my head and replaced with: will I be followed? Where would he pop-up next? Even without Rudolpho being in plain view, I was now self-conscious about every move I made. I couldn't help but wonder if I should go on the defensive. Waiting around like prey to be stalked wasn't really the M.O. I wished to adopt with him. Suddenly I realized, I had no M.O., where he was concerned. That, would have to be remedied, I concluded.

Slipping into a hot bath I tried to relax and let the last twenty-four hours melt away. Dressing in a white cotton sundress and sandals, I headed for the boardwalk.

It was always a nice stroll for me. The shops, the eateries, almost made me feel…normal. Locals intermingled with flocks of tourists, selling, and buying T-shirts and small curios. I perused some of the clothing stores and debated buying a long flowing skirt in an array of colors. As much as I tried to enjoy what had once brought me comfort, I had this gnawing inside.

True, I was like a dog that hadn't been properly socialized. I didn't try to make friends, wasn't even sure I wanted them. But watching all the groups of friends, and couples pass me by, laughing and joking, I wondered if I was missing some deep part of the human experience. I could speak well enough to get a man to drop his drawers, and disarm him. But this wasn't much of an accomplishment considering the men I interacted with, and spoke to, were there for this reason. I was more like a big, well wrapped Christmas present that turned out to be socks. But even before, when I was a happily married woman, I had no friends to speak of. I wasn't a member of the PTA, didn't belong to a book club. Hell, I wasn't even part of the neighborhood watch. Derrick had been my whole life. And even though I didn't miss him, not even a smidgen, I did sometimes miss having someone to talk to, someone who could make me laugh. Someone to watch mother-nature do her thing with, whether that be a sunset or a storm, I thought as I watched the incoming grey clouds gathering.

Feeling a little too wonky, and wondering if I was close to my menstrual cycle, I decided to head back home. I'd watch a funny movie, eat good cheese, salami, and sourdough bread, drink a couple glasses of wine, and just try to shut my mind off.

As I turned the corner of my street, I saw someone walking back up the side of house from my backyard. It was him, Rudolpho. I sneaked behind a neighbor's hedge and watched him. What had he been doing in my backyard? Walking up to the front door, he knocked and waited for someone to answer. I couldn't really be shocked that he was there. He admitted that he had followed me home the first night we met. I was surprised it took him this long to try and invade my most personal of spaces…well, almost my most personal. But I reminded myself, he had already been there, too.

He stood on the porch…just waiting. His wandering around my house had caught the eye of the nice elderly man living next door. He said something to Rudolpho. I watched Rudolpho nod and say something back before getting into his black Jeep. When his Jeep disappeared in the opposite direction, I continued to my house.

"Good afternoon," I said a little loudly to Mr. Draper who was hard of hearing.

As he turned toward me, he smiled. "Oh, good morning, Audra," he said. "You just missed someone who was looking for you."

"I did?" I acted surprised.

"I asked his name," Mr. Draper nodded his bald head, "but I couldn't hear what the man said."

"That's okay, I'm sure he'll be back," I forced a smile.

"He drove a Jeep…personalized plate," Mr. Draper added.

My brow furrowed, did good ol' Mr. Draper remember his license plate? "Yeah? Do you remember what it was?" I asked.

"Sure, it was all letters, R-U-D-E-L-F," he jutted out his chin. "Mean anything to you?"

I slowly shook my head, "I can't say that it does," I shrugged. "Thank you though," I smiled, and headed for my front door.

So…Rudolpho knew my real name by now. It wasn't that hard to get public information. I decided that I should do a little snooping, too.

The house had warmed with the heat of the day, but rain was coming, I could smell it in the air.

Changing into a pair of booty shorts and a white tank top, I got comfortable. Pulling out my laptop I went to the DMV plate search. I had to agree to all these computer demands of not using the information for fraudulent or illegal purposes. I hit the accept button and waited. It only took a few moments before I had the legal owners name; Tyler Whitmore. Looking at the screen, my head shot back. Was he *that* Tyler Whitmore? Son to the computer mogul, William Whitmore? The address, which was not fully disclosed, simply read Naples, Fl.

I sat back and let my thoughts go for a walk; Tyler Whitmore…a killer…stalking unfaithful married women…stalking me? W.T.H., I wondered. It's not like I didn't think the rich and privileged were capable of murder, look at the Menendez brothers and hundreds of others. But…he had a lot more riding on his not being found out, than I did. Then again, he could also afford the very best lawyers, who were sure to be great at manifesting reasonable doubt. That's *if* charges were ever brought against him, in the first place. In a lot of ways, his last name made him an untouchable.

Needing verification; I brought up family photos from old news articles. As I scrolled, there were pictures of his father, his mother, followed by three step mothers, an older sibling; a brother, who sadly died in a plane crash just over a year ago and then…him.

There he stood in a three piece Armani suit, dripping with female attention from all sides. His hair was pushed away from his dark blue eyes. He was sporting that smile that made my mind go to a dark, warm place, deep inside.

Looking at all the women, fawning all over him, the question in my head changed back to, why me? He obviously had no trouble finding a date or whatever his little heart (or any other parts of him for that matter), may desire. Was he slumming? I mean, I'm no slouch, well off enough to take good care of myself for the rest of my life. But I certainly wasn't in the same category financially or socially as young Mr. Whitmore. How did he stay under the radar, I wondered? But then I realized that I hadn't had any idea who he was when we met. I knew the name. It graced plaques on buildings, park benches, museums and so on, that were owned by Whitmore Inc. Maybe being the son of a rich mogul wasn't like having movie star status. Maybe you only stood-out, in your own circle?

I did a quick search and found out that his father was left a widower when Tyler was five. Two years later, his father married the first in a slew of step-mothers. The divorces were quite public…all cheating wives, according to the articles. "Hmmm." It seemed like Father Whitmore's sperm was only potent one time after fifty, having his son Tyler at the age of fifty-two. I had to assume his mother was much younger than his father. Looking back through old public records I found out that she was twenty-five years his junior.

"Go Mr. Whitmore," I said to no one.

As I went back over old records I saw that Tyler had no run-ins with law. That didn't mean he hadn't done anything wrong. Obviously, I knew better. But what would old man Whitmore be willing to pay to keep his child out of jail, out of media.

Back to the question that now plagued me…why me?

Cutting up some cheese, salami and grabbing a sleeve of crackers, I decided to open a bottle of red wine. Taking my full glass, and what would be considered my dinner back to my couch, I searched for a movie that made me happy. Deciding on an old favorite I got comfortable and pushed play.

Lightening lit up the sky, and thunder rumbled as an evening storm passed through. I was about an hour into Shrek when the doorbell buzzed. My eyes shot to the door, what were the chances it wasn't him?

Looking through my peephole, I saw his tiny image bounce back at me. I let out a deep breath and opened the door. There he stood; black T-shirt, well-worn jeans, and a pair of black boots. Pushing his dampened hair away from his face, he smiled. That smile could be the death of me, I thought. I don't know why, It wasn't his M.O., but I suddenly wondered if he was in fact there to kill me. It wasn't a completely irrational thought. I mean, I was a loose end for him every bit as much as he was for me. And…he had deviated before where I was concerned.

"So…Audra, how are you?" he used my real name, grinning.

"I'm well Tyler, how are you?" I returned the same shit-eating grin.

"May I?" he asked.

I paused considering how this could play out. Finally I opened the door wide and gave him the *welcome* hand gesture. He moved past me and looked around as I closed the door behind him.

Turning to look me up and down, he hovered over my breasts for a moment before visually moving down to that spot where my thighs met. "Nice place," he said.

I wasn't sure if he meant my home, or my honey-pot, from the way he stared. I cocked my head and waited for his eyes to meet mine.

Raising his eyes, he said, "I love the old bungalow style homes," letting the possible innuendo wash away.

"Really, I'd think it was a little small by your standards."

"Ah, I see you've been doing some research. But that will only tell you what my father likes, or what he possesses. I require less to be happy. Why, I even own a small piece of property around here. It's more to my liking," he took a few more steps, continuing to look around.

"Oh, yeah? Close to here, huh?" I asked.

"Very close," he smiled. "A newly acquired piece of proper-ty," he spun to face me. "I have a renter at the moment," one side of his face pulled up into a cockeyed grin.

"Is that true?" my brows lifted in mock surprise.

"Yeah, I stopped by to see my renter earlier today…bring her the new rental agreement…but she wasn't home."

"Damn shame," I said.

"We haven't met yet. Well not formally," he added. I stuck

my tongue in my cheek as he extended his hand to me. "Tyler Whitmore and you are?" his eyes twinkled.

I stared at his hand for a moment before reluctantly bringing mine to his, "Audra Murphy."

"What a beautiful name," he turned away from me, and went back to looking around. "I like the way you've decorated. Very comfortable," he strolled around my living room as I feigned interest. "I see the kitchen," he pointed. "Is it up to your needs?"

I nodded, "It works well for me."

And I assume that's the bathroom," he walked toward a darkened room down the hall to the right. "How's your plumbing?"

"It's fine, thank you."

"And that room?" he pointed before moving down the hallway to the closed door on the left, "What room is this, Audra?"

I stared at him for a moment, before saying matter-of-factly, "That would be my bedroom, Tyler."

"Ah," he nodded. "So this is where you lay your head at night."

"Sometimes," I answered.

"Oh?" his brow lifted. "Do you spend many nights away from your own bed?" he queried.

My tongue shot into my cheek. "Actually, I spend many nights…on my couch. I get a good cross breeze when I open the windows."

"No air-conditioning?" his brow furrowed.

I gave a slow shake of my head, "Like you said, it's an old house. I'm lucky to have heating, even though it's not nearly as beneficial here."

He nodded, "So back to this room," he put his palm against the closed door. "You mind if I take a look…see if there's any damage that needs to be fixed?"

"Oh," I nodded, slitting my eyes, "you're here to access damage?"

"Well, it *IS* an investment. I like to take care of my investments," he looked me up and down.

"Be my guest."

I watched him disappear into my bedroom. If I was unnerved by his stalking me to Dango's, him buying my home; this really pissed me off.

I heard him call out from the bedroom, "I like the color scheme. I didn't peg you for a romantic."

"Then you were right."

"But red is the color of passion," he added.

"It's also the color of blood," I said under my breath. "It's my favorite color," I said loud enough for him to hear.

"I like the oversized furniture…especially the bed. I think all beds should be four-poster."

I could hear his footfalls returning on the wood floor. Peeking out of the room, "Your bed's at a good height," he winked.

I smirked. I was quite sure what *height* he was referring to.

"It seems I've made a sound investment." As he walked toward me, he asked, "Your thoughts?"

"It's well built."

"*Mmm,* that's exactly what I was thinking," he sucked his lower lip like he had done when the taste of me was still fresh there.

"Why?" I asked.

"Why do I think it's well built?" he asked coyly.

"Why did you buy my house?" I clarified.

"Why do you think?" his brow furrowed. "What are your thoughts?" he folded his arms across his chest.

We stared, sizing each other up. "Would be quite a trophy," I suggested the path of reason between two serial killers.

"Ah…that it would," he nodded and began pacing. "If I kept trophies, I guess that would be a logical thought."

I stayed silent.

"But I don't," he shook his head ever so slightly.

"Then I really can't fathom a logical guess," I told him.

"Really?" he drew slowly nearer until we stood a foot apart. "Are you sure you can't think of any other reason?" Reaching out, he wrapped one arm around my waist, pulling me against him.

"I have no desire to be kept," I said coolly, through a tightened jaw.

"I can't imagine a woman like you could be kept," he stared down into my eyes. "I just want an excuse to be close to you…to see you."

"So this little uninvited drop-by, won't be the last?"

"I would prefer to be invited," he leaned his head down and kissed my neck just above my collar bone.

Damn that spot, I thought to myself as my eyes automatically fell closed.

"I have needs," he said between soft kisses.

"And from what I've learned about you, you have a fan-club ready and waiting to fulfill those needs." I was trying to keep my thoughts clear, but I kept seeing flashes of him…on his knees.

"No. I have a fan-club of women who like my social status. Women who like the idea of what I am heir to. When I did my homework…finding out all I could about you," his eyes met mine, "I found that you had more than enough money to live a completely different life if you chose. Yet...you choose this," he looked around. "I like that about you."

I stayed silent.

"In my world...everything is status and the way people see you. Wear the right clothes, drive the right car, live in the right zip-code...it's all a façade. Nothing DEEP resides within what money can buy," he brought his fingertip to my lips, outlining them slowly. "I enjoy the things...that can't be bought."

"So you bought my house?" I tried not to laugh at the glaring contradiction.

"Well I still expect you to pay rent," he grinned.

"I wouldn't have it any other way."

Letting his eyes roam over my body, he changed the subject, "I like your little shorts." Reaching out, he rubbed the thin cotton material at my thighs between his thumb and forefinger. "I like your legs," he leaned his head down again, softly brushing his lips over my chest.

I was pretty sure how he liked my legs...open. "Do you really think this is a good idea?" I breathed out, trying not to enjoy his hot breath and moist lips on my skin.

He lifted his head to look down at me, "This is the best Idea I've had...since I fucked you last."

"Who's the romantic, now?" I asked.

"Would you like it better if I said made love to you?" his eyes held mine.

"Absolutely not."

"Good...because I want to fuck you, Audra," he said before kissing me hard.

He had no idea what hearing these words meant to me. It

was like an earlier wrong, was being set right. I let his kiss envelop me, surrendering to it.

"Call me Lila," I whispered, as I wrapped my arms around his neck. Scooping me up into his arms, he carried me to the bedroom.

The first thing that stole my attention from him was that he had lit my candle while he was in here supposedly looking around for *damage*. I couldn't help but wonder what was it with him and the candles? But more importantly, he knew we would end up in here. What an easy slut he must think me. This thought would normally shut me down, end the moment in a heartbeat. But if I was being honest with myself, I was quite easy…for him. I had had a taste of him. I had felt him hard inside me. He had caused a craving I had never felt before. I knew he would bring me the satisfaction I needed.

Laying me down on the bed he backed away. I just waited to see what he would do next. Walking over to my bedroom door, where my silk bathrobe hung, he pulled the tie from the waist loops. Holding the tie, he moved to the side of the bed where I lay, questioning my current decision to open the door to him.

"Do you trust me?" he asked, his midnight blue eyes dancing in the candlelight.

"Not exactly," I looked at the tie, being pulled tight in both hands like an instrument of strangulation.

He nodded and grinned back, "You will."

I would have felt better if my gun were lying on the bedside table. But I did take some comfort in the fact that it was just a few inches down in the drawer beneath. Not that I had any delusions of my being able to win in a hand to hand struggle with him. I had to admit, if only to myself, it was a little sick just how much of a turn on it was to not to know if I could trust him. The fact that this was my version of thrill seeking…was a bit twisted to say the least.

"Tie me up?" he said.

"Why would I want to do that?"

"I want to see what you do with me, when you have full control."

I cocked my head. He was giving full control…to me? Was this nothing more than him trying to prove that he trusted me? Or, was he really turned on by the thought of what I would do to him, if it were left to my own imagination?

Standing there in front of me, he waited to be controlled. "Take off your shirt," I ordered. I watched as he pulled the black T off over his head. He was chiseled and defined in all the right ways. I obviously noticed before, but sometimes, you think you may have imagined something better than it was. This was not the case. Which would also mean that I hadn't *mentally exaggerated* what his jeans were having trouble keeping concealed. I bit my bottom lip, knowing exactly what he had to offer me.

"Now the pants." My eyes warmed over; anticipating the view that made every part of my body, applaud.

Tyler grinned, unbuttoning his 501's slowly, released his already hard-candy member from its denim prison. Seeing him standing at full attention, my mouth began to water.

"Lay down," I demanded. "Diagonally," I added.

He lay himself down and scooted across the bed until his head lined up with the far post.

"Arms up," I told him.

I crawled up his body, straddling him. Purposely I pushed my crotch down on his erection. His hips instinctively pushed his pelvis up. His engorged erection searched out my hot-spot. A low moan escaped him as I withdrew her point of entry from his swollen tip.

Wrapping his wrists, tight, he gave a little pull to show me that he was in fact bound.

"Do you trust me?" I asked, looking deep into his eyes.

"Indubitably," he said, smiling from ear to ear.

His use of this word took me out of character and made me giggle a little.

Reaching across him, I let my hard as steel nipple that was trying to poke through the fabric of my tank top, brush over his face, as I reached across him to my night table. Opening the drawer, there she sat; my 40 cal. A sense of peace filled me. But I was going for something a little less destructive now. Pulling a black paisley bandana from the drawer, I held it up for his approval.

"You're going to bind my legs, too?" he questioned.

Shaking my head ever so slightly, "Blindfold," I smiled.

"Hmm…" escaped his lips as his brow furrowed.

"You don't trust me," my head cocked to one side.

"I just…really like seeing you; watching you," he admitted. "Those sweet lips…your tits." His gaze wandered down to where my happy place lay on top of his erection, "Everything," he whispered. "But we can do it your way. I just have one request."

"I thought I had been given full control?"

"It's only a request," he whispered. "You have the right of refusal."

I thought about it, "What is your request?"

"Undress for me, first?" his eyes twinkled.

Seemed like an understandable request. But I say this because women aren't as visual as men. I could picture everything he had done to me, and I to him, like I was watching it on a movie screen. Suddenly I felt sorry for his gender's difficulty in reliving a memory; storing it for playtime.

Moving myself off the bed, I stood and turned my ass to him. Looking over my shoulder, I hooked my thumbs inside the waistband of my little shorts. Bending at the hips, I worked them down, one inch at a time until they hit the floor.

"I want to lick you from stem to stern," he said. "Will you spread for me?"

"One request, huh?"

"Please," he whispered.

I liked it when he said please. I liked when a man was courteous before fucking me; dirty while in the act of, and quickly leaving soon after. Spreading my legs a little wider, I bent my body forward then slowly reached for my ankles; the proper way to take a spanking. Only, right now, he could only envision the act. Looking back at him, pushing my tooshie up for his approval, he made a hungry noise.

"I want to take you from behind," he said. "Show me your tits?"

"Awfully demanding for a bound man, aren't you?" I stood upright, turning to face him.

"I like the view," he offered.

I was fully aware of just how much he liked the view. Every hard inch of him, screamed this truth to me.

"Please," he said again.

With a grin, I pulled my tank top over my head, covering the girls with my hands. Rubbing and kneading them, I envisioned his hands, his mouth, ravenously attacking them. I had always been submissive, and I had more than liked it that way. Being held tight, held down, seen as the instrument of his fantasies, was the ammo I had always craved. But this, this in control (with a few requests), knowing it was me, my body and how I would use it, that made him lose control, held its own massive appeal. I would do some of what he asked, yet, I, my body, still ran the show.

"Show me how hard they are," he pled.

Walking to him I leaned over and let my nipple lightly graze his lips. His mouth searched, as I pulled away. "You look with your eyes," I said as I mounted him again. Backing down his body, I let my nipples barely brush his flesh as I went, watching them leave every hair on his body, standing on end.

He writhed a little, his breathing faster, "Fuck I want you."

Twisting my body around to mount him backward, one leg on each side of him, I gently rubbed my girl and her slippery wetness against the head of his cock. Giving him the full view, I looked over my shoulder. Tyler watched intently as I slid myself across his shaft.

"God, you're so wet." He pushed his hips up, again.

That, I was. The thoughts running in my head, the deviation from my sexual M.O. as a *submissive*, had ignited a new form of play.

"I want to be inside," he moaned.

I shook my head at him, holding up the blindfold. Changing my mount to face him, I slid up his body. He whimpered a little as I lay it across his eyes, tying it behind his head.

I looked at him, a real life fantasy. A gorgeous man, naked, erect, blindfolded, and bound…mmm, what a beautiful toy I had at my fingertips. Now the only question was…would I be a taker or a giver? Even in this position, I could be the giver if I did everything he asked of me.

I ran my finger lightly over his lips, watching his mouth search out the origin of sensation. He pressed his tongue to the tip then wrapped his lips around it, sucking. I watched, as he sucked with such need, doing that one thing I well remembered him doing to my little swollen clit. His actions conveyed his wants. Seems being the giver could be sexy as hell. I'll give him what I want. The thought brought a devilish grin to my face.

I traced my fingertip down his chin, down his neck, watching his flesh rise in tiny bumps. I continued lightly down his chest, to his stomach, all the way to the line of hair that pointed to his pussy pounder. Leaning down, I let my tongue just graze this line. His skin was soft. His scent driving me back to a shared memory where he was in charge of my desire, my release.

"I'll be right back," I told him.

"What?" he asked, now showing a modicum of the fear one would expect knowing that the woman who had you bound, was in fact a murderer. I couldn't help but grin.

Returning a moment later, I shook the glass I was holding making a clinking noise.

I could see his head turn slightly toward the noise, trying to place the sound.

Pulling an ice cube from the glass, I brought it to his lips. Watching him lick at it put me in mind of him licking something else. He let his tongue tickle it, swirling, before wrapping his lips around the melting cube and gently sucking. Dragging it down his chin, over his Adam's apple, it left tiny droplets from the heat radiating off his skin. I dragged it down to his chest. His nipple hardened as I pulled the cold over it, letting it drip and drip and drip as he writhed. Just watching him arch, made me bite my bottom lip. When I brought the heat of my mouth to his nipple's rescue, his jaw fell open with a low groan. Warm then cold, then warm again, made his body tense with pleasure, then relax with relief. And I was in control of both.

I put the melting cube in my mouth and worked my way down his stomach. I loved that line between his muscles that separated his eight pack. I spent time just listening to his breathing accelerate from the cold, followed by a relieved pant, when the ice was removed. Skipping over his impressive and rock hard girth, I let the cube drip down onto his balls.

Drawing in breath of shock, his hips thrust and shook. Sucking on the cube, until my tongue was freezing, I dragged it from the underside of his cold-tightened sack, in one long motion up to the base of his member. Over, and over again, I lapped them, the pressure increasing with every pass. His body twitched and shifted, his breath caught in his throat between moans of approval.

"Oh fuck, baby," sprang from his lips, over and over.

Moving all the way up the shaft, I let the tiny cube drop from my mouth, swirling my freezing tongue around the head of his dick. His hips rocked, arching to push himself up, the way he would when he wanted to be deeper inside. My own wetness began to trickle. I wondered if he was picturing coming in my mouth. I knew I was.

Dipping a finger inside my warm creaminess, I reached out and pulled it slowly across his bottom lip. One timid lick of his tongue brought a low growl from deep inside him. Hungrily, he went to work, sucking away my gift.

"I love the way you taste," he whispered.

Pulling my finger away from him, he let out another whimper. I slid back down his body and turned to mount him backward. I moved my hips back, placing my wetness just within reach of his waiting lips then pulled slightly away as his breathing increased, his tongue searching for her. I let him have a quick taste, before moving away again.

"Fuck baby, you're going to make me come without ever getting inside you," he whispered desperately.

This comment pulled a grin across my face. "Is that true?" I asked before immediately pushing my mouth down on his cock. His hips pushed up, thrusting himself deep.

"Oh God," he cried out. "Let me taste you again, please," he pled.

I was in control. I could bring him pleasure, torture, it was my choice. As I hovered just out of mouth's reach, I could feel his hot panting breath on her; craning his neck to find her.

"Please," he pled.

I slowly eased my body into position to give him another small taste. His head bolted upward, his tongue going wild, worshiping the whole area as I went back to work on his member.

Up and down I worked as he lapped, licked, and flicked at my happy spot. Swollen and wet, I felt my excitement, my passion, building quickly. I was almost there, as he thrust all of himself into my mouth again. He was driven by his own need. I felt him deep in my throat. His moan muffled as he kept sucking me. Feeling his body begin to shake from below mine, my own beginning to shake above his...this was it. We were going to explode into each other's mouths.

All the sudden, his hands broke free from their silk restraint. Ripping the blindfold from his eyes, he grabbed my hips, holding on tight as he pushed me over the edge. Hard we came, my scream muffled by a throat-full of him, his moan lost in my love patch. The taste of him, his excitement mingled with the pleasure his talented tongue delivered, made me gush.

As he held me there, his arms wrapped around my thighs, licking me clean, I twitched, uncontrollably. The sensitivity was too much as I tried to escape his grasp. In the blink of an eye, he sat up. Moving me forward, he pulled his body from beneath mine.

Placing a palm on my low back, he guided me down onto my stomach. Turning my head to look back at him, I saw him grab his cock; still fully erect and wanting more. Pulling my ass up by my hips, I waited on my hands and knees. Reaching both his hands between my legs, he spread them wide.

"May I?" he asked, just grazing me with the tip.

I smiled back at him, "You may," both of us pretending I was still in control.

Pushing the head inside of me, I gasped, shocked that he still stood at full attention. Again he pushed, letting my wetness invite him in. He buried himself inside, deeper, and deeper until he filled my space, completely. From behind, he was hitting that illusive spot. The one that made me wince with pain and howl with pleasure. Over and over he tapped it, sending shocks of excitement through my whole body. A different sensation was building. A different release was coming.

My control may have been taken from me, but I could still demand from this vantage. Looking back over my shoulder, my jaw quivering, I growled to him, "Smack it…hard."

Biting into his lower lip and never missing a beat, he pulled back his hand and clapped it hard across my ass. Oh, that sound! It was as exquisite as the feeling that shot through my whole body.

"Ah," I cried out from the welcome sting. Head turned up to the heavens, I yelled, "Again." Again I felt the sting that I craved.

I felt his fingertip playing at my backdoor. Pushing my hips back a little, I silently gave him permission. Filling me from both sides, I slammed my ass back into him, panting like a wild animal. He had unlocked an unexplored piece of my sexuality. Pleasure, pain, pleasure, pain; he balanced me so well between the two. He was the master at keeping me somewhere between moaning and screaming, as he continued to pound that spot. The pleasure and pain rose to an almost unbearable point, yet my movements silently begged him not to stop, not to slow. I was there. Not a sound could I utter as my G-spot exploded. Shaking, my body was vibrating so hard. As I gushed, I thought my legs were going to give out.

"I'm going to come," I heard him warn.

"Inside," I instructed through a shaky breath.

"Inside?"

I looked back and nodded to him, "Deep," I ordered, grabbing between my legs to cup his balls; rubbing and kneading them. I watched his eyes close. His head fell back, as he fucked deeper and deeper toward his grand finale. Biting his bottom lip, the euphoria transforming his face; this was the sexiest thing I had ever seen. I could feel every pump of his juice, staying as deep inside of me as our bodies would allow.

"I love fucking you, baby! I love fucking you!" he said over, and over again.

Falling on top of me, we crashed onto the bed. He placed exhausted kisses on the back of my neck between shaking breaths. Normally, this would have put me on edge, but I was too drained, too spent, to analyze my fears at the moment.

here are you going?" he asked as I Army-crawled my body out from underneath his.

"Water!" I rasped, as though I had spent months on a dessert isle.

Standing naked in front of my open fridge, was a welcome feeling to my overheated body. I grabbed one of those small bottles of water, and downed it. Grabbing two more, I walked back into my bedroom. He was sprawled in all his glory across my bed, glowing. Handing him the bottle, he grinned up at me.

"I do love fucking you," he said to me.

I forced a tight smile.

"What's that face for? Is it me saying *fucking,* that bothers you?" he asked.

"No," I laughed and gave a little shake of my head.

"Then what's wrong?" he looked perplexed.

"It's nothing, really," I shook my head some more.

"No, it's something. And I'd like you to *tell* me if I did something wrong. Was it the ass thing?" he pondered a guess.

"Did it seem like I had a problem with that?" I stared at him.

He grinned and shook his head, "No. So what is it, then?"

"It's…it's you saying you *LOVE* fucking me," I exaggerated the word.

He gave me the confused face again, "I DO LOVE FUCKING YOU! Can't you tell?"

"It's the word…the L word. It just makes me a little… uncomfortable…that's all," I gave him a shrug.

"Well…I guess I could say I *LIKE* fucking you. Really doesn't express how much I enjoy it…doesn't give it the merit it deserves. But if it makes you uncomfortable, I won't say it anymore," he shrugged his shoulders.

I gave him a curt nod, "Okay then."

"Sorry about your tie," he held up the two pieces of silk that used to be one.

"Don't worry about it," I laughed.

"So I take it you're on the pill?" he asked.

"No," I said blankly as I pulled up my booty-shorts.

Tyler looked around, "You do know I wasn't wearing a condom, right?"

"We've already exchanged too many body fluids to worry about that now," I told him.

"I'm not worried about that," he explained. "But what about pregnancy?" his brow lifted.

I pulled my shirt down over my head, "You don't have to worry about that, either."

"Why…are you barren, or something?" Without a thought, he threw the word out there. The word that once left a dent in my heart.

"Actually, I am," I said, before I turned and walked out of the room.

In the kitchen I poured myself a glass of wine. When I turned around, he was standing there, leaning against the doorway.

"Wine?" I asked him.

He nodded, "Please."

I felt his eyes on me as I filled a glass for him, as well.

"I'm really sorry," his eyes met mine when I turned toward him. "When I said that, I didn't mean to sound…brazen."

I forced a laugh, "It's okay. It's not a big deal," I shrugged.

"Right," he said like he understood that I didn't want to have this conversation.

A moment passed while I re-corked the wine and cleaned a small spill with a napkin.

"So, what side of the bed do you like to sleep on?" he leisurely sipped his wine as my eyes rounded.

"Excuse me?" I needed him to repeat himself.

"The bed. I like to sleep close to the window when I'm alone. But if I sleep next to someone, I like to be closest to the door. It's a man-thing," he explained.

"Ugh," was all that made its way through my lips. If I understood him correctly, he wanted to stay the night…with me…in my bed?

"Seriously, either side will be fine," he shrugged.

I tried not to laugh at the audacity of the thought. "Why would you want to stay…here?"

He stared at me, "Because," he chose his words carefully, "I don't want you to think that I got what I wanted from you, and then just bailed out?"

"Oh," I laughed, "not an issue," I shook my head at him. "You don't have to worry about that, either."

"You say that a lot," he pointed out. "Either you really aren't like other women, or you're going out of your way to make me think you're not," his brow furrowed.

"It's nothing personal. I just like sleeping alone. I'm used to it. And I think a lot of women feel the same way I do."

"Not the ones I've met. More than once I've been called an asshole, and more, for lacing up my boots, too soon after coming."

"Well, you won't get any of that, from me," I assured him.

Walking him to the front door, he turned to face me, "I really do..." he caught himself, "...enjoy fucking you," he leaned in, putting a soft kiss on my neck.

My eyes fell closed as he hovered there for a moment.

"Sleep well," he whispered before turning and walking to his Jeep.

"You too," I said to his backside before closing the door.

Leaning against the door, I couldn't help but acknowledge the truth; *I really am a broken toy.* I had always been an introvert. So saying; *"Lots of women feel like I do,"* was ridiculous. It wasn't like I *knew* what *lots of women* thought, much less, wanted. I did know most women weren't serial killers. And if the romantic movies, books, and greeting cards were correct, most people did look for some kind of meaningful relationship. They wanted someone to hold during the night. Whether it was love, friendship, hell even a cat. But the norm...was not me.

What I did know for sure; I had enjoyed stepping a foot over the line of my normally submissive behavior. My husband had never really asked what I fantasized about, what I wanted. And the one time I tried to release the little devil in me, I was chastised and left humiliated.

I didn't have a lot of personal experience with men; that was true. So to play with someone who wanted me to take some control, someone who liked seeing me express my wants and desires…this was a whole new playing field for me. I rubbed the hand-shaped welt on my ass, with a naughty little grin. But I still didn't want anything more from him, and somehow I had to make that clear.

Walking back into my bedroom, I could still smell him there. A mixture of cologne, sweat and hot sex, lingered. The fact that the scent of him, us, made me swoon with fresh thoughts and wants, bothered me. Immediately I stripped the sheets from my bed and hurried them into the washing machine like they were contaminated. Setting the machine to the longest and hottest wash cycle, I decided I would sleep on the couch.

I was awoken by voices outside my living room window. Looking at my wall clock, my face squished up; 7am? Who the hell would be in my front yard at 7am? Looking through the window, I saw Tyler talking to a man in a dark blue uniform holding a clipboard. Opening the front door, Tyler turned his eyes to me, "I'll be right back," he told the gentleman.

"What's going on?" I asked as he approached.

"Having air conditioning installed," he said.

"Don't you think you could have discussed this with me?"

"Over a cup of coffee? I'd love to." He waited for me to open the door and invite him in.

Pushing brew on my single server coffee machine, I said, "This isn't necessary."

"Well, you never know, it may be for my next tenant," he

shrugged. "Or if you had company," he offered as if it was an afterthought.

"Already thinking ahead, huh?" I stared at him.

"A good business man does that," a hint of a smile pulled up one cheek into a smirk.

"So what are your thoughts…thinking ahead?" I handed him a cup of coffee.

He licked his lips as I continued to stare blank faced. "I'd like to watch you hunt again."

At this comment, a laugh escaped me, "Yeah, because it went so well the first time."

"Technically…I saved your life," he said. "The man was a killer, who intended to kill you," he reminded me.

"Yes," I nodded back, "but you didn't yell out, "*That guy is a killer*." You yelled out, "*Don't you DARE suck another man's dick*," I reminded him.

"I did," he nodded, matter-of-factly.

"So why would this time be any different?"

"Well, do you suck other men's dicks?" he did a palms-up.

"No," I gave him the palms-up, back.

"Now that I know this…it won't be a problem," he shook his head.

"I guess my question is…why would it have been a problem in the first place?"

His eyes rounded, "Are you okay with me licking someone else's pussy?" he questioned.

I had to admit, we didn't use fluffy words to describe our parts or actions.

My first thought disturbed me; *I'd fucking kill her…and possibly, him.* But what I said was, "Of course I'm okay with it.

You and I are just having a good time; fulfilling a *need,*" I offered.

I watched his tongue move into his cheek, "Oh, is that what it is?"

"I can't imagine why you'd think it's anything more than that," I said calmly.

The smile stretching across his face conveyed unsaid words. There was a *fuck you,* in that smile. "Well, okay then. I guess I'll see ya later, Audra," he walked out the door and closed it behind him.

When the door shut, the reality of my words hit me hard. What had I done? In the very best case scenario, I may be forced to share my candy. And in the very worst, I may have gotten myself cut off from my candy-man, completely. "Fuck!" I said to no one, as I heard his Jeep drive off.

I let out a sigh. It was better for us to make the break. We had very little control when it came to our desire for one other, and I like feeling in charge. He was throwing me all off kilter, I told myself. Now I could just go back to just being me.

5

*S*ix days passed, and no sign of Tyler. It may have been the fact that I hadn't left my house, given him anyplace where he could accidentally bump into me. It wasn't like I missed him. I did however miss what he did to me, with me, for me. I hated that he had awakened this sleeping beast. The thought of him, inside me, had caused a need to be reborn. A need that was now remedied, by me giving myself carpel tunnel syndrome. I tried everything else I could think of cleaning until there was nothing left to be cleaned, a hot bath, a cold shower, hell, even yoga. But every time I pulled my legs up over my head, I pictured him between them. And *Downward Dog,* was no better. It was possible I was handling this the wrong way Maybe… I needed to hunt.

As I dressed for a night of hunting, enjoying the thought of my new central air (it would take another day or so to get the unit installed), I played Nina Simone.

It wasn't that I was down, really. I just couldn't get into the right frame of mind. Nina was a big help when I felt…melancholy; or didn't feel sexy. And considering this was what I used as bait, I was worried about how it would affect my ability to catch my prey.

This is for the best, I kept telling myself. Tyler had been getting far too comfortable, too familiar. Still, I couldn't stop thinking about him. I knew they had meetings for this shit, but I wasn't a sex addict, I was a *him* addict. I had been married too long not to know how it worked. The first year is all passion, experimentation. By the end of the second year, sex is something you did when the cable went out. And by the end of the fifth year, sex was something you did, with someone else, apparently. Being honest, even the first year with my husband, hadn't been as good as the first night with Tyler.

One of the only girl tricks I knew was, when you don't feel sexy, fake it. I loaded my girls into a black, pushup bra and synched them up. Pulling on my black thigh high pantyhose, fastening my garter belt to them, always helped feed the *sexy.*. Next I shimmied into a low-cut, black, form fitting dress. The four inch red heels were starting to have an effect on me, as well. I always liked the way heels made me feel. I lined my top lashes with black, and winged the ends. Black mascara, red lips, brown contacts, and a long black Betty Page wig with big rolled bangs, completed the look I was going for. I clipped one side of the wig back with a big red flower barrette. Grabbing my tiny clutch purse, just big enough for a prepaid credit card, old ID in my married name, breath mints and my 40Cal, I headed out on the prowl.

I had decided on a rockabilly club just a few miles away. The crowd was thirty-ish. Tonight I wanted to draw a handsome man into my web. It could have been an ego thing. It could have been the desire to see if someone else would look at me like he had. Like somehow I could break his spell with one true look of desire, over debauchery. I called a cab and had it pick me up a few blocks away from my bungalow.

I was off to a great start, the cabby kept stealing glances of me in the rearview mirror. Usually I didn't like this much attention. But tonight it was necessary.

Walking into the club, I realized how intimate it was. Forty people or so, moved about; it wasn't as crowded as I had hoped. Retro signs hung on the walls with pictures of old bands and album covers woven in between. The bar was a circle in the middle of the room. Also not my favorite. I preferred to be facing a mirror, not an old guy with a thinning pompadour and a button up shirt made for someone a bit more svelte, than his girth boasted.

Looking down the bar to see what I would be drinking tonight, I grinned. Boilermakers; this, I could do. Ordering myself a shot of whiskey and a beer back, I started to feel in my element. Until Tyler walked in, that is. Had he just been waiting to see where I would pop-up?

Our eyes met momentarily and if there was any fire, it wasn't the good kind. He did look delicious in a pair of crisp 501's and a white T-shirt. His boots: polished, hair slicked back. He was exactly the kind of guy you would expect to find at a club like this one. Women shifted and turned in their seats, as he walked by.

Tyler let his focus be drawn away and walked to the other end of the bar, out of my clear line of sight. If I wanted to be coy with my glances, it wouldn't be easy. When the music stopped I could hear a woman two stools down, talking to her friend.

"That guy, right there...now that's yummy," said the blonde with the big liberty curls and high ponytail.

I glanced in her direction. She was pretty in a kind of dime-store-floozy, way. She wore a pink, pearl buttoned sweater that well-advertised her huge breasts, and a black pencil skirt that gave her a nice round ass. But the scarf tied around her neck that hung to the side, please. It was all a little too Sandy from Grease.

I watched her slip off the stool, "Okay," she told her friend, "if I give you the thumbs up, you're on your own."

A mousy little thing with big blue eyes under black curls said, "You're married, Ashley!"

"Don't be such a shoulder angel. What Darren doesn't know, won't ever hurt him," she smiled.

I watched her friend shake her head in disgust.

Being nonchalant, I turned my head like I was trying to see what the band was doing. I saw this Ashley person saunter up to Tyler, as I spun my head back to my drink.

I wondered if I should leave. It was obvious that he had followed me here hoping that I would see him flirting with another woman and lose my cool. I hated it when men worked overtime to try and prove their point. Just as I got ready to leave, a young man sat down beside me.

"May I buy you a drink?" he asked.

I turned my attention to him; blonde faux hawk, deep dark eyes, wearing a Stray Cats shirt, 501's and a big smile. He couldn't have been more than twenty-five years old.

I licked my lips as I looked down. A white gold band on the wedding finger of his left hand, made me smile.

"Absolutely," I told him, leaning my chin on my palm.

He ordered me a second round and asked, "So, you from around here?"

I smiled, "I am. You?" I asked.

"Just visiting. It's my cousin's bachelor party," he pointed to a group of men acting like drunken assholes. All of them had score cards that they held up for every woman who walked by.

I nodded, "Ah, fun crowd," I raised my brows. "So I see you're already married," I pointed to the ring.

"I am," he smiled. "She's the love of my life."

He was still talking, but I could feel…something. I could feel him…passing behind me. As Tyler walked past me on his way to the restroom, he looked back over his shoulder.

I went back to my conversation.

"That's why I can't stand to hang out with them," the man before me said. "They just don't care that they took vows."

"So, I have to ask; why would you buy a drink for a woman sitting alone at a bar?" I tilted my head.

"You looked almost as miserable as me," he shrugged. "Oh God, I hope I didn't offend you," his eyes showed me that clearly this wasn't his intention. "It's just…"

"No," I cut him off and smiled, "you didn't. In fact, I'd like to buy you a drink."

"Well, two is usually my limit," he nodded down at his empty glass, "but…what the heck! Thank you."

Me and this young man, whose name was Steve, sat for an hour as he told me all about his wife, and two little girls. On his phone, he showed me picture after picture of the loves of his life. My night wasn't turning out how I expected. But this Steve guy reminded me that there are good men out there, and that they're taken.

Soon enough, I had hit my limit and was ready to call it a night, kill or no kill. Saying goodnight to Steve, and wishing him well with the merry band of idiots, I headed for the back-door. The plan was to go home and sleep in my bed. I was already outside when I heard Steve calling after me.

"You forgot your purse," he said handing it to me. I thanked him then he started walking back toward the bar door. Just then, Tyler and tonight's bimbo, passed by Steve heading out into the alley.

"Oh hey, hi Lila," Tyler said to me with a wink. The pink scarf woman was draped over him like a cheap drunken suit. "Where'd your friend go?" he looked back at the closed door.

"Back to the bachelor party," I offered. "He's a happily married man," I smirked.

"You know this chick?" the blond piped up, clearly a few drunken steps behind the sober conversation.

"Yeah…she's a…old friend," Tyler had to hold the woman around the waist to keep her upright as she wobbled in her heels.

"Like I'm a friend," she tried to whisper to him in a seductive manner.

"Something like that," he told her.

"You two have a good night," I said, and turned to leave.

"You didn't really stick your dick in that, did you?" the drunken woman asked. "She's like…a 7…if that!" she laughed until she snorted.

I could feel his eyes on me as I walked away. I wouldn't give him the satisfaction of knowing that this woman, and I use the term loosely, bothered me in any way. Part of me even enjoyed the thought that he would have to feign his interest in her, until he could find a good kill spot. He wasn't really an *out in the open,* kind of guy. He probably already had a room and was luring her back there right now. Jealously tried to rear its ugly head. Would he fuck her first? I pushed the thought away and hailed a cab at the end of the next street.

It was still early when I arrived home, not yet would the carriage turn back into a pumpkin. I slipped off my hunting clothes and threw on a pair of booty shorts and tank top; my go-to comfort clothing.

Opening a bottle of red wine, I sunk into my couch and turned on the TV to try and drown out the thoughts I knew were manifesting.

"A '7'," I thought, "If that?" If I was a seven, what the hell did she think she was? I was toned, and tight. Gravity hadn't kicked my ass yet, or made me its bitch, I told myself. But if that's what he wants to stick his dick in, so be it. I had better things to do. This is what I told myself while I watched an infomercial for a 1,200.00 dollar vacuum cleaner.

I pulled my ass to my room after my third glass of wine. I figured those three plus the three Boilermakers I had at the bar, should make it possible to sleep in my bed without thoughts of him.

When I woke, I brewed a cup of coffee and retrieved the morning paper from my doorstep.

"Surprise-surprise," I said looking at the headline. The body of a woman had been found. As I read on, my brow furrowed. It was definitely the blond from the night before, but she had been killed behind the club in the alley. Also, she had been stabbed in the heart, not had her throat slit. This wasn't his M.O. at all. Was he shaking things up a bit? Had he just decided that one minute more with the drunken whore was too much to bear? I read on, *signs of sexual activity were present.* Not gonna lie…that stung a little. Shaking it off, I told myself, although our tryst had been fun…much needed…fucking mind blowing…(I shook my head to bring my thoughts back where they belonged), it was over now and I could resume being whoever the hell I was before I met him. This is what I had decided when my doorbell rang. 8am on a Sunday morning? It was either him, or the Jehovah Witness's started trying to convert very early these days.

Looking through the peephole, there he stood flowers in hand. For a moment I debated just walking back to the couch, but curiosity was gnawing away at my insides.

I opened the door and stared at him.

"Good morning," he said like I was being impolite by not starting a conversation.

"Good morning. Was there a problem with my rent check?" I knew it was catty, and petty, but I was having a hard time faking *happy*.

A forced smile pulled across his face, "Are you going to invite me in?" he held out the bundle of Stargazer Lilies.

Taking the flowers, I opened the door with a sigh, "Sure."

I had forgotten that I had left the newspaper on the table. I saw him raise a brow as he walked past the article. "Anything good in the paper today?" he asked as I went to put the flowers in a vase.

"Oh, haven't you read the paper?" I asked sarcastically.

"Actually I read it over breakfast," we stared at each other.

"Seems our friendly neighborhood slasher, has changed his M.O.," I faked another smile.

Tyler's brow furrowed, "Wait a minute…you don't think that was me, do you?"

I sighed, was he going to try to lie to me? I shook my head, "That IS the woman you were with, isn't it?"

He nodded, "Yeah, I was. But then her husband showed up and a huge scene erupted. Last thing I saw, was the two of them heading for the backdoor."

I wasn't sure I believed him and it showed all over my face.

"Look, right here," he pointed at the paper, "it says there were signs of sexual activity."

Funny, that was the part that made me make this face, I thought. "Yeah…I read it," I confirmed.

"Well then…wait! You don't really think I would have fucked HER, do you?"

"Well wasn't that kind of what you said you planned on doing?"

"I said no such thing. I asked you if it would bother you *IF* I did. Just because you made it painfully clear that you would not in fact be bothered, doesn't mean I would do it," he informed me.

"Is this the part where I'm supposed to say I know you better than that?" I gave him a palms-up.

"No. This is the part where you decide whether or not you will trust me, and my word, just enough to NOT make me *that guy* in your head," his face contorted with anger and frustration.

I took a deep breath, "You know I have trust issues," I reminded him.

"I know and I get it. But you are treating me like every other piece of shit you've ever known, ever met and that's not gonna work for me. And if you were going to be pissed if I slept with another woman, why can't you just say so? I get the whole *I don't need you,* attitude, you've got goin' on. I even respect it! But this I don't *WANT* you shit, is gonna get old," he warned.

I took a deep breath and tried to figure out what to say, what to do next. "So you didn't go to that club, latch on to that bimbo, in hopes that it would in fact, make me jealous?"

"Of course I did, I can admit that. But I had no intention of fucking her," he shook his head. "I was just gonna do…what I do. And for the record, you, and me, we both work the same way. She's supposed to think she's gonna get dick. So if it looked like she was going to, I was doing what I do, what we do, correctly."

There was some logic to this, even though I was trying desperately to find a reason why he was wrong.

"So…did you?" he asked.

"Did I what?" I asked as if I wasn't following his train of thought.

"Did you get jealous?" his eyes held mine.

This was so uncomfortable for me. Did I admit that I had, which I did. Or do I push him even further away, with my refusal to be honest with him, and with myself?

His brow lifted waiting for the answer.

"I'd think the trouble I'm having expressing the way I felt about the situation, should be telling," I shrugged.

"No," his eyes rounded. "I'm going to have to hear the words," his head nodded.

I stuck my tongue in my cheek, "Are you really this needy?" I asked.

"Are you really this infuriating?" he threw a question back at me.

I put my head back and sighed, "Okay…fine…I was a little…"

"A lot," he cut me off.

"A little," I repeated through a tightened jaw, "uncomfortable with the thought of you…fucking her."

"Oh, so close, but the word I'm looking for starts with a J," he grinned.

"You're enjoying the fuck out of this," I huffed.

"Little bit," he confirmed.

"Fine, fuck! I was jealous. Are you happy now?" I blurted out throwing my hands up in the air.

He smiled then, crossing the distance between us to take me in an embrace. "See, you didn't burst into flames or choke to death on the words…"

I was not a fan of emotions. And of all of them, jealously was the one I liked least. Jealously was a form of weakness in my opinion. And the thought of being *SEEN* as weak…was a prelude to a homicide…his.

He held me tight and I felt both content (which really bothered me), and a gnawing desire to run (which was more *me* on every level).

"This still doesn't change the fact that I'm not looking for, nor do I want, a relationship," I told him.

"I know, I know," he whispered in a soothing voice dripping with condescension.

I let out an irritated sigh, "How long are we gonna do this *holding* thing?"

"Just until you hold me back," he whispered again.

My upper lip, curled, into a snarl, "Fine," I said and wrapped my arms around him.

When he let me go, he had the satisfied look of *winning*. Little did he know, he shouldn't think of me as a prize. I was still just a beautifully wrapped box of socks.

"So what's on the agenda tonight?" he questioned.

I was confused and it showed, "I plan on ordering a pizza, watching *Despicable Me* and falling asleep on my couch."

Now he wore the confused face, "You're not hunting tonight?"

I shook my head.

"Why not?" his brow furrowed.

"Because I only hunt…when I feel like hunting. And I don't feel like hunting."

"So…it's not because I want to watch you hunt?" he asked for clarification.

I grinned, "No, it has nothing to do with you."

Tyler stayed a bit longer then said he had something to do for his father and asked if he could come back later.

I was already feeling the *run like hell,* rearing its ugly head. "How about a night to myself?" I asked.

"Sure," he never batted an eye and I was grateful for that.

This whole business of him asking me what my plans were, was just a little too much like…dating. We had a couple things in common, that's true enough. And both of those things brought me a much needed and enjoyable release. But the thought that we would *make plans, hangout,* that was just too weird.

As I made it through my day, dusting vacuuming and scrubbing my already immaculate home, I chastised myself for just how many times my thoughts traveled back to Tyler; the smell of him, the feeling of his hands on my body, that sexy spot on his low back, where I could feel his hips rocking…the spot that I had held onto for dear life as he pushed himself deep inside me.

"Dammit!" I yelled and threw the worn out cleaning sponge. Peeling off my scrubbing gloves, I sat on my couch with my head in my hands. What was happening to me?

I stared at the phone, almost *willing it* to ring. I knew there was a phone number on my new rental agreement. But was it the number for a rental company, or was it his number. I knew there was only one way to find out…and now I had to decide if I was sure I wanted to find out. Pulling on a skirt and a halter top, I decided I needed retail therapy…with a happy ending.

As I looked at all the shower massagers, priced from reasonable, to *it would be more cost effective to pick up some 'random' in a bar*, I read about what each one of them brought to the party.

One had three settings, including pulse. Another had ten different settings; pulse, vibrate, spray…the list went on and on. My eyes rounded, was I really going to try to convince myself that this thing could be an actual substitute for passionate fingertips pressed into my flesh, a warm mouth sucking on my nipples, a talented tongue working my happy spot. I hated the needing he had caused to run amuck in me. But I did prefer this option to arthritic fingers, I thought, as I looked down at the water massager in my hand.

Parking and scurrying up to my front door, I saw Tyler's Jeep pulling up with an A/C van behind him. What the hell was he doing here? What happened to my night alone? I wanted to put away my purchase before he entered my house. Wishing I had bought more than just the massager, I stashed the bag in the bathroom and closed the door.

"Hi," Tyler said, as I opened the door. "I'm really sorry about this but the A/C company got the unit in, and said it was either today, or next Friday. I hope you don't mind me telling them to go ahead and get it done?"

"No, that's fine," I answered as nonchalantly as possible.

"You okay?" he asked. "You seem a little…jumpy."

I hated him thinking he could *read me* in the slightest. I hated it even more that he was right. "I'm fine. I was just expecting some alone time. Ya know, to get some things done."

Tyler reiterated, "Once again, I'm sorry."

Forcing a smile, I said, "It's fine. Can I get you something to drink?"

"Actually, do you mind if I use your restroom?"

Staring at him I couldn't help but wonder how weird it would seem if I asked him to use the one at the gas station five blocks away. "Of course," I said, hoping that he wasn't nosey enough to go looking through the bag sitting next to the tub. The bag that contained my pathetic substitution for him.

I don't know why I was so uptight. Why should it matter if he found the shower massager? I mean, I'm a grown ass woman, and I'm allowed to satisfy my own needs. Then I realized that I didn't want him to know I had needs. I had given into my needing during our first meeting, but it had been over a year for me. I could justify having needs at that point. But, I had cast myself as a woman who wasn't controlled by her needs; at least not for extended periods of time. Now I was the woman who had been done, and done well, a few times, and was still out purchasing a pulsating friend with nine pleasure settings.

As I went back and forth about how I felt about my new awaking desires, I noticed he had been in the bathroom a long time. We weren't *there,* were we? Like in the couples zone where you are privy to each other's privy habits? I knew I wasn't. And if I had to do that, while he was here, I would go to the gas station!

After a bit, I heard the faucet go on for a moment, and then off. He washes his hands, I thought. I do like that in a man. When he stepped out of the restroom, he held my bag at his side. My eyes slit as he walked toward me, grinning.

"I hope you don't mind, but I went ahead and installed your shower massager." the devil in him, winked at me.

Not being sure what to say, I just gave my head a little shake. I refused to blush or show any signs of embarrassment.

Drawing closer, so close our bodies almost touched, his lips brushed my ear, "I'd give you almost anything…just to watch you use it."

His hot breath made all the hair on my body stand on end; a chill ran down my spine.

"And I'd give you everything else…if you'd let me help," he added.

"I don't need you to give me anything," I let him know.

Putting his fingertips to my jaw, he said, "I disagree."

I turned my head to face him, our lips so close, they momentarily grazed each other. Slowly I brought my fingertip to his mouth, tracing the line from top to bottom in a circle.

His tongue licked my finger as it moved across his bottom lip. "Are you going to kiss me?" his eyes held mine.

We stared for a moment longer, "No."

"Fine," he said as he moved my hand so he could press his lips to mine.

Pulling away slightly, our eyes locked again, mine never flinching. His hand moved up to the back of my neck, holding me. Whatever I had said, my eyes, my breathing, contradicted my words in every way.

Again he moved forward, his full lips, warm against mine as they met once, again. Softly kissing all around them, from Cupid's bow to my full bottom lip, our mouths barely touched. My nipples hardened and stood at full attention. Without thought, a low moan of approval escaped me. Slowly pulling his tongue across my lips, I felt mine part slightly.

"Tell me to stop…if that's what you want. Is that what you want?"

I considered what I wanted versus what I wanted to admit. My head shook ever so slightly, "*No.*" As he brought his lips closer to mine; our shared breath, excited me in every way. I knew…I wanted him. Melting into him; into his kiss, I gave myself away, again. His tongue met mine. The taste of him, was seduction. Then he did that one thing; the one he had done to my happy spot until she exploded. The one that would start my building of want, of need, anew. My mind went back to that moment. My legs shook uncontrollably. I remembered how I tried to slide away from him. How he had held open my quivering thighs and licked me clean, only to cause another gushing.

Down my neck, he kissed. My head fell back to give him full access to my go spot. Cupping my breast, his fingertips rolled and squeezed my nipple between them. The sensation of his touch, his kiss, shooting through my whole body, I felt the familiar warmth, felt myself swelling with a *needing* that needed to be met. Immediately wet and wanting, I could feel myself begin to pulsate.

I could hear the workers, heaving my new A/C unit onto the roof.

I knew what this moment had made of me; a yearning, needing wreck. Purely out of curiosity, I rubbed my palm across the engorged bulge in his pants.

"We're going to have to wait," I told him, breathlessly.

"Why?" he kept right on about his business. Which, at the moment, was me, and my rock hard nipples.

I pointed to the ceiling.

"Are you modest?" he grinned. "Afraid they may hear us?"

"No," I shook my head. "I'd just like to give you my full attention."

Hearing it put this way, Tyler nodded. "Can't fault you for that," he smiled and ran his hand between my legs. "Promise?" he petted over the top of my skirt.

"Promise what?" I asked, rubbing him in return. Our mouths so close to one another, they grazed as we spoke.

"Promise that you'll give me your full attention later," his hand slid under my skirt, in search of wetness. Finding her moist and ready, his finger slid between her folds, massaging.

I took in a deep breath, and tightened my grip on him.

"Promise," he repeated. His eyes burning into mine as he lightly circled my clit.

I hesitated just to see what he would do.

Sliding his hand further down, he pushed a finger inside me, "Promise."

I panted, my breath trembling, "Promise," I whispered.

As soon as he wouldn't make an enlarged spectacle of himself, Tyler headed outside to oversee the new A/C unit being installed. Little thought had been given to the fact that the installer would have to install the new thermostat inside the house. Being grateful that we wouldn't be pulled from our play to open the door, I stole glances at Tyler. Everything that had been put in motion was on the forefront of my brain. I couldn't stop thinking about his lips, his hands, everything he had to offer. I swallowed hard as my mouth watered with the thought of him.

The nice HVAC man stood in front of us telling us how this new thermostat worked. I nodded all the appropriate responses as every word was drowned out by my own thoughts, memories. Setting the thermostat to 72 degrees, the tech headed for the door.

As soon as the gentleman stepped outside, I pushed Tyler up against the closed door. Dropping to my knees, pulling apart the button-fly of his jeans, I didn't even let him take off his shoes. His bared ass pushed against the door, he moaned as my lips, my tongue wrapped around the head of his member.

His fingers curled into my hair just as the doorbell rang.

Looking up into his eyes, surprised but not stopping, he yelled out, "Who is it?"

The nice man who had installed the A/C unit, said, "I'm sorry, sir, I didn't get your signature."

I tried not to laugh as I swung with his turning body. Shifting positions, Tyler cracked the door, leaning his head and one arm, out, as I stayed crouched behind the door, sucking hard. Retrieving the clipboard, Tyler pulled his upper body back inside and signed as quickly as he could, while thrusting and trying to control his breathing.

Swirling my tongue around and around the tip, his breath came faster and faster, "Oh God," he said as he handed the clipboard back through the cracked door.

"Ugh, have a good day, sir," said the man.

Tyler had hit his limit of control, "Oh, God, yes!" he closed the door. Pulling me off my knees he said, "You're a bad girl!" he admonished playfully. "Bathroom now!" He shuffled me backward, trying not to trip over his jeans still wrapped around his ankles.

Turning on the shower, he then turned to me. Pulling off his shirt, then his shoes, he kicked his pants off onto the floor. "Undress…slowly," he said.

I raised a brow to him. So, I guess he's in control this time.

Watching him grip his swollen cock, I wanted it back in my mouth. I wanted to finish what I had started. But watching him, his hand moving up and down as he watched me undress, it was a lovely view.

I untied the belled knot holding up my skirt, and let it fall.

"Mmmm, no panties…just the way I like you," he chewed on his bottom lip.

Pulling my tank top off over my head, the hand working his cock moved slower, the strokes longer.

"This is how I see you…in my mind…when I jack off," he gave a low moan.

I smiled and bit into my own lip. The thought that he thought of me when he touched himself; that I was what *worked* for him, was one of the sexiest things I had ever heard.

"Do you have any idea…how many positions, how many rooms, how many times, I've had you, in my head?" his breathing increased.

Oh, if he only knew, I thought. I had become a finger-banging-wreck since the first night me met.

Standing there naked, my nipples hard, swelling in all the right places, he asked, "Will you touch yourself for me?"

I smiled coyly, "Where?" I asked, bringing my hands to my breast, slowly rubbing them. "Here?" I cupped them, rolling, and pinching my hard nipples between my fingertips.

His rubbing slowed, both of us just enjoying our view. Long strokes, up and down he worked, sucking his bottom lip the way he did when my cream touched him there.

"What about here?" my fingertips slid slowly down my breasts, curving around my ribs to follow the line of my stomach. I stopped as my fingers hit my mound. "Should I touch here?" I asked.

Tyler nodded.

"Tell me what you want," I held his gaze.

"I want to see how you touch yourself…when I'm not around. I want to watch…how you please yourself."

The thought; what I did to myself when I thought of him, was enough to make me moan out loud. Leaning myself back, my back against the wall, I pulled one foot up to rest on the sink. Giving him the full view, two fingers made the peace sign, sliding between *my lovely's* lips. Working, my fingers slid around my engorged pearl. Up and down, they moved in a V, trapping my clit between them as they squeezed. My eyes fell closed, savoring the sensation, the look of pure indulgence painted on my face.

His voice brought me back, my eyes slowly opened. "What are you thinking, right now?" he whispered.

A huge smile pulled at my cheeks, "I'm thinking about you… touching me like this," the speed of my finger-work, increased. "I think about your tongue…your head between my legs. That circle thing you do…the one that's sure to bring me there," my fingers began to circle as they acted out a delicious memory.

"Show me," he requested. "Closer," he dropped to his knees.

I nodded to him and slowly crossed the distance between us, I stood directly in front of him, spreading slightly for visual access to my hidden jewel. My fingers began to work again. My head fell back, as I allowed myself to be brought closer and closer to that point; the one that caused heaving breaths on the inhale, and rolling rhythmic grunts on the exhale.

He watched, so intently, his mouth watering. "Inside," he looked up into my eyes as he grabbed me by my hips. Sliding my legs further apart, he pulled me closer, so I could stand above his face.

I worked my fingers down again, sliding them back and forth from hood to pot. Dipping my middle finger inside, I moaned, as my thumb worked in circles on my clit.

Watching him, watching me, he had the look of hunger. Swallowing hard over and over, I knew his appetite was growing. Tyler was a true practitioner and lover of cunnilingus. Even if I hadn't had proof of this, I would have seen it in the way his mouth watered.

"Is that how you do it?" he asked.

I looked down at him and nodded slowly. "This is how I do it."

"What do you think about?" his hand slowed as his grip tightened around the shaft.

I smiled, reaching out to pull my fingertips across his lips, "Your mouth on me."

"Where," he asked in a whisper.

With my free hand, I drew his mouth to my breast.

Taking my nipple in his mouth, he began to suck, making my head roll back, thoroughly enjoying the line between pleasure and pain. His moan, the vibration of it on me as he sucked, drove me wild.

He was enjoying holding my gaze as his tongue swirled and lapped between long hard sucks. "Where else do you picture my mouth?"

I smiled, a moan escaping me as I looked down at my hand, fingers still working.

Sliding between my open legs, he rested his head back on the toilet lid. Watching my hands working, as I stood straddled above, I didn't have to wonder if he liked his view.

Grabbing my ass with both hands, his fingers kneaded into my flesh as his excitement doubled. My hips start to rock as I brought myself closer and closer. I could see the desire in his eyes, feel it in his increasing grip. His appetite for her, hit its breaking point.

Quickly he moved my hand and brought his mouth to my mound. Teetering a little with the jolt of being pulled to him, his lips disappeared between her lips. I steadied my palms on the toilet tank and held on for dear life as he licked with frenzy. I had already been so close, just watching him, thinking of him and what I knew he was going to do to me.

Staring down at him, feeling him, my legs began to shake. My breathing was shallow and quickened as he brought me there. His hands tightened around my hips, fingertips searing into my flesh. Those intense eyes; I wanted to grab him, to dig my fingers into his hair, pull his mouth harder against me. But in this position, I was merely a passenger along for a fucking blissful ride. As I came, my head rolled forward, my jaw dropped open. A moan, loud enough to shake walls, and wake the dead, escaped me again and again.

As I stood there, squirming, legs still vibrating from what he had done to me, he smiled, "Lay down," he pointed to the tub.

I grinned, thinking of how our rolls had changed. Both enticed and curious by where his sexual imagination would take me; take us, I obeyed his request. Had he thought about what he wanted to do to me, how he wanted to *have me*, while he was installing his less than comparable stand in? Had he pictured this moment in his head?

On my back, knees bent up and opened wide open, he sucked at his lower lip while he took in his view. Turning the massager to pulse, he aimed the steaming warm water at my toes.

I smiled, still lost in my own thoughts.

Slowly he pulled the stream upward; up the inside of my calf, to my knee. As he brought the spray up my inner thigh, I let out a delicious sound of approval. Skipping over my V, he moved the spray to just above my mound. The warmth ran down, tickling my pearl as it tricked. My hips instinctively tucked, from the sensitivity he had already gifted me. Up my stomach he crept, the water spray lightly raining down splashed droplets on my nipple. My whole body was becoming engaged once again, in this slow seduction. All my *needing* spots waiting to be hit with the pulsating action while he lit the rest of me on fire. It was like sweet torture, to feel the water teasing but not engaging. I writhed trying to catch the stream where I wanted to feel it, just to have him move it away with a devilish grin.

"What do you want?" he asked.

I moaned and writhed some more.

"Do you want it here?" he pulled the pulsating stream to my nipple.

The water finally hitting it in hard bursts, felt amazing. I nodded my approval.

Taking my other nipple in his mouth he sucked as I began to *want* again.

I could feel the water being slowly guided back down my body. Down my stomach to rest on my inner thigh, I arched again. It was so close to where I wanted it to be. He let the water stream down between my legs, tickling as it once again lapped my clit before being moved away. The sensation he manifested in me had become my addiction.

"Here," he leaned over to kiss my lips as he finally took aim at my pearl.

I moaned into his kiss. The pulse of the water: hitting my freshly swollen clit, again, and again, drove me wild. The warmth of the bursts, strong and steady, made my pelvis rock upward in search of the rapture she now demanded.

Tyler moved himself into another position. One hand held onto the massager, while the other slid a finger in and out of my slippery self. My eyes rolled back, my body shook, my hips pushed up, working for every feeling he offered me. Ah, how selfish she had become from his attention, the thought popped into my head momentarily.

But as impressive as it was, I knew the massager would never be a worthy adversary for him. But the way he used it, the way he watched, swallowing hard, licking his lips, while he aimed the pulsating water between my legs, would be a mind blowing memory I could indulge myself with anytime I wanted.

His fingers still deep inside, I emitted tiny moans with every tap of my G-spot until I could barely breathe. I could tell how excited he had become watching. But it wasn't working fast enough for his liking. Not nearly as fast as he could get me there. Shutting off the water, two of his fingers dove back inside, while his thumb circled and rubbed my jewel.

"You like it like this, don't you?" he asked.

"Yes," I whimpered the word.

"Tell me…what else can I do for you?"

It felt so good, he felt so good, as his fingertips double tapped deep inside. I had been so close and this was all I needed. Hearing him ask me what I wanted. Knowing he would do anything I wished. There again, "Ah, right there!" I turned my face to the wall of the tub. My eyes squeezed closed, praying he didn't move, or slow.

"Come for me," he whispered.

Make me, I thought. *Make me.* He had me, oh, I knew he had me. My legs slammed against the sides of the tub, as I wailed, "Fuck, baby! Fuck, Baby!" As my wild wail was reduced to tiny whimpers of pure delight, I let out a giggle.

"God, I…" Tyler stopped himself before he said the dreaded word; the one that had threatened to shut me down before. "Watching you come…it's the sexiest fucking thing…I've ever seen," he whispered. Leaning over, his hand gently moved my jaw, so he could kiss me long and deep. I melted into him. I was totally spent, exhausted, euphoric.

"I want to be inside you," he said. "I need to be inside you." His eyes burned with the fire he couldn't deny if he tried.

I nodded my approval, but I did hope he didn't expect my rubbery legs to hold me up, too long.

Pulling my wobbling self out of the tub with his assistance, he brought me down to my knees on the floor with him. Bending me into the downward dog position over the tub wall, he took a long lick of me, from stem to stern. Rubbing his cock back and forth around my slippery opening, teasing me, he asked, "Do you want me inside you?"

A moan escaped me.

"Do you want me inside you?" he asked again, needing confirmation.

Looking over my shoulder, the feeling of him tipping the hole, knowing how good he would feel, "I want you inside me. I want you, you…" he pushed the head in, halting my words as I waited for the next thrust that would bring him an inch deeper. I felt her struggle slightly against his girth. He slowed, working just the tip in and out as he waited for her to welcome him.

My breath was pushed from me as she gave a little more, and then a little more.

Again he pushed. Again she warmed for him, giving him entry. Inch by magnificent inch, he buried himself deep until our bodies were finally base to base. Slowly he began to pick up the pace. His hips slamming against my ass cheeks, I began to howl.

His body thrust into mine. My own, pushed back against his, wanting to feel him hard and deep inside me. He knew what I was asking for. My body pleading to be taken, fully. I pushed my hands against the shower wall for support as he slammed himself inside me. This was the hardest he had ever fucked me; more animal than anything I had ever experienced, and I was mad for it…for him.

Grabbing me by my shoulders, he pulled me back, harder, and faster, ramming his cock into me. There was pain…but it was mind blowing. My body jarred, over and over. My face, my lips, had gone numb from having my breath shortened between pants of pain and pleasure. Growling like a wild animal, he asked me where I wanted it. No words escaped my lips. I couldn't speak.

"I'm ready…now?" he asked.

I turned my head to see him; right there, on the edge, waiting for me to *okay*, his finale. "Now! NOW!" the sound that came out of me was broken and halting.

Pulling himself out of her tight warmth, I felt like I was finally able to take in a full breath. Squeezing my round ass cheeks tightly together around his cock, he thrust himself up and down between them. Roaring again, his juice released. Shooting all over my back and ass, he called out,. "You're a sweet fuck, Audra. You're my sweet fuck, baby."

As soon as he released his hands from my shoulders, I crumpled forward over the tub wall, panting until I could slow my breathing.

Grabbing the towel off the rack beside him, he wiped me clean. I turned my head just in time to see him fall back. Laying across my floor, he was trying to regain his own breath.

"I know you hate hearing it, and I am sorry in advance, but I cannot seriously just *LIKE* fucking you," he exhaled.

He was right; I hated hearing it, the L word. But I'd be a liar if I said I only *LIKED* fucking him, too. I was addicted: from the way he kissed, to the scent of him, to the way he felt in every part of my body. I hated the fact, as much as I loved the feeling.

Standing, I felt pain. It was the kind of pain you have when you can feel your insides. Letting out a tiny moan past my dry lips, he said, "Don't get me started."

"Aren't you spent?" my breathing still faster than normal. Wobbly and light headed, I said, "I feel like I've been pounded into submission."

A smile pulled across his face, "What can I say? You're a craving, unlike anything I've ever wanted."

Some part of me; a part I wasn't capable of admitting existed, wanted to believe him. Grinning to myself, I stepped over his body and went in search of water.

I had the second bottle open by the time Tyler peeled his body off the bathroom floor and walked into the kitchen.

"Can I have one of those?"

Walking to the fridge, I grabbed him a bottle of his own. Handing it to him, he searched my eyes, "You okay?"

I gave him a half grin, "Fine. Why?"

"I was just worried that maybe I…hurt you."

Was his ego attached to the question…a size thing, maybe? I couldn't believe that he had any insecurity in that department. "I'm fine," I repeated.

"You just…" he paused to rephrase the comment, "I get a little overzealous with you."

I bit my lower lip, remembering.

"And you," he continued, "you get silent afterward."

Laughing I asked, "What are we supposed to talk about? Neither of us has a job, and what we do have in common…," my brows raised.

Tyler's smile pulled up both of his cheeks.

"Our other hobby," I added, "is best left…unspoken."

"I bet we have a lot in common," his brow furrowed.

Skeptically I raised my brows back at him, "Like what?"

"Like…what kind of music, do you like?" he leaned against my counter.

"Jazz and Blues," I answered.

"Huh…anything else?"

I shook my head, "Not really. You?"

"More the stuff I grew up on, Grunge, Alternative."

"Huh," I returned.

"Favorite food?" he threw the question out there.

"Italian. You?"

"Mexican."

"We keep swinging at the ball," I laughed.

"You like baseball?" he sounded hopeful.

Shaking my head I answered, "Not even a little."

"Okay," he put his palms up, like he had finally found our groove. "If you could go anywhere in the world, where would you go?"

I had to laugh at his desperation of finding one thing. "Probably Colorado,"

"Do you ski?"

There was that hope in his voice, again. "Nope."

"Then why would you want to go to Colorado?" he wondered out loud.

"I love the snow and mountains. You?"

"Not a fan of snow, or cold, but I do like to ski. He changed gears, "I like to go to New Orleans during Marti Gras." Just saying this made him happy. I could see it on his face. "You ever been?"

My head shook.

"Have you ever wanted to go?" his brows rose.

I winced and continued shaking my head. "I can't stand crowds," I gave him a palms-up.

Tyler cocked his head, like he was trying to add me up.

"I think it's safe to say, we don't have a lot in common."

"Well," he pushed his fingers through his hair, "did you and your husband, have a lot in common?"

Just the mention of Derrick's previous existence made my body go ridged. I hated to even think of him. After a moment of remembering the music at our wedding, our vacation house in Big Bear, taking an Italian cooking course, I nodded. "Yeah, we did."

Tyler lifted his brows and his palms to me, "So…maybe it's not always a good thing?"

Slowly I began to nod. Tyler had plucked a cord in me; the one that said having things in common, didn't always equal happiness. The few things Derrick and I didn't have in common, were much harder for me to accept. Loyalty, honesty, worthiness. I was lost in this thought, until Tyler brought me back.

"I'm sorry. I wasn't trying to drudge up memories." His hand wrapped around mine. "I'd just like to get to know you a little better."

Warning signs flashed. I wasn't comfortable with the idea of letting anyone in; in my thoughts, or fears, dreams or hopes. These were mine. "I'll let you ask me one question."

"One?" his eyes rounded. "Wow, you won't make this easy will you?"

I couldn't blame him for asking this, either. But, I had been more than *easy* for him since the night we met. It may have given him a false sense of who I really am.

"I guess I better make it a good one?" Tyler gave a small

shake of his head. Thinking for a minute, he rolled questions around in his mind. I stood there, trying not to become impatient. As time passed, I began to worry about what I had agreed to answer.

Suddenly, his eyes turned to mine, "What's your favorite form of torture?."

I'll admit, if anyone else had asked me this question, I would have been wary to say the least. But we, he, and I, were the same animal. Staring into his dark blue eyes, twinkling with mischief, I knew exactly what it was. Biting into my bottom lip, I pondered whether I could reveal so much of myself to him. Finally, I decided to be brave, fearless, "You."

A tiny grin pulled up one cheek as he closed the short distance between us. Pushing my hair back from my face, cradling my jaw in his palms, he brought his lips to mine. I could tell by the way he kissed me. I had said too much. This kiss wasn't the ferocious attack I knew, craved even. This was slow, deep, and dripping with a beast I refused to name.

When he pulled back from our kiss, I didn't know where to go from there. Was he going to try and cuddle again, get mushy weird? Kissing usually led to sex, but right now, my insides were aching.

"You hungry?" he asked.

I hadn't given food any thought, but once he mentioned it, I began to nod.

"I know the best Italian restaurant in Florida," he grinned.

"Do I have to get dressed up?" I asked, my voice making it clear that this was a deal-breaker.

"Nope, it's a come-as-you-are kind of place. You may want to bring a sweater, though."

I weighed the appeal of a good Italian meal, to lying on the couch eating cheese and crackers. They both had their pros, in my book. "Okay," I nodded.

"Great, I'll pick you up in an hour," he smiled.

This confused me. Why would he ask if I was hungry, then expect me to wait an hour to go eat? I just said "okay." I figured I needed a shower, and possibly even a nap. Great sex is exhausting…who knew?

6

I submerged into the tub, letting the hot water do its best to relax my mind. But truthfully, I now had two places in my home that I couldn't keep myself from thinking of him. This realization did make me want to kill something; a cheating husband, or a bottle of Cabernet, either would work. How did I get here? I wondered. What were the odds that two people with the same rare and twisted pastime, would end up meeting? Divine intervention; I shook my head at the possibility that The Divine intervened for people like us. If there was a God, and I was still on the fence about his existence, I didn't think I would be held in his good graces. The more I pondered, the more I questioned our *CHANCE* meeting. He had known the serial killer, The Piano Man. Was there a chance that I had been on a *radar* of sorts…his? As soon as the thought presented itself, it was dismissed. I was a *nobody*. And not just in his world, but in the world at large.

Dressed and ready to go, I sat and watched a little TV, trying to separate my suspicions from my thought pattern.

When the bell rang, I answered the door. There he stood in

501's and a hoodie. Oddly enough he looked delicious dressed down. My paranoid thoughts that I had let run wild, disappeared somewhere in his smile.

"Do you have a sweater?" he asked.

Grabbing my sweater and purse, we headed to the Jeep. Driving up the coast, he pushed play on his CD player. Lena Horne began to sing, "I've Got a Right to Sing the Blues," forcing my brow to rise.

"Thought I'd give Jazz a try," he grinned.

Pulling off on a dark deserted dirt road leading down to the ocean, there was a clearing. He threw the Jeep in park and smiled.

"What are we doing here?" I questioned as he jumped out of the driver's seat.

The serial killer in me went on alert as he stepped to the back of his Jeep and popped the trunk. "Come on," he said.

Carrying a bundle of firewood, and a blanket, he headed toward the water.

By the time I made it down the little path of sand, he had already spread the blanket and was arranging the wood for a fire.

"Go ahead, take a seat," he said as he headed back to the jeep.

Watching him walk away, I wondered what the hell was happening. I agreed to dinner, not a date, and this felt…*date-ish*.

Coming back down the path, he had a second bundle of wood and a picnic basket.

"Best Italian restaurant in Florida, huh?" I asked.

"Actually," he said, unloading a bottle of wine and two glasses, "the food is from the best Italian restaurant in Florida."

"So why didn't we go to the restaurant?" I wondered out loud.

"Well," he handed me a glass of Chianti, "I wanted you to have the best meal in town."

I nodded, "Okay."

"But because this IS the best in town, it's also packed to the gills from the moment they open their doors, until they flip the *open* sign to *closed*."

I just stared, slowly cracking a grin.

"I know you don't like crowds," he winked.

"Ah, I gave you a few pieces of personal information and you're using them against me."

"I choose to think you gave a few pieces of personal information, and I'm using them to accommodate you," he explained.

I laughed out loud, "I'll give you that one. This is very accommodating. Thank you."

As he opened one of the metal *to-go* containers, he started me off with antipasto salad and garlic bread while he built a fire.

There wasn't a lot of idle chatter as we began the meal, but I was waiting for it.

At last, Tyler asked, "What's your favorite memory?"

I didn't want to answer questions about me; my thoughts, feelings. Especially since as of late, it was him and what he did with me, how he made my body feel. Exhausted, spent and content, being the words I would have used to describe our time together. Aside from him, I would have to crawl back through so many memories that were once happy, but now left a bitter taste in my mouth. I honestly wasn't even *happy* when I killed. It was more of a great release. It was sort of like an orgasm, without any emotions attached. It did the job on one level, but was completely devoid of another. I had been quiet for so long, Tyler looked worried that with this one question, he had shut me down completely.

"I'm sorry, I just…ya know…" he stammered. His blue eyes dropped to the ground.

"It's okay," I let out a deep breath. I knew he had done his research on me. I knew he had to know that I had lost both of my parents, far too young. And it was too painful for me to speak of them. I had lost my husband, and didn't wish to speak of him. The look on his face made me feel…if I had to guess, bad for him. After another moment, I said, "I do have a cherished memory. He shifted his body to give me his full attention. Before my husband died, I went to our cabin in Big Bear, alone. I wasn't sure how I'd feel about all the quiet. Having no one to speak to for days."

"Did it bother you?" he asked.

My brows lifted as my head began to shake, "No. I sat out on our third story patio…just relaxing in a rocking chair with a glass of wine. Then it started to snow." I could see the memory in my mind's eye. "On top of a mountain, surrounded by huge pine trees, I looked out from our cabin…down the winding road to the town below. It was beautiful, calm, serene. I finally acknowledged just how much I loved being alone."

"It didn't take any getting used to?" Tyler seemed confused as to whether he thought this was even possible.

"My husband had been slowly preparing me to be alone, for years," I admitted. I was ready to change the focus of this conversation. "What about you? What's a great memory of yours?"

He grinned at me, sucking on his lower lip.

"Something else."

Tyler laughed, "I'm going to say moving out on my own."

My brows rose, "Was this recent?"

"Pretty much. My father has always wanted to keep a tight

hold on me. He used to have a tight hold on both of us, but my brother passed away a little over a year ago."

I knew this, and wouldn't pretend like I didn't. "Your father rules with an iron fist?"

"More like his bank account. He told me if I wanted to move out, I was cut off. It was kind of his last ditch effort to keep me under his thumb."

"And you did it anyway? Wow."

"What wow?" he grinned.

"It's just a lot to give up," I said honestly.

"Freedom to be my own man, and be treated as an adult, is worth more to me."

Self-respect, honor, Independence. These qualities I respected. I was beginning to see him in a different light.

"Plus, it's not like I'd be broke without his money. Mom left my brother and me a healthy trust fund."

Okay so maybe he wasn't completely destitute without daddy. Still it was a lot of money to walk away from. Especially now that he was the sole heir.

"Truthfully, my father has always been a very loving man. But after my mother died, he became so overprotective of me and my brother. It bordered on controlling. Then when my brother passed…" Tyler shook his head. "He would never threaten to take his love away; he'd never say anything so heartless. So instead he went with the only other threat he could use as a bargaining tool. Unfortunately, he also raised his sons to believe that money wasn't everything," Tyler grinned. "It seems his desire to raise sons that were ethical, determined and self-sufficient, may have backfired."

I wondered if Tyler's conscience over killing cheating wives ever bothered him. Admittedly, my kills never weighed heavily on my mind.

It wasn't until after Derrick died (and I found out that even his own wife couldn't trust him), that I wondered what else he may have been involved in. He made quite a few steps above a good living. I never had to worry about finances. As he always said, "I got this!" Which was now the epitome of, "*Don't you worry your pretty little head about it.*"

I ate heartily; Chicken Parmesan, Fettuccini Alfredo, but Tyler's words lay heavy on my mind. This was exactly what I had tried to avoid by living as I always had; as an introvert. But now, I was starting to…feel something for him.

I caught myself wondering what his home life must have been like. The loss of his mother. The parade of step mothers, half, or even one third the age of his father. The divorces. Being well loved, but admittedly controlled. I wouldn't have expected someone like him to be so…grounded. Yet, I told myself, it was pretty early in the game to assume I knew all the plays.

"More wine?" he asked as the empty glass hovered halfway to my mouth.

Shaking my head a bit to bring me out of my thoughts, "Yes please," I said. I held out my empty glass for a refill.

"You seem to be lost in thought? Everything okay?" his brow furrowed.

Looking at him sidelong, I asked, "I'm trying to figure out what you want from me. Why you're trying to get closer to me. I'm not lying when I say I don't want a relationship. So what are you hoping will happen between us?"

He looked almost offended as his brow lifted, and his head shook, "Can't I just be fascinated by you? I mean, I don't know how long you've been," he stopped, trying to figure out how to phrase what I was, "…this way, or what clicked to make you who you are. But I've been alone, one foot in the light and the other in the dark, for long enough to know…we're a rare breed."

He spoke as if we were a different species from the rest of the world. I imagine it would feel that way for someone who had been raised in very social circles. My head cocked as I considered how difficult this must have been for him. *Constantly* being surrounded by people, yet not having even *one* soul, you could confide in? I at least had the luxury of anonymity.

"When I met you, looked down the barrel of your gun, I felt like we were kindred souls. Really," his eyes flashed. "Have you ever wondered what the chances were, that we would meet? Or…what about the fact that neither of us killed the other. Considering that's what we were there to do."

I had to admit…it wasn't like we collected Elvis memorabilia or hunted deer. Our commonality was probably the rarest of all hobbies. Well, except for those people who eat the people they kill, or wear their skin. I assume in the U.S., this was the rarest of the rare. Funny how a killer, such as I, can consider someone else's *kill* in poor taste.

I began to nod, "I have considered our meeting, not to mention the way it ended up…"

"Fate," he said, staring deep into my eyes.

I cracked a smile, "Yeah, I was leaning more toward a one in a million chance."

"Think about it," he shifted his body so that our crossed knees touched. "We have the same code. We only kill adulterers."

I nodded.

"Then there's that fact that we ARE both hunters, killers," his eyes bore into mine.

My eyes studied his; was it madness I saw there, or passion? "Okay, maybe a one in a billion chance."

Swallowing hard again, he looked like he was trying to decide whether or not, to tell me something. I hated that anything could pop out of his mouth at this point. But I also hated to stifle him any more than I already had. "Just say it," I finally told him.

"On my life," he started, "I swear, I've never met anyone who drives me like you do. It's in your scent." He looked baffled, and his head shook ever so slightly. "It's in the way your eyes make me want to tell you all my secrets. It's in the way you taste…the way your body fits mine. The thought of you, in any, and all capacities." he paused. "It starts a hunger…I can't explain."

I wanted to look away, but he caught my jaw and scooted his body even closer to mine. "You are not just a want for me, Audra. I feel you under my skin. In my veins. You are my need," he whispered. His eyes searched mine. I was afraid of what he would see there. Leaning in close, our lips met. He drew the breath from me that I had been holding since he started talking this way.

I wanted to pull away, tell him he was reading too much into *US*. I wanted to viciously cut any tie that binds. But, I too, had felt the pull. He created in me a stirring, a yearning that I found myself unable to explain, but also unable to deny. His scent, his smile, the anticipation of him, his touch, his kiss, the way his body felt inside of mine, it was all synergy.

He moved forward slowly, pressing his chest against me. Leaning me back, he lay his body on top of mine.

Silently we stared into each other's eyes. I had trusted before and it led me down a tortured path. I didn't want to do this, again. I didn't want to give myself freely, only to be discarded, abandoned. His eyes; I didn't want to believe what I saw there; what I felt. There was no humor present now. All joking aside; I saw his need. The thought scared the hell out of me, and I knew I couldn't hide it either. I knew he saw my truth. Suddenly he brought his lips to mine.

All the passion his kiss conveyed, all the needing, was returned to him in my kiss. As our desire drove us, I wanted to give myself up to this feeling, this belonging. But somewhere, in the back of my mind, fear reared her head. I could almost hear her whisper in my ear; *this one is going hurt.*

Our kiss slowed. His tongue met mine with a gentle mingling. It wasn't the urgent *needing* I had experienced with him before. This was almost timid; the way you approach something that can leave you bruised and beaten. He feared me, too. His hands didn't grope with the fury that had driven us in previous encounters; they caressed my body, my curves. My hands ran down his back, holding him close to me. I could feel his interest peaking between my legs, as his erection reacted to our fusing.

The sensation of our bodies, the way we fit together, it was undeniable. Pushing himself against my happy spot, his slow rhythmic grinding caused a *warmth* to dampen my panties. I couldn't deny it, and couldn't stop, as I began to grind myself up against him in slow unison. This was breeding a different kind of ache inside me. Our kiss was never ending. Over and over, our tongues twisted together. I had forgotten what this kind of kiss was like, too. This wasn't animalistic, with nothing more than a need to be sated. I felt more than my physical desire for him. I felt a connection that was deeper than the lust I knew we shared. I could feel him solid against me, as he tried to keep his body rocking slowly against mine. My legs instinctively wrapped around him, giving him full access to the spot that would bring me *there*. I felt the familiar building inside me as we made out like teenagers.

As my breathing increased, my mind was being drawn back to a time when this was the closest I'd allow myself to go. Back when I was still a scared virgin, experiencing my first impending orgasm. I was there again, wanting, pulsating. But no longer was I a frightened virgin, scared by my body's reaction. I knew what was coming. And I loved it. It was his kiss that was driving me there. And what I felt in his kiss, was pure ecstasy. His body arched so he could stare down into my eyes as I stood on the edge about to dive over.

Coming, I moaned again and again. Unlike the girl I had once been, I didn't stifle my moment of pleasure, embarrassed by my own excitement. Instead, I let him know just where he took me; how he, his kiss, his body, satisfied me.

Burying his head in my neck, I heard him *release* as he rubbed himself against me. His orgasm punctuated by the moaning of my name. I loved to hear my name fall from his lips, mingling with his bated breath.

When my senses returned, I buried my head in his neck and began to laugh from beneath him.

Laughing with me he said, "I cannot remember the last time I came in my jeans."

Now I wasn't as uncomfortable just lying there beneath him, as I had been. Even though this thought bounced around in my head a bit, I told myself that it wasn't comfort. it was just the afterglow that kept me from retreating to a neutral corner. Then just as I put away the fear of being intwined with another's body, he ruined my new attempt at a peaceful physical interaction.

"I'd like you to meet my father."

Feeling my body tense, I started to wiggle free from underneath him. "Why?" I asked.

Sensing my immediate retreat, he said, "He's having a thing at his house and I'm expected to attend."

I stared at him, searching for any response other than just *no*.

"I'm expected to be there," he repeated. "And I'm supposed to bring a date."

I continued to stare like he was speaking a foreign language.

"Look, I know how you feel about the whole relationship thing. And I promise you, this isn't where I'm going with this. I just don't want to spend the whole night with Mitzi and Bitsy attached to my hip." His head shook like the thought was just too much to bear.

I winced and bit my lower lip. My head beginning to shake a little, "I understand your predicament, I do. But I don't really *do* social events. I mean, I don't know if you've noticed," I gave him a palms-up, "I'm kind of a solitary person."

"I know, and I *do* get it, but it would be a huge favor."

I resisted the urge to say, "You're damn right, it would be!" I felt very put on the spot. I almost wished he would have given me a date for this…whatever it was, so I could say I was busy that night. But he *DID* know me well enough to know that I never had plans to do anything but hunt. I thought about this; what could I say? I'm washing my hair that night? I looked away from him as I tried to come up with something, anything. When I looked up, he was giving me the face.

"What is that?" I pointed to the look.

"Puppy dog eyes," he raised his palms.

"Don't do that," I informed him.

"Why, is it working?"

"No, it's creeping me out," my head rattled around.

"Come on," he pleaded. "Do this for me, and I'll owe you one. Whatever you want!"

As I rolled this thought around in my head, I began to stare off into space, thinking about what I could ask for. What I could want, that he hadn't already given me?

"Well?" he looked hopeful.

Reluctantly, I told him, "Fine. But, I reserve the right to ask for my *anything,* as you offered, until I see what kind of hell this turns out to be. Deal?"

Tyler's eyes slit as a grin pulled up one side of his face, "Deal," we shook hands.

.

7

Tucking myself in on the couch, I wondered just how bad this party could go. I had of course gone to several of Derrick's work parties. I had done the normal schmoozing that was required by the wives of firm members. But I willingly did these things as a good and dutiful wife. Now that I had no reason for forced conversations or interactions, the thought of doing so seemed like nothing more than an unnecessary reason to make myself uncomfortable. Then there was the fact that for all our romping, we knew very little about each other. Except for the shred of internet scanning I had done on Tyler and his family, I knew little. I didn't know if he had once had a long term relationship, if he rode horses, or had been a star athlete. I knew damn near nothing, except for our shared hobby (which I deemed unsuitable for dinner conversation), and the unexplainable infatuation we felt for one another.

Hopping out of my makeshift couch bed, I grabbed my laptop and searched Tyler's known past. Maybe this would give me some more input? Or at least help me answer basic questions that were sure to arise from catty women competing for his attention.

Scrolling through, he was almost predictable for a young man raised in an affluent family. Tyler played Polo and tennis, took fencing lessons, and enjoyed racing cars. He spent his sophomore year at the most prestigious school in France.

My mind immediately went to the thought of him speaking French while he took me. In my mind, this was sexy as hell. That was until I pictured him yelling out, *"Oui, oiu, oui."* I shook my head to clear the image that had suddenly lost all sex appeal.

I figured this was enough to get me through one night. All this *getting to know you* crap, was supposed to be reserved for *relationships,* which was already out of my comfort zone. But learning bits and pieces this way, seemed almost creepy. I had to wonder then, what the hell did the internet have to say about me, so I Googled myself.

The first thing that flashed on the screen was a picture of Derrick's car being raised from the shallow ravine that claimed his life, as well as the woman who had her head in his lap. The front of the car was smashed, blood splattered across the inside of the windshield. Staring at it, I tried to feel...anything. Nothing came, so I set the attempt at *feelings* aside.

There were other sites that claimed to have more information on me: lineage, birthday, places I had lived, arrest records (which of course, there were none). My whole life read as a tombstone. Just the basics, born and waiting to die. So, did Tyler have more information on me than this? And if so, how? Circling my discomfort level a second, and a third time, I put the laptop away and slept.

When my A/C kicked on at 7 am, I grinned realizing that I could do my normal routine. Pressing brew on my coffee maker,

I then went to retrieve the morning paper. Coffee in hand and very content with having my alone time, I opened the paper to see the headline:

LOCAL SOCALITE FOUND DEAD IN HER NAPALS HOME

Mitzi Gardner, of the Naples Gardeners,' was found dead this morning in her Naples home. Mitzi was 35 years old and engaged to Trey Maylin of Palm Beach Fl, the heir of the Maylin Corporation.

Mitzi's body was discovered early this morning by her maid. As of now, the details of her death are being withheld from the public. One detective did go on record, saying that Ms. Gardner's death has been ruled a homicide.

There was more about poor Mitzi; about her young life, family ties, schooling, and so on. My mind had gone somewhere else, though. Tyler. One of the reasons Tyler had vocalized for wanting me on his arm for this shindig, was to avoid spending the night, avoiding a woman named Mitzi.

I was sure that the *Mitzi,* who now lay on a slab at the morgue, was probably one of a few Mitzi's in the Naples area. Still, If she had been engaged, as good as married, and she was still trying to work her claws into Tyler, would he see that as unfaithful? For me, this line was a little blurry, I admitted. I knew that people changed their minds about their betrothed; broke-up, ran away. I guess in my mind, they weren't adulterers until the *I Dos'* were said. Were they cheaters, assholes, letches? Yes. But not true adulterers. Then again, I had to assume there were many different interpretations of the same code.

I knew the afternoon would get hot and muggy. It was still

early enough, that I decided to take a beach stroll and enjoy the sunshine while I could. My feet, burying themselves in the sand, was one of my favorite feelings. As I slipped off my sandals and walked the shoreline, I enjoyed the waves stretching out to splash my toes. Deep breaths of ocean air, was a form of meditation for me.

Walking up my street I wasn't as surprised as I wish I could have been to see Tyler's Jeep parked in front of my house. The memory of hiding in the bushes until he drove away entered my mind. The phrase *we are always one decision away from a completely different life*, rolled over and over in my head. What if we had never slept together, never hunted each other, never met? Hell, what if I had never moved to Florida?

When Tyler saw me, he jumped from the driver's side of the Jeep. Rushing around to the passenger door, he removed what looked like garment bags.

"You moving in?" I asked sarcastically.

"Are you asking me to?" he flashed that amazing smile I was sure had been kryptonite for many women and some victims.

"Nope," I smiled back.

"I brought some gowns I thought you might like to try on."

My brow furrowing, I asked, "Are you under the impression that I can't afford to buy my own gown?"

Tyler's head shook, "Why do some people look at a gift and search for the poison arrow? I'll never understand this flaw in human behavior."

This comment left my eyes round, "And now you're calling me flawed?"

Tyler cracked a grin that derailed my defensiveness. "I'm well aware of your ability to take care of yourself…financially… emotionally…mentally…"

My brow rose, "You forgot physically."

"Maybe so, but I bet having someone else do it, is way more satisfying than your shower massager."

Despite not wanting to, I laughed, "I'll give you that one."

Holding up the bags, he said, "These were my mother's gowns. I wondered if maybe you'd like to wear one of them?"

My face squished up at the thought, "No offense, but…" I wanted to tell him how creepy this was, without pointing out that the person who would think this was okay, was also on a different level of creepy than me.

"They've never been worn," his head shook. "She had lots of gowns gifted to her by some of the greatest designers ever known."

"Your dad…kept them?" I don't know why, but it plucked a string in my heart.

"Mom's suite has been left just as it was before she passed."

I had to admit, I was a little envious of his father's love for her. I almost wished that I had at least once in my life, been loved this way by someone; was the love of someone's life.

"Look, if it's too…weird, I'll understand, but you really need to see the Valentino."

As we headed inside the bungalow, I asked, "What makes you think your mother and I would wear the same size?"

"Because, she was also a ten with a size six frame."

At this, I had to smile.

As Tyler presented each gown one by one, my eyes popped a few times. He was correct, his mother had exquisite taste. And right again, I fell in love with the strapless, floor length, red Valentino.

Modeling the dress, which fit like it had been made for me, Tyler drew in a breath, his eyes warmed as I spun in a circle.

"You are so beautiful," he said with more than an ounce of awe.

Smiling at him, I knew I felt beautiful. "So when is this shindig?" I put my hands on my hips.

"Tonight," Tyler nodded.

"What? Why didn't you tell me this, last night?"

I figured if I gave you too much notice, you'd have time to come up with an excuse why you couldn't make it," he gave me his best shit-eating-grin.

My face squished up. I had to give him that one, too. I had already been working on how to make the *I have to wash my hair* excuse, seem vital, somehow.

"Will you wear the Valentino, then?" he asked.

I let out a long sigh, "Yes."

"I'll be here at 6pm to pick you up," he smiled and headed for the door.

Looking in the mirror I wondered out loud, "Should I wear a wig?" I cocked my head back and forth, contemplating.

"No," his head shook. "I like the real you, best."

8

The more I thought about tonight, the less excited I became. If Tyler didn't want to spend time with these people, his people according to his upbringing, why the hell would I?

But at 4pm, I put myself in the tub, shaved all the stuff that could be seen while dressed, including some stuff that couldn't. Clean and hair-free, I painted my toenails as close to the same color red as the dress I would be wearing. Slipping on my black strapless bra and panty set, complete with thigh highs and garter belt, I looked in the mirror. To me, I looked dangerous. Like I was going hunting. I knew the exquisitely designed Valentino, in its richest red, would go a long way to making me feel more elegant.

I did the smoky eye thing, but a little less bold than I usually would have for a night out hunting. Curling my black bob, I gave myself some height at the crown, and a little wave at the ends. Now for the finishing touch; lips lined and filled with a bold red.

Transferring what I needed from my purse into a little black clutch, all I had to do was slip on my four inch black heels, and I was ready to go.

When the doorbell rang, I had no idea what awaited me on the other side. Opening the door, there stood a driver.

He was a huge man. Not really tall, per say. We saw almost eye to eye. But what he lacked in height, he made up for in width. His bull-like shoulders, had almost consumed his neck. I'd guess him around late fifties, with full head of slicked back gray hair.

"Miss Murphy?" he said in a thick New York accent that made me cock my head. "I'm here to take you to the Whitmore Party." Seeing my coat wrapped around my arm he said, "May I?"

Handing it to him, I turned away so he could assist me. I was confused. Where was Tyler? So when I turned around, I asked, "Is Mr. Whitmore, Tyler Whitmore," I clarified, "in the car?"

"No ma'am, he sent me to pick you up."

"And you are?" I held out my hand.

"Simon," the man said, taking my hand in his.

In the back of the limo I went over our conversation. Tyler had definitely said *HE* would pick me up at six. I wasn't happy about the thought of entering this party alone, but I had agreed to go.

The driver called from the front seat, "Mr. Whitmore picked out some driving music for you…if you'd like."

My eyes slit, wondering what he thought could make up for his absence. "Sure, thank you, Simon."

"There's also a bar back there, if you'd like a drink," he said into the rearview mirror.

Finding the whiskey bottle, I poured myself a healthy double and sat back, seething pissed.

As Muddy Waters' *I Just Want to Make Love to You* began to play, one side of my mouth curved into a grin. "Bold choice," I said under my breath.

An hour on the road, I was sure the Valentino would be a wrinkled mess by the time we arrived at wherever the hell we were going. Just as I poured myself another whiskey, we pulled off the freeway.

"We should be there in another twenty minutes or so," Simon said.

By now, I had already heard the full Muddy Waters album, and was a quarter of the way through a B.B. King. If I had any patience left, it was ONLY from the expensive booze and good music.

Turning down a private lane, we passed through the open double security gate and pulled up behind a line of cars waiting to drop off their passengers.

Scooting across the seat toward the front of the limo, I leaned over the driver's seat to get a better look out of the windshield. Simon looked in my direction as I inspected the huge French Chateau style mansion.

It was impressive to say the least. Three stories high, built of stone. The windows were huge arches set symmetrically on each side, on each floor. The grounds: lush green grass and shaped hedges, surrounded a huge marble fountain of a woman dancing naked while looking to the stars.

"First time here?" Simon asked.

"Yeah," I said, less than thrilled. "You?" I looked at him.

"No ma'am, I'm Mr. Whitmore's private driver."

I nodded, looking back at the house we were slowly

approaching. "How did you get this detail; picking up Tyler's date an hour and more, away?"

His head turned to me, "He wouldn't trust anyone else to pick you up," he said matter-of-factly.

I wasn't sure what to make of this comment. Was I supposed to take this as a compliment? Did the driver? Or did Tyler think this man was persuasive enough to change my mind if I suddenly found that I had a pounding headache that would prevent me from attending the ball?

From three cars behind, I could see the open front doors of the Chateau, and two men taking coats and bags from the incoming guests.

"I'm kind of surprised they didn't postpone the party," I cocked my head at the driver. "I heard about Mitzi. She was a part of this circle, wasn't she?"

Simon stiffened a bit, "Well, yes she was, but Mr. Whitmore would never postpone this party."

I stayed silent, hoping this trick would work on him, the way it had on my therapist. Who, I assumed, was now in therapy, herself.

"You see," he continued, "today is the anniversary of Mrs. Whitmore's passing.

My brow furrowed a bit, I knew there had been several Mrs. Whitmores. But I only knew of one that had passed on: Tyler's mother, the first Mrs. Whitmore. "He must have really loved her," I said looking down at the dress I was wearing.

"Like no other," he confirmed. "Not any before…or any after."

I sat back and waited for the limo to pull to the front of the line where nice gentlemen in full tails assisted the women out of their cars.

It seemed odd to me, that if you loved someone so much, that you would celebrate the anniversary of their passing with a party. But I wasn't going to pretend that I had any idea how someone should act. Given the fact that I hadn't mourned the passing of my husband for even one second, clearly, I wasn't the one to decide what the proper reaction should be for anyone else.

As we pulled up to the red carpet, an attendant opened my door. I just sat there. It wasn't until the gentleman looked inside that Simon turned his head and asked me, "Is everything okay, Miss?"

I looked from the doorman to Simon, back to the front door. Blowing out a deep breath, "Yeah. Here I go."

Simon grinned at me, "You'll be fine, Miss. Have a good night."

I didn't understand this man comforting me. Did he sense my apprehension. Or was it the air of new money wafting off me that had alerted him to my level of discomfort. Either way, I gave him a smile before letting the attendant take my hand, and assist me from the limo. I noticed curious eyes turning my way. Throwing my shoulders back and lifting my jaw, I started up the stairs on the young man's arm. At the door he gave me a grin and a low bow. Another man rushed forward to take my coat as I glanced around at my surroundings.

The foyer was a large domed room with a huge walk-in closet to my left where all personal items of the guests would be stored. The marble floor stretched off down the long and wide hallway. Following the elderly couple who had arrived before me, I walked through a large sitting room.

Several paintings covered the vast walls with what I assumed were family members. I spied one of a younger Mr. Whitmore;

his arm around a beautiful even younger, young thing. Her hair was a chestnut brown with big curls. Her dark blue eyes were almond shaped, and fetching. Now I knew from which side of the family Tyler had received the eyes that had captivated me. Further along I walked, passing by a painting of the whole family: Mr. and Mrs., Tyler, and the older brother, who I would guess was to be about nine in this piece of work. Hard as I tried, I couldn't figure out who he looked like. Tyler had features of both of his parents. But his older brother; I could see a bit of his mother in him, I guess. I couldn't help but wonder if all these paintings had hung here for the following Mrs. Whitmores' to behold.

The two big arched wooden doors at the end of the large sitting room were opened as I approached. Looking down a massive flight of marble stairs at the ball room, packed with people dressed to the nines, was below. Chandeliers hung every twenty feet or so, across a seemingly endless ceiling. Immense paintings, circa 1700's-1800's, of people dressed in the finest frocks of the period, graced the walls. I wondered exactly what this room had seen in its heyday.

Standing on the landing, looking out at the sea of unknowns, I wondered where he was. At the far end of the room below, sitting as if on a throne, was Mr. Whitmore. He had to be eighty years old. People approached the sitting man as if he were a king. To his side, I spied Tyler bending to whisper something in his father's ear. As he stood, I saw him in all his delicious glory. The traditional black tuxedo, drew my eyes to his broad shoulders. I let my gaze be drawn down his V shaped torso, and lower. I knew the deliciousness that lay beneath the garment. His light brown hair had been pushed back away from his eyes, making them even more fetching.

Like a predator with his prey, his head rose. His eyes found me at once. His full focus, was me. I watched him take in a deep breath before placing his hand over his heart. The women who had surrounded him, turned their heads, following the direction of his gaze. He bent to whisper something in his father's ear, then stepped down off the dais, walking toward me. I let him get half way across the room, just watching him watching me, before I started down the staircase.

The immediate yearning he caused to stir inside me was both exciting and frightening. *I don't want this.* It was nothing more than a flicker of thought that disappeared as soon as he brought my hand to his lips.

He leaned in and whispered in my ear, "You look amazing."

"You just saw me in this gown a few hours ago," I pointed out.

"You're mistaken."

I looked at him questioningly.

"I've been picturing you in this gown, all day," he grinned.

With this, my lips curled into a grin.

Leaning in close again, his hot breath on my neck, "I've been picturing you out of it, as well." Oddly enough, I felt the heat of a blush warm my cheeks.

"Come, I'd like you to meet my father." He drew me forward by the hand through the sea of onlookers. A small crowd circled the man on the throne. He laughed gaily, enjoying being the center of attention. As I stepped onto the dais, Mr. Whitmore turned his attention to me.

I smiled as Tyler waited for the conversation to end so he could introduce me. But even as Mr. Whitmore listened to the conclusion of the other man's story, his eyes traveled to me. A look of shock spread across his face. He turned questioning eyes to Tyler.

Now my eyes darted to Tyler, wondering what I had done wrong: Was it the dress? Was he shocked to see the dress of his beloved deceased wife on some unknown woman? I now shared in Mr. Whitmore's discomfort. He had all but stopped listening to the man prattling on before him. Noticing, the older gentleman who had been talking, went mute. Now everyone's eyes followed Mr. Whitmore's…to me.

"Father," Tyler began, "this is Audra. Audra Murphy," he smiled at me.

But all his father could do was stare then repeat, "Murphy?" his eyes searched his son's.

Tyler gave his father a slow nod.

Coming back to himself, Mr. Whitmore stood and extended his hand, "You must forgive me. Your beauty…it knocked me off guard." His eyes seemed to soften. "Welcome to my home." Taking my hand in his, he brought it to his lips for a kiss.

"Thank you, sir. I am pleased to meet you," I said, finding my smile.

"And I, you," he gave a curt nod. "Please enjoy the evening," he motioned to a man carrying a tray of champagne and offered me a glass.

"Thank you," I said taking the flute in my hand.

"I'm going to introduce her around," Tyler told his father as he took my hand in his.

Moving away from his father, I asked Tyler, "Was it the dress?"

"It was," Tyler nodded. "Didn't I tell you…you look stunning?" he smiled.

There were people everywhere, dripping with diamonds and

attitude. I never felt uncomfortable around the rich. I had rubbed shoulders with them all too often before my husband died. Unlike some people, I didn't envy their money. The things that couldn't be bought always meant the most to me. My husband had been a materialist. At the time, I thought this was his only flaw. And it was one I could live with, just as easily as without. But it seemed that people from *old money* were a far different breed than the *nouveau riche*.

It was like I was being presented to a club that wasn't accepting new members at this time. Women looked down their noses at me. Even the few that managed to smile did it with a hint of venom; loathing or amusement.

The men…well…their reactions were a bit more varied. Some looked completely unimpressed by my existence. Others looked far too interested, wondering if I belonged there. Afterall, what would a man with everything in the palm of his hand, be doing with a woman like me? I couldn't fault anyone for that thought. I myself had once wondered the same. And still there was another group: a group that looked at me as if perhaps I was a trophy. One that could be won.

Taking me aside, Tyler whispered, "And now do you see…?"

I cocked my head, "What am I seeing?" I questioned.

He leaned in close, "Why you fascinate me."

Our eyes locked; there was that hunger again. I not only saw it, I felt it.

Grabbing my hand for a quick kiss, Tyler asked if I would be okay if he excused himself for a moment.

I had to grin, "I'll be fine," I assured him. The truth was, I didn't give a damn what these people thought of me.

As soon as he disappeared from my side, women began to flock. Some followed him as he cut through the crowd of ball gowns and tuxedos. Another group of mid twenty-something's, made their way over to me.

As three women approached, I offered the most genuine of smiles. They looked like triplets who weren't identical: Same long, flowing blonde hair, same height, same tanned skin, and over-done make-up….same nose.

"I see you've caught the eye of young Mr. Whitmore," said one of the women, whose young face and body looked pulled tight and sculpted by a surgeon's scalpel.

"Well…for the moment," her friend offered. All three laughed that throaty laugh that was better described as a guffaw.

"We didn't mean to offend," said #2. "It's just sometimes the men in out circle forget their upbringing, and go off to slum. Again, no offense," she forced a sticky smile.

One side of my cheeks pulled up into a cockeyes grin, and I gave a little shake of my head. "None taken. I am thoroughly enjoying my young Mr. Whitmore moment."

"Are you from around here?" clone number #3 asked.

"Los Angeles," I offered.

All three women exchanged amused looks, "That seems fitting," the first woman squished up her nose at me. I would just rather kill myself than have to admit something as trashy as being from Los Angeles."

I cocked my head, like something had caught my eye. Reaching out, I tried to wipe something from the tip of her nose.

"What are you doing?" she backed away, quickly, horrified that my peasant hand might touch her.

"Oh, I'm sorry, I thought you had a mascara smudge on your nose. The lighting in here is tricky," I smiled. But it's just a shadow…from that little wrinkle right there," I leaned in and pointed.

The other two women took in deep offended breaths as the first woman clasp a hand across her face to hide her flaw. As I turned and walked away from them, I heard the bashing of my character, begin.

I was never a fan of mean girls. Even if I weren't a complete introvert, I would never have been an asshole just because I could be. I watched from a few feet away as the women made their way to another group of women who were waiting to be offended by the ladies' interaction with me.

Tyler was coming back through the crowd. I felt his eyes on me long before I ever saw him approaching.

"Having fun," he asked raising his brow.

"Top shelf," I raised my champagne glass to him.

Amused by my response, he asked, "Will you dance with me?"

Looking around the huge room, I was suddenly aware that no one was dancing. I smiled, "Sure."

Setting down my glass, he led me onto the floor. One hand cupped my hip as his other brought me into a proper frame.

"Listen," Tyler said. "Listen to the words." One hand raised into the air, giving someone, somewhere, a cue. After a moment, a song began to play: Take Me to Church, by Hozier.

From the very first words, I began to grin. As he glided me slowly around and around in a proper Waltz, his eyes locked on mine. I knew this was something he meant for me to not just hear, but to understand. My heart began to pound hard as the words made me aware, captivated me.

Others moved from the floor, watching as we glided. The

acceptable distance between us, the frame of polite interaction, was lost as he pulled my body closer to his.

The chorus rang out, and he picked up our pace. The words hit me with a deep awareness. They conveyed everything I had been feeling, everything I couldn't explain. I was to be made aware, to understand, that everything I had tried not to feel, not to want, he felt as well. The wanting, and the needing. The passion, the desire to *worship* one another; everything the song revealed of his soul's drive, I found *living* in his dark blue eyes that never left mine. The burning was there. I felt it in every inch of my body. My own eyes sparked, as I envisioned his body, his hands, his mouth, using me as his idol. I would allow him to use me for his absolution, and penance alike. I would become the chalice for his thirst. And when I dropped to my knees, I knew I would praise him until I received every last drop he offered.

Others were watching, but somewhere in my mind, everything, everyone else, faded, like a picture with a blurred background.

When the music slowed, he brought me into a deep dip and held me there breathing harder than the dance could boast all the credit for. Drowning himself in my eyes, he searched for my understanding of what he was offering me. All he needed was one sign that I knew; that I too, *wanted* in this way. A slow nod of my head, gave him the confirmation he sought.

A sense of knowing pulled a smile across his face. Lifting me to a standing position, he leaned in and pressed a tender kiss to my lips. The chill that ran through my entire body felt more like a bolt of lightning that had started in my chest and branched its way through me.

As he led me off the dance floor, the looks we received were different now. Some of shock at our less than proper music, less than proper display. Others looked confused or even a little envious.

When Mr. Whitmore quickly stood from his throne, our attention was drawn to him. I couldn't even pretend to know what he was thinking as he beckoned Tyler forward with a curl of his fingers. He didn't look pleased.

Tyler nodded to him, then turned back to me, "Will you excuse me, again?" Still a little breathless, he said, "I won't be long," giving my hand a squeeze.

"Of course," I smiled. I found it odd that I did care what made Mr. Whitmore look so appalled. I could easily assume that this particular song had never been played at a Whitmore Ball. And even though our dance wasn't a typical waltz, it's wasn't exactly risqué, either. "I think I'll step outside and get some air," I said before he hurried off.

I watched as Tyler made his way to his father. Mr. Whitmore pointed to another room to have a private discussion with his son. Mr. Whitmore's eyes shot to me; cold, angry eyes.

Taking a deep breath I turned and made my escape to the back patio, as tongues wagged behind cupped hands.

Stepping onto the rounded patio surrounded by beautiful urns of blooming flowers, and four two person marble benches set in a half moon pattern, I took a breath of fresh air. The full moon was just rising and stars were having trouble trying to outshine her glow just to be seen.

As I turned, a handsome man approached. He was tall and trim, with blonde slicked back hair and a grin that screamed cocky. Pulling a gold case from his inside breast pocket, he retrieved a cigarette and put it to his lips. Without a word, he offered one to me as he closed the distance between us.

"Thank you," I said as I reached into the case. Putting the cigarette to my lips, he reached out his lighter, igniting the flame.

"My name is Daniel Gaines," he offered.

"I blew out a plume of smoke before I extended my hand, "Nice to meet you, I'm Audra…"

He cut me off, "Audra Murphy," his brow rose.

I couldn't tell why he wore a smirk. Was it my last name? Was it the fact that Murphy wasn't an affluent family name from old money?

"I'm sorry, have we met?" I knew the question was ridiculous, given the fact that the men I had met, well, most of them, I had killed.

"We've never had the pleasure…but I know all about you," he pushed smoke from his lungs.

"Do you?" I cocked my head, intrigued by his comment.

"Well, what I need to know," he smirked.

"Pray tell," I took another drag of my cigarette.

"Well, you're Tyler's new toy," he eyed me waiting for some reaction he wouldn't receive.

"Am I?" I grinned.

"I will admit though, I think you're my favorite as of yet," he licked his lips as he scanned my body, "and the Valentino…a nice touch."

"Oh, do you like it?" I stared at him, my hands moving slowly down the sides of my body.

"*Mmm,*" his eyes warmed as he began to nod, slowly.

"Well, maybe when I'm done using it, Tyler will let you borrow it?"

"See, I was thinking something along those lines, as well," he moved closer into my personal space.

"Were you?" my eyes slit.

He nodded again, eye fucking every part of me.

"Tell me…what are you thinking?"

Moving in close enough to whisper in my ear, he said, "I was hoping…Tyler might let me have you…when he's done. We are very old friends, he and I." He reached out his hand, slowly grazing the curve of my breast with his fingertips.

I chuckled, looking down at his ringed wedding finger, "I'm afraid that I'm really not that kind of woman," I said as I slid away from his touch.

His stare turned to stone, "I hope you aren't under the erroneous notion that you mean anything to him. I do so hate to see a woman who is obviously intelligent in her own right, her own world…not realize that she's completely out of her league, with this one. You are nothing more than a game to him, Audra."

"Oh," I nodded, "so your recommendation is to…?"

"I say ride it out…until he loses interest…and then…," he moved in close to whisper in my ear, "…let someone else fill your…*emptiness*," he hissed. "He'll never *CHOOSE* you, Miss Murphy," Daniel said with absolute certainty.

Just then, Tyler stepped out onto the patio. His head cocked, as Daniel moved quickly out of my personal space.

"Daniel, nice to see you," Tyler said walking to my side, and wrapping his arm around me, "I see you've met Audra?"

"I have," he nodded to me. "We've been having a delightful conversation, haven't we?"

"Delightful," I agreed through a tightened jaw.

"Again, nice to meet you," he brought my hand to his lips for a kiss that made my stomach turn. "Tyler, I'll be seeing you at the club. Now if the two of you will excuse me, I must be getting back to my wife. After the show you two put on, she'll want me to parade her around the dance floor, I'm sure," Daniel exited the patio.

Tyler reached for my cigarette and took a drag before handing it back to me. "Everything okay?".

"I'm fine," I looked at him sidelong. "Everything okay with you?"

"Fine," he nodded, avoiding my eyes.

"Really? Your father didn't look any too pleased with our dance. At least I choose to think it was the dance."

Tyler gave a deep sigh, "My father likes to keep his circle…small."

"Small," I smirked and nodded my head, "And I assume there's no room for a woman without social standing or pedigree. I mean, you can dress a woman in Valentino, but she's still nothing more than a well-dressed pauper, right?"

"To some, maybe," his eyes flashed.

"Why did you bring me here?".

We stared at each other while an elderly couple slowly made their way out onto the patio.

Grabbing the cigarette from my fingers, he pitched it into an ashcan before taking my arm and leading me past them. Down a long hallway, he hurried me, before escorting me into a darkened room. When he turned on the light, we were in a huge study.

Mahogany bookshelves lined two walls. Two wingback leather bound chairs faced a massive fireplace. Behind them sat an oversized desk sitting on top of an even larger oriental rug. Tyler motioned to the couch against the far wall.

I'd rather stand," I said, walking over to lean myself against the desk.

"Fine," he nodded curtly.

For a moment, neither of us said a word. He seemed to be gathering his thoughts on the last question I had asked him; *"Why did you bring me here?"*

Finally taking a deep breath he said, "I brought you here so you could see *why*."

"Why what, exactly?" I shook my head.

He stayed silent.

"I didn't ask for this," I began. "In fact, I told you…from the beginning…I wasn't asking you for anything! Didn't want anything from you!" my head shook harder. "If you knew how others would see me, treat me…how your father was going to see me…" my eyes rounded, "why did you put me through all of this nonsense?"

His eyes flashed hot as a white flame as he crossed the room to where I stood, "You think I care how *they* see you…what *they* think of you? That dance…that song…" his head shook madly, "didn't you understand it?"

My eyes narrowed, admittedly not understanding what that song had to do with anyone else, or their perceptions. Why he had chosen here, now, to express himself?

"I was *presenting* you to them. *ALL* of them! My father included!"

"As what?" I fumed, "Your favorite plaything?"

Tyler's face contorted, he looked pained by the insinuation I had hurled at him. Closing the last bit of distance between us, he grabbed me by the arms and stared down into my angered face.

"I was presenting you…as *mine*. *You* are who I want. *You* are who I choose!" he swallowed. His eyes bore into mine. His breathing increasing from the icing-over he was watching form in them. Shaking his head, he said "No!" before kissing me hard.

My head cocking back, I flared, "What if I don't *want* you to choose me?" His eyes seared into mine, searching for the truth. I knew what he would see there, what I couldn't hide. But still, I was scared; wounded.

As I tried to make my face, my eyes, my body seem unreceptive to him, his head began to shake, "Don't do this!"

I tried to pull away. I wanted to pull myself back from him, and the spell he had cast over me. But he held tighter. I wanted to fight it, if only to prove that my feelings for him weren't exactly what I feared they had become. The rush of emotions, my need, I felt it. I tried to look away as pools began to well in my eyes. I knew what he stirred was drowning me inside. He had melted the ice in my veins, giving him access to my froze over heart.

Lifting my chin, he said, "Look at me, Audra!" A tear fell as I met his frightened eyes with my own. Wiping the tear from my cheek with his fingertip, he repeated his plea, "Don't do this," he whispered. "Don't pull away from me!"

I could see it there, in his eyes. I saw fear. Real and raw, it presented itself to me. Swallowing hard, he tried to read my thoughts and feelings. What was he seeing there, through the gateway to my soul? I could feel myself crumbling as my gaze dropped to the floor.

"No," his head began to shake. Raising my chin, forcing me to see him as he threatened to crumble with me, he whispered, "I need you. I need you!" his lips crashed into mine.

As the sweetness of his mouth filled mine, I knew, I needed him too. There was no use fighting it. His kiss would overpower me. Hold me captive, just as it had since we first met. My arms circled his neck, allowing myself to be devoured. My inner struggle was between what I wanted most, with my whole body and soul, and what I feared more than anything. But my fear was being cast aside by his yearning…as well as my own.

Tyler's arms encircled my waist, pulling me so close, so tight I could feel his heart beating against me.

"I need you," he said again.

"I want you," I whispered, frightened by how the meaning behind these words, speaking them out loud, would change me. They had to.

His body relaxed, knowing that I had just offered my surrender. Reaching down, he gathered and pulled the skirt of the Valentino up over my hips. Grabbing me under my ass cheeks, he lifted me unto the desk. I thrust my fingers into his hair, pulling him back into my kiss, as he worked frantically at his zipper. My legs encircled his waist, wanting him more now than ever before.

Grasping his erection in one hand, he pulled my little black panties aside with the other.

I leaned back a little, while holding on tight around his neck, bracing myself for the pleasure I knew was coming.

As he pushed inside me, he grunted out a breath at the resistance she offered him. Pushing again, my eyes fell closed, my head fell back. He didn't wait for her to welcome him. Inching his way inside her by sheer force, he took full control of his need to fill her space completely, to claim me, as his.

He lay my body down across the desk. Raising my legs onto his shoulders, he seized my hips, pulling my ass just to the edge. Thrusting again and again, the head of his cock forcing its way into me, repeatedly. He groaned, "I need to feel all of you. I need to be deep inside."

The pleasure of the pain, the look on his face, the words he spoke, made my body react. I could feel her *warm* for him. Soon his ridged pushes were welcomed by the wetted desire he fueled in me. Our eyes fixed on each other, it was there. I saw it in his eyes, it was there. Surely he had gone mad with desire to claim me as his. This thought made me swell. Finally I felt the base of him as his body slammed against mine.

Every inch of him felt like a gift. My eyes closed as my breath came faster.

"Tell me," his request no more than a breathless whisper.

My lips parted, but no words were spoken as I panted. I bit into my lower lip, wondering if I could.

He repeated his request with more need, "Tell me, Audra… tell me you're mine!"

I panted harder and faster, driven forward by all the feelings and emotions he had awakened in me. I wanted to, more than anything…I want to, I told myself.

"Tell me," he growled, knowing how close he had brought me, "Tell me you're mine!"

His repeated request becoming a demand of his needs; the needing he knew I shared. Finally, I let out an uncontrollable wail, as I took the dive. I could feel my pussy begin to contract around him, pulsating. Crying out, my voice quavering, "I'm yours… I'm yours… I'm yours," my whole body shuddered and convulsed while he watched me release…everything.

Hearing my words, the look on his face changed from one of uncertainty to one of absolute *knowing*. He pulled me up into his arms, holding me tight against him, his lips found mine. Passionately, we kissed through the euphoria of his ejaculation. His explosion, so hard, so deep inside of me, I whimpered as I felt him filling me.

Dizzied, I lay back across the desk with Tyler coming down on top of me. Burying his head in my neck, he tried to regain his breath. Dropping his head to my breast, I felt as though he would be able to see my heart threatening to burst from my chest.

I lay beneath him, sated in every way, when a low snap drew my attention. Turning my head toward the cracked door, I spied Daniel lighting a cigarette. His stare was cold, and hard as my lips pulled up into a wicked grin.

"You're mine," Tyler repeated over, and over again, as he placed innumerable kisses on my neck and chest.

Never looking away from Daniel, I confirmed one more time just in case he had missed the grand finale, "I'm yours, Tyler. I'm yours."

As Daniel disappeared into the darkness, Tyler brought his lips to mine, soft and sweet. "Let's get out of here,"

"Don't you want to stay for the rest of the ball?"

Smiling he answered without hesitation, "No."

9

On the long drive back to my house, he reached across his center console to take my hand in his. "I saw you speaking to some of the ladies…"

You mean the Stepford Wives?"

"Yeah, them," he laughed. "How did that go? Or should I even ask?"

"Let's just say I'm sure I made a lasting impression," I gave his hand a squeeze

I still couldn't help feeling the gnawing of doubt trying to rise in me; why had he pursued me so? I made it clear that I wasn't looking for, didn't want a relationship. I guess the mixed signals from my open legs, could have played against my words. We still knew so little about each other though. Maybe we would get to know each other, then decide against this whole *mine* thing. I wasn't an impulsive creature. Everything I did had to be well planned. How had he snuck under my radar?

Then there was Daniel. He spelled it out for me; *he'll never choose you*. What if this WAS a game for Tyler? Just bending me to his will. He could make me want him, crave him, just to abandon me later. But, I did know something his rich shoulder-rubbers didn't. He and I, we were of the same breed, enjoyed the same pastime. One, I'm sure, no one else would ever understand.

Tyler broke me from my thoughts, "Can I ask you a question?"

"Oh God, I hate that question," I said.

"You don't even know what I'm going to ask," he laughed.

"No, I mean the *can I ask you a question*, question," I shook my head. "No one ever knows what they're agreeing to talk about when someone asks this of them."

Tyler nodded, "Good point. I'll just ask and you can decide if you'll tell me, or choose not to answer."

I let out a sigh, "Okay, hit me with it!"

"When did you start hunting?" Tyler asked seriously.

I knew one day we'd talk about it: my breaking point, when I shattered. I sat mute long enough to make Tyler wonder if this was one of those things I wouldn't talk about.

"When my husband died," I began. "I found out in a horrifying way that he had been cheating on me. In fact, the act of cheating directly led to his death."

Tyler nodded, keeping his eyes on the road.

"I was living inside the world he had created for me. A world that made me into the woman I was. What I thought, what I felt, what I believed, what I was completely certain of…it wasn't real. None of it was real. In one moment, my house of cards, came tumbling down."

"So…that's when you were born?"

I had never heard it put this way. But as I rolled the wording around in my head, I began to nod, "Yes."

"So, was your first kill here in Florida?"

"Yes," I confirmed. "What about you?" I figured tit for tat.

"Mine started much younger and all of them were here."

I had had a question stirring that I wanted to ask, so I did. "I heard about Mitzi. Was she…one of yours?" I asked.

"No," his head shook. "I know better than to hunt in my circle, even though many of them may be *more than deserving*, according to my code. Plus, Mitzi wasn't married."

I was oddly relieved to hear Mitzi hadn't been one his. That would have meant our codes were slightly skewed and could have caused a moral dilemma for me. But that Daniel guy? He fit my code. And, I wasn't a part of his circle, as he so enjoyed pointing out. My gun would be too quick for the death I wanted him to experience.

Even though it made me a little uptight to speak so openly about things better left in the dark quiet room inside myself, it was nice knowing I *COULD* discuss these things without judgment. Doesn't everyone hope to find someone they can be real with, unguarded?

"Is this, tonight, going to change things between you and your father?" I asked.

His dark blue eyes shot to mine, "Unlikely. But you asked the wrong question."

"I did?" my brow rose.

"You should have asked if I care what anyone else thinks. I don't," he squeezed my hand again. "My father wishes for my happiness."

The rest of the drive was quiet. I just enjoyed the view of the moon and stars, the feeling of Tyler's hand in mine. As we pulled up in front of the house, I wondered if I was supposed to ask him inside. This was the part I disliked about our shifted roles with each other. Not knowing what to do. Just a week ago I would have waved goodbye to him from my front door. Now I wondered what being *his* meant. How did this change…everything?

Pulling open the passenger door, Tyler reached out for my hand. The smile he wore, one of pure calm, contentment. He wasn't feeling what I was. Walking me to the front door, I struggled with the thought again; do I invite him in?

Pushing my door open, he put his hand on the curve of my back, gently moving me inside, with him following closely ay my heels.

I don't know why I was so nervous. It was like this small shift in the way we thought of each other made me self-conscious. Now, all the sudden, I was afraid to make the wrong move, say the wrong thing.

Tyler wrapped an arm around my waist, pulling my body backward against his and squeezed me. I let out a contented sigh as he put warm kisses on my bare shoulder. Moving his way up my neck, my flesh rose.

Turning my body to face him, he cupped my face and drew me into the kiss that had on many occasions made me forget I had boundaries. Melting into him, the feeling of his lips on mine; so warm and sweet as he stroked my tongue with his. I couldn't tell which of his kisses drove me deeper: the frenzied kiss of needing, or the passionate kiss of wanting.

"Bedroom?" he asked smiling into my eyes.

I grinned and whispered, "Do you want to fuck me, Tyler?"

His head shook slightly, "No."

As our lips met again, he walked me backward into my bedroom.

His hand rose to caress my cheek. My eyes drew closed, enjoying the sensation of his touch, his palm following my jaw line slowly. My lips parted as he traced them with his thumb.

Cupping lightly, his hand moved down my neck, inch by inch, coming to rest over my heart. Opening my eyes, he was staring down into them, just watching my reaction, my body's reaction to him. Every hair stood on end. Chills hardened some parts, while warming others. Every part of me enjoyed his attention.

Circling me, his warm breath on the back of my neck, drew out a low moan. Placing puckered lips to my bared shoulder, fired off another round of chills. I felt the Valentino's zipper being pulled slowly down. Tyler's hands followed the curves of my body, my hips, making the dress fall to the floor.

Wrapping his arms around me, he pulled me back into him and held me there for a moment, just breathing together. I hadn't been this content in...I couldn't remember how long. I could feel his body solid against mine, hard and strong. Bending down to pull me up into a cradle, he lifted me into his arms, walking me to the bed.

My eyes softened, watching him unbutton his tuxedo shirt. I knew what lay beneath the expensive clothes and my mouth began to water at the sight of his bare chest. Releasing his zipper, I grinned as his pants fell. He was so beautiful to behold; every inch of him.

Moving to where I lay, he touched my face again before leaning in to softly kiss me. My arms circled his neck; just craving his kiss. This was a whole other feeling. One I didn't remember.

Sliding my panties off, he took his time running his hand back up my leg, just caressing every inch of me. He put one kiss above the mound between my legs. Another kiss was placed just above the last. His warm lips ran the rest of the way up my body, not concentrating on any of my go spots, but following my midline until meeting my mouth again.

Resting his body down on top of mine, my hands slid down his sides, wrapping their way around him. Holding someone had become a foreign thought for me. But now, I craved the feeling of his weight on top of me, his arms around me.

My fingertips slid down his muscular back, as I kissed the soft skin of his neck. Tyler let out a low sigh of approval before moving his mouth back to mine. I wanted him, but in a different way now. This was the kind of wanting I didn't think I was capable of anymore; the one I had feared. The kind of wanting that wasn't just propelled by the body's desire. This was deeper. I could see it in his eyes.

Bringing my arms over my head, he interlocked his fingers with mine, our palms pushed against each other. His hands were burning hot, his energy radiating from them.

My legs fell open, giving him the access we both wanted. I could feel myself moisten around the tip of his cock, like a wet kiss. Working the head of him in, my eyes fell closed, just enjoying the sensation he gave me. He felt so amazing. Pressing himself further into me, he let out a pleased *"Mmm."* His breathing was deep and slowed. Propelling himself further, he pushed to the end of me, his body fused against mine.

Moaning blissfully, Tyler knew he was right where I wanted him. Raising his devilish grin to me, he bore in again, making my breath quiver as it escaped my body. Seeing the way he looked at me while he pushed his body against my favorite spot, it was full of his hunger to see me sated. He would do anything to bring me there, to gift me this. This knowing multiplied my own appetite to bring him there with me.

Whispering, he said, "I am yours, Audra."

I knew this. I felt it in every look, every touch, every kiss.

My body worked with his, grinding my pussy down his shaft from underneath.

I felt the tickle of my orgasm building, but it wasn't just physical. I felt emotions, running wild in me, mingling with the pleasure he brought. Something I hadn't felt in years. Maybe not ever, not like this. The connection I had with him…the belonging, scared me, then faded away like a shooting star. My moan wasn't one of bated breath, but one of an intense emotional purification.

"I'm yours, Tyler," I whispered in his ear.

Pulling his head up to look into my eyes, his face revealed the *knowing* he had hoped to find. He understood what these words meant to me…to us. He pushed again, watching my slow, beautiful escalation, feeding his own. Our shared bliss, mounting, "Come with me," he requested.

Pulling me to the edge with him, my hands tightened in his, my legs began to shake. I felt myself going over as I emitted low, soft moans of pure ecstasy. The only thing better than feeling my own release, was feeling him release at the same moment. He pushed so hard against my body, so deep, he felt like a part of me. I felt his gush flowing with mine.

Holding him in my arms, listening to each other's contented exhales, we enjoyed the euphoria. The weight of his body was so welcome, as I ran my fingertips down his spine. A while passed before he rolled his body off mine and he pulled me into the nook of his arm. Holding me tight; my head lying on his chest, he squeezed me closer. I was certain I had never felt this way before.

Putting a soft kiss on my forehead, he said softly, "I will *NEVER* fuck you again, Audra."

I swallowed hard. With that one declaration, I felt my

stomach drop, my eyes began to burn. I squeezed him tight, but didn't know how to respond. Finally, I said quietly, "Please don't say that," my head shook slightly. I knew he didn't understand why I said this, why his comment had caused me to go ridged. And I didn't want to explain that my husband had chosen to take a mistress in some small part, because he couldn't fuck his wife.

For a while we just stayed there, my body curled against his as he petted me. I had that feeling...that I needed to say something, but I couldn't. I was going over the way we met, the desire I once had to never feel *everything* I now felt. How had it changed so quickly? What if...his saying this was his way of saying he saw me as...more; that we shared something deeper. Had I just pushed him away without thinking, without trying? He had been able to fuck me, and he fucked me well. I had to face the fact that if I let old fears, old scars, rule the way I thought and responded to him, I would ruin everything, before it even started. My husband was dead. And all the insecurities, anger, and pain he bore into me, needed to die with him.

Suddenly Tyler's voice pulled me from my intense thoughts, "Tell me something about you," he asked.

My eyes met his, "You know me," I replied then looked quickly away, worried that he would see this new storm raging inside.

"No," he gave a quick shake of his head. "I know your favorite food...your favorite color...I know what you like me to do to you."

I bit my lower lip, raising my eyes slowly back to his.

"I want to know something deeper," he said, reaching out to outline my lips with his fingertip. "Tell me something I can't learn…by simply being near you. Tell me something you're afraid to say out loud," he whispered.

I felt my eyes cloud over, like the fear of saying this aloud could swallow me whole. Taking a deep breath, trying to swallow my fear, I took a leap of faith. "I think I'm falling in love with you."

Again, he searched my eyes for the truth. Finding it there, slow dancing with my inhibitions. My fear of rejection, of misreading the situation, of putting myself in the most vulnerable position, he saw them all. He pulled me closer, kissing me over, and over, again. Slowly the trepidation that threatened to overtake me, sent me into a panic, dissolved.

Pulling me on top to straddle him, staring up into my eyes, he said, "I've been falling…since the moment I first laid eyes on you."

This brought a skeptical look to my face.

"Don't make that face," he said seriously. "I really have been."

"Ever since you found out I was a hunter?" one side of my mouth pulled into a grin.

"Yes," he reached up to push a lock of my dark hair behind my ear, "but even before then."

I smiled and shook my head.

"I've only become more obsessed, more intrigued…"

My head cocked to one side as I pondered his words.

"I've *BEEN* falling in love with you, Audra…this whole time," his palm caressed my cheek.

I brought my hand to his and held it there, just feeling his warmth. He was real, and what he said, matched the sincerity on his face. Kissing his palm lightly over and over, I let out a heavy breath and beamed from ear to ear.

Moving his hand down between my legs, he moved his half-swollen self from between them. "Look what you do to me!"

Looking down I smiled bigger. Slowly I began rubbing myself up his shaft to where the head of him found my creamy wetness. I felt him hardening from her slightest attention. I held his gaze, rocking myself forward and back, until his hips began to arch upward, trying to find his way inside. Lifting myself up just enough to pull him into position, I lowered myself onto the tip. Sliding slowly down, until our bodies met again.

His face stretched into that smile I loved. He leaned back against my headboard, just enjoying the show.

The look on his face showed it, but I still loved hearing it. "I love seeing myself inside you," he sat up so I could lean further back. Extending my legs on each side of him, I leaned back and locked my arms down on the bed behind me. Arching to give him the best possible view, I began to grind in a circle.

"I love watching the way she sucks him," he licked his lips. Reaching out, his thumb rubbed circles over my throbbing clit.

"She likes sucking him," I offered.

He watched as I slid myself up and down the shaft. His eyes warmed over, biting his lower lip, he was held captive. Seeing himself filling her; from the tip to base. Knowing how much she loved him, how well she showed him.

"Her kiss is so tight."

Hearing him refer to her *kiss* was such a sexy thought for me. I just watched him watching us. He was in rapture from what was presented to him; thinking, feeling. My other lips were growing jealous for the feel of him, the taste of him. I put a finger to my mouth, "Here?" I asked.

The smile that pulled across his face said it all.

I moved down his body to put my other lips to work. My

tongue licked form base to head, sucking the taste of us from him. He was rock hard when he said, "I want to see you. I want to see your lips around me."

Raising myself from his cock, I moved to bow at his side. On my hands and knees, he watched as my lips wrapped around him, praising him.

Tyler's hand moved up the back of my thigh to my ass, squeezing, kneading as his excitement grew anew. Moving his fingertips between my thighs, my legs spread wider to give him full access. Finding the wetness and warmth, he slid his finger inside me. He let out a contented moan just feeling her, the way she tightened and pulsated from his affections. There was no doubt he belonged there.

Rubbing his balls in my hand, I massaged, gently squeezing, waiting for that moment he hit the brink.

He asked, "Do you want me…to come?"

I moaned my own yearning to taste him, leading him over to where his reward lay. His hips thrust, once twice, finally grunting through his release, filling my mouth, running down the back of my throat.

I made the sound we all make when we get a taste of our favorite thing. As his body shook, I sucked, not wanting to miss a drop, refusing to. Licking my lips, I told him, "I get so hungry for you."

Tyler smiled as he gave me the come-here finger curl. I made my way to his waiting mouth for a kiss. I was more than sated, but then he whispered to me.

"I want your legs around my neck," he licked his lips. Pulling my leg over his body to straddle him again, he then slid down between them.

Holding onto my spread thighs, he placed kisses, one after

another, on my little gem. Slowly, each pucker was punctuated with a light sucking before puckering again.

"I love kissing her," he kissed and kissed again. "She's so good to me…sucking my cock like she does."

I was throbbing as his tongue returned to add a little more pressure…a little more suction. His pace increased, as did my pleasure.

He moaned, "That's my girl…that's my sweet little fuck," he whispered to my pussy before pressing his mouth hard against her. Kissing her long and hard; the same way he kissed my mouth.

I took in a deep breath as my excitement doubled.

Swirling against her, the tip of his tongue worked, faster and faster. I was being thrown into a frenzy of pure ecstasy. I braced one hand against the wall to steady myself. The other hand reached down, cradling his head between my thighs as I moaned. "Baby, right there, she loves you, right there," I panted. "Tyler, yes!" was repeated, again, and again, until the point of no return. My body convulsed. Seeing sparkles behind my closed eyes, colors dancing, I wondered if I would pass out. I wondered…but I didn't care.

Pulling me back down to cradle me in his arms, I asked, breathlessly, "So what would you call that?"

Tyler thought for a moment then smiled broadly, "Worship."

Drained, but beyond content, I curled into the nook of his arm. I couldn't believe how different each orgasm with him felt. From just release, to explosion, to…whatever I was feeling now, they all hit me, satisfied me completely, in completely different ways.

I never expected to fall asleep. Much less did I expect to wake with my head on his chest. I assumed that all men snored loudly. My father had sleep apnea. And when I was young, I worried that he would just stop breathing and never start again. My husband snored so loud that I had to make sure I fell asleep before him, or I would wind up in the guest bedroom at 3am. But Tyler, his snore was quiet, his breathing just barely audible. It was soothing.

Tyler stirred, pulling me closer to him, "Good morning," he whispered, putting a kiss on the top of my head.

"Good morning," I returned.

"Are you hungry? I feel like I haven't eaten in days."

"It's all that energy you've expended," I joked.

"Well, I'd like to burn more," he raised my chin so our lips met. "And to do that, I'm going to need food. Are you a breakfast person?"

I shook my head, "I'm a coffee person."

"How about, we start with coffee, and then I'll take you to brunch?" he suggested.

I hid my grin, "Sounds good."

Pushing brew on my coffee maker, I offered him the first cup. "Cream? Sugar?".

"Black," he took the cup with a smile.

"Well, you're easy," I grinned.

"I am for you," he winked.

I retrieved the paper from my doorstep and headed back to grab my own coffee. Unfolding the previous day's news, I started on page one.

There was an update on Mitzi's case. Strangulation was the official cause of death. There were signs of sexual activity, but they had ruled out rape.

My brow furrowed, how could they rule out rape, I wondered. I had a feeling that even though totally consensual, I myself had some tenderness, possible tears or abrasions from our usual version of sex; animalistic. Not to mention, some men were just more blessed than others, making even the consensual, look and feel forced. I couldn't help but wonder if this was erotic asphyxiation.

Tyler returned from the bedroom wearing nothing but his tuxedo pants and a smile. My eyes traveled down his tanned, well sculpted torso. "Anything good in the paper?" he asked, taking a sip of his coffee.

"There's more about Mitzi. She apparently had consensual sex before being strangled."

Tyler's brow furrowed, "Does that mean they're looking at her fiancé?"

I scanned the rest of the article. "It doesn't say. Why?" I set my cup down.

"Well, I know her fiancé Trey. He's a good guy…upstanding," Tyler looked confused.

"Is there a chance it was auto-erotic?" I lifted my brow to him.

"I'm not going to pretend to know her habits, or fetishes, but I'd actually be shocked if it was."

My head shook, "No. It doesn't say anything about Trey, or even if they have a person of interest."

"I can't imagine there would be," Tyler's brow lifted. "In these circles they're probably staying pretty tight-lipped on the case. I mean, the people who would normally be the first questioned, come from wealthy families that would sue for any touch of slander."

"It is different in your world, isn't it?" I stared at the article.

"Their world," Tyler corrected. "I've worked hard to separate myself from what I was born into."

"So…any thoughts? Anybody you would suspect?"

"Well, it's not like a common street killer…like us," he added, "to choose a home with security cameras, an alarm system…in a gated community?" His head shook "Whoever did this, knew about the security, the risk involved. They'd have to, to have not been caught on camera."

"So if this wasn't Trey, it would have to be either a worker at the estate, someone who worked for the security company, or…" I raised my brows.

"Or one of the upper-crust," Tyler filled in the blank I had left floating in the air.

I nodded, "Those do look like the only likely suspects."

"Does it say whether or not anything was taken from the house?" he questioned.

"No, but like you said, probably keeping a tight-lip on the evidence," I shrugged.

Tyler nodded, "Mitzi was a huge pain in the ass. I won't pretend she wasn't. But being pompous isn't really a murder-able offense in these circles."

"Hmm," I said.

"Hmm, what?" he asked.

"Just wondering how well we really know anyone? I mean, if I had met you on the street, instead of the way we did," I grinned, "I would never have pegged you for a killer."

Tyler nodded his head after considering what I had said, "I would never have pegged you, either."

We just sat there quietly for a moment: Me, pondering the fact that I hadn't perceived the intentions of The Piano Man; nor he, mine. Thinking about how badly that could have ended for me, I reached out and squeezed Tyler's hand.

"So, what's your pleasure today?" Tyler broke me from my thoughts.

I thought about it, "I don't know," my head shook.

"Did…you feel like hunting?" he asked.

Slowly beginning to shake my head, I told him, "I really don't. You?" I asked.

His brows lifted, "Nope."

This didn't seem too odd to me. In the year that I had lived here, I only acquired six kills. I guess Tyler would have been number seven, but even that would indicate that I only *hunted*, only killed, when the need arose in me. Maybe he was this way, too. Of course, he had admitted to having twelve under his belt, but he had also started long before I did.

"You know what, I'd like to take you somewhere special today," he said. "You could use a change of pace," he added.

"You're not taking me back to Naples, are you?" I looked at him sidelong.

Tyler laughed, "No, I'd like to take you to one of my favorite places. You game?"

Seeing as how I didn't have the drive to hunt, the house was clean and I couldn't find any viable excuse, I nodded.

"Okay, go get some comfortable clothes on, and I'll be back in an hour to pick you up," he put a kiss on my cheek and headed to the bedroom to retrieve the rest of his tuxedo from the night before.

After Tyler left, I decided to go get clean and make myself as ready as I could for an excursion I knew nothing about.

Opening my medicine cabinet to grab my toothbrush and paste, I noticed that mine wasn't the only toothbrush in the holder. A blue brush sat next to my red one. Furrowing my brow, I thought; he had expected to stay the night last night?

The blue intruder hadn't been here yesterday. Was it wishful thinking that had made him pack for an oral hygiene moment at my house, or had he been manipulating the outcome of events? Was this just part of a presumptuous nature; was this pre-destined in his mind, or was he just optimistic?

Teeth brushed, face washed, I jumped in the shower to clean off the scent from a night of pleasure.

When Tyler knocked on the door, I was a little surprised that it was quickly followed by him letting himself inside. I couldn't hide the look of concern this brought to my face.

"Sorry, I wasn't sure if you'd hear me if you were in the bath-room," he reasoned.

I decided to joke instead of cornering him about the walk-in, not to mention the toothbrush. "Were you hoping to catch me in the shower?" I asked.

"I'm always hoping to catch you in varying stages of undress," he grinned. "You ready?"

"I didn't know how to dress, is this okay?" I asked spinning in long skirt and a tank top.

"You're perfect," he winked. "Come on," he ushered me to the door.

In the Jeep, we started off going north to the 75 then headed west. When Tyler started to play music he knew I would enjoy, I asked him to play me some of his favorite music, instead. Grinning, he asked me to grab Sublime's 40 Oz. to Freedom disk. It wasn't bad, I enjoyed the rhythm, and the lyrics made me laugh.

An hour or so later, we pulled off the main road and headed into the Everglades National Park.

"So, ugh, you brought me out to the Everglades?" my brow rose.

Tyler laughed again, "May not seem like the best place to take people like us, but I guarantee you, you're going to love this."

I nodded, amused by him thinking he knew me well enough to make this assumption.

Pulling up to a dock of sorts, Tyler got out of the Jeep to talk to a man about an air-boat rental.

"You're the one that called the other day?" I overheard the man say.

The man seemed about forty-something, thick around the middle, wearing overalls over an ill-fitting homemade muscle shirt, and a ball cap that read, "*I Like Tuna.*"

"Yeah, it turns out we had a day off sooner than I thought," I heard Tyler tell him as I approached.

Staring at Tyler for an explanation, he just wrapped an arm around me and smiled as he squeezed me closer to him.

Now I was a little more on guard; not that I thought I would end up crocodile chum, but that this was a date, and it had been planned for the supposedly unknown future.

"You know how to work one of these things?" the man asked Tyler, as my eyes widened.

We were going out…unattended…into a swamp…on a little boat?

"I do," Tyler handed the man a wad of bills.

"There's a GPS…just in case you get lost out there. You can get turned around pretty easily with the shifting," the man warned.

Admittedly, until now, this wasn't even on the list of places I didn't want to get lost.

As Tyler moved us down a narrow path of water, he saw the look on my face. "You don't like boats?" he yelled over the sound of the fan.

I gave my head a shake, "It's not the boat," I yelled. "It's the water. More accurately, it's the things that live in the water!"

Grinning he said, "I'm not gonna let anything happen to you. I promise."

It wasn't *HIS* intentions I questioned. It was the intentions of starving water beasts with huge teeth. What if their intentions trumped his?

"Just try to relax and enjoy the scenery!" Tyler suggested.

Taking a deep breath, I retrained my focus. As we passed by tall reeds and patches of swampland, birds took off in all directions, flying for safety. The sheer number of them amazed me; not to mention the colors. I had never seen some of these species. I let the sun beat down on my shoulders and the wind whip my hair back. Releasing a deep breath, I began to smile.

Turning the boat down another offshoot of water surrounded by marshland, I reminded myself to hold on. Tyler did seem to know where he wanted to go, making turns without stopping or even slowing at times. I had lost track of the right, left, rights we had taken, quite a ways back. The space, or water, we had covered did make me realize just how easily done it would be to lose yourself, lose your direction, in this vast swamp.

Another right and I saw a large patch of trees ahead, hanging over the waterway. As Tyler slowed the boat, we floated forward.

The encircled tree lined cove was canopied, and blocked out the sunlight. It was like we entered a different world. Huge dragonflies skimmed the water. I could see the shells and tiny heads of swimming turtles breaking the surface. Surrounded by moss covered cypress trees, the quiet was broken only by the sounds of birds in the distance, and insects chirping and buzzing.

"Listen," he said as he made his way down from his perch to take the seat next to me.

I couldn't hide the look of awe on my face. "It's beautiful," as my eyes drawn in every direction.

Tyler smiled while watching my reaction.

"How?" I threw the incomplete question out to him.

"I come here a lot," he looked around, enjoying the view. "We started coming here when I was young."

"I guess I didn't picture your dad…as an Everglades kind of

guy," I joked.

"Oh, he wasn't," Tyler shook his head. "But my brother," he began, "he was uncomfortable with all the socializing expected in our circles; parties, balls, events. He hated them and was truly miserable in all social settings."

"A true introvert, huh?"

"That he was," Tyler smiled with a nod of his head.

"Sounds like we would have understood each other very well," I grinned.

"I believe you would have," he gave me a squeeze. "My dad struck a deal with Joel. That was my brother, Joel. Dad told him for every hour he spent doing something he hated for appearance sake, he would bring him here, or anywhere else he wanted to go, for the same amount of time."

I thought about this, "That seems like a good bargain. That was nice of your father, to give your brother the downtime he craved…needed," I added.

Tyler nodded again, "It was a need, too. Joel would spend hours, days, working alone on toy models and reading. Sometimes he just sat there, no TV, no music…just enjoying the quiet."

This made me wonder, "How was he with you…growing up? I mean, did he play ball with you, or board games…anything?"

"He did," Tyler began, "but when he needed to be alone, I didn't press for his attention. I'm six years younger than him, so luckily I did have some friends my own age, ya know, to play with. But when Joel felt like being a kid, I was the one he would seek out," he smiled.

I could see the pain in his eyes, the loss. I knew it well.

"He was my best friend. I told him all of my secrets and he told me all of his," Tyler grinned. "We trusted each other."

"If you don't mind my asking…" I couldn't even bring forth the words.

"It was a plane crash. That was another solitary pastime dad allowed him to have. He learned how to fly as soon as he was old enough. He said the world was beautiful…when you could step away from it."

I nodded like this made perfect sense to me.

"Then one day, he took off on a solitary flight. We still don't know for sure what happened, but his plane went down in the Ocean. There were a lot of people who saw the crash from shore."

I tried not to wince.

"Dad had divers sent down to the crash. They retrieved his body," Tyler looked lost in a memory that made my heart hurt for him.

"I'm so sorry," I said, reaching out my hand to his. "Truly, I am."

Tyler let out a sigh, "You know, he was the smartest person I've ever known. I wish I would have known just how smart, a little sooner."

I didn't know what this meant, but didn't want to interrupt, either.

"Anyway, dad and I have come out here a few times since he passed. We just sit here quietly, and enjoy all the sights and sounds that used to make Joel happy."

"Well, he chose an amazing spot," I looked around. "Thank you for sharing his place with me."

"I knew you'd appreciate it, his place," he smiled then leaned in to kiss my cheek. Pulling me closer, we just sat there quietly for the next hour or so.

Slowly moving out of what had been his brother's happy-place, we headed back to the dock.

"Ya made it," said the man coming out of a little shack.

"We did," Tyler smiled as he helped me onto the dock. "I thank you for the use of her," he pointed to the airboat."

"Anytime," the man reached out to shake Tyler's hand.

"And please tell your father, Tyler Whitmore, says hello."

The man nodded, "Will do."

On the way out of the park, Tyler asked, "So Miss Coffee, you hungry yet?"

"Famished," I admitted.

Pulling off at a lookout with a bench, Tyler asked if this was an okay place for me to eat. I had to laugh. He was so worried about making sure I was comfortable. "This is great," I told him as I hopped out of the Jeep.

The bench faced open marshland that was alive with activity. I loved watching the birds, listening to them calling and chatting to each other.

Grabbing a picnic basket out of the trunk, Tyler walked over to the bench. Salami and peppers with provolone cheese and Italian dressing on hoagie rolls and macaroni salad, was a great meal indeed.

"Very good," I answered, covering my mouth when Tyler asked how I liked the sandwich. I had to admit, Tyler had done his homework on me. I should reciprocate by learning about some of his favorite things.

"So what do you like to do for fun?" I inquired.

Tyler's eyes sparkled and danced as one side of his mouth drew up into a naughty grin.

"Besides that!" I laughed. "Hobbies."

"I used to like racing cars. But it's almost like I grew out of it since my biggest fan passed away."

I nodded, understanding what it meant to lose someone who used to cheer for you.

"I guess I used to do a lot of things; surfed, shot skeet, rode horses, mountain biked."

"You don't do any of those things anymore?" my head cocked to the side.

He gave a quick shake of his head, "Not really."

"Do you miss any of them?" Not that I did any of those things, but I'd be willing to try. Well, any of them but the surfing, that is.

"I've had a lot to keep me busy this year," he told me.

"Like what?" I wondered out loud.

"There were a couple of projects that needed my attention. Work stuff for my dad. But that's over now."

I nodded. I assumed that whatever his dad had him doing was for one of the many companies his father owned.

"I like hiking, now. It's good exercise, and it helps clear my mind," Tyler nodded.

Ah, I thought. This, I could do.

A moment passed before I turned my head to him and asked, "Why Rudolpho?"

Laughing, he asked, "What do you mean. Rudolpho is a great name! I mean it may not be as good as Lila, but..."

I had to laugh back, "My favorite flowers are lilacs..." I turned my palms up at him, and shrugged.

"So lilacs became Lila," he nodded.

"Yep...my alter ego."

"Funny you put it that way...alter ego," his head bobbed up and down.

"Why?" I was still laughing at his expression.

"Because, Rudolpho, was supposed to be Rude-elf."

My eyes squinted, "I'm not following," I admitted.

"It was supposed to be my character's name. I was an elf. A high elf," he said, like that was totally different than any another kind of elf.

With this comment, my lips pursed as I tried not to laugh out loud. "Your character," I repeated.

Letting out a sigh, Tyler said, "Joel and I…used to…have characters."

"Like…roll-playing?" I giggled.

"Yes, like roll-playing," he laughed like hc was embarrassed. "Like I said, he was always in his head, and roll-playing, helped him use his imagination instead of just always succumbing to the realism and logic of this world. It was a way to bring him out of himself."

I nodded, "Okay, I get that, but….how did you get Rudolpho from Rude-elf?"

"I was young when we started playing," he explained. "I didn't spell well," his head shook as he started to grin again.

My brow raised, "Okay."

"Well, I spelled it, R-U-D-O-L-F. When Joel saw it, he asked, "As in the reindeer?""

Now I couldn't hide my laughter. I cupped my face to hide a giggle.

"So then when I said, "No, Rude-elf," Joel said, "*Oh*," he gave me a shrug. "And that's it, that's how I became Rudolpho, at five years old," he said with reddening cheeks.

Seeing his embarrassment, but noting he was still laughing at himself, and the memory, warmed my heart. Leaning in, I told him, "Well, I like your alter ego." I put a kiss on his cheek and grinned from ear to ear. "Rudolpho," I said in the sexiest voice I could muster, making him laugh harder.

Heading back to my house, the sun still high in the sky, Tyler asked if I would like to go for a walk on the beach.

It was warm out, muggy, but with the off shore breeze that made Florida livable for me. Heading down to the boardwalk, Tyler reached out to take my hand in his. This small act, holding hands, would have seemed foreign, uncomfortable, just a couple weeks ago. Now, even though it still felt…odd to me, I realized that I didn't pull away. I didn't want to. How had this happened? I wondered again. It wasn't like me. I didn't believe in whirlwind romance, or being swept off my feet. That kind of take on life, a partner, was for people who had their heads stuck in the clouds. It wasn't reasonable for anyone who was ruled by logic, or had it thrust on them. And I was this girl, now? The one who chose to dismiss logic?

Walking the shoreline for a long while in silence, Tyler finally spoke, "Where do you see yourself in twenty years?"

I pondered the question. The truth was, I hadn't really given any thought to the future, and I told him so.

Nodding Tyler rolled this around in his mind.

What about you?" I asked wondering if he had his life all planned out.

"Well, I know I could never live away from this," he turned to look at the ocean.

On some level, I had to agree. I had now lived on both sides of the United States and the only thing they had in common was an ocean nearby.

Out of nowhere, Tyler asked, "Would you like to see my home?"

It seemed odd to me, only now, that I hadn't questioned where he lived. I hadn't seen where he lived, or had even cared to. My world, up until now, was just my home, where I existed.

"Sure," I said, wondering in what kind of lavish place he laid his head.

As we walked back up the boardwalk, I could see the sign for Dango's, my favorite hole in the wall for a pulled pork sandwich. I remembered our encounter there and a blush rose to my cheeks as he grinned down at me.

Turning down a small walkway between two homes turned into businesses, he headed up the back stairs to the second story over a surf shop. If I looked confused, it's because I was. It wasn't the fact that his home wasn't up to his financial status. It was because of how close in proximity it was to my home. I had passed by this surf shop almost daily on my walks, for over a year.

As he unlocked the door, I asked, "How long have you lived here?"

"About nine months," he said holding the door open so I could step inside.

The wood floors of the tiny one bedroom had been refinished and shined with the glow of being highly waxed. His white couch and armchair were overstuffed. A large entertainment unit sitting across from the bay window that looked out to the ocean, held a huge TV with a slew of books surrounding it. Checking out some of the titles, I noticed that most were psychology: abnormal psych, applied behavior, developmental and even neuropsychology.

"You're a psychology buff?" The thought wasn't too surprising, to be honest. I mean a serial killer who studied or used psychology, wasn't much of a stretch. My eyes were drawn to a psychological study of serial killers. Tyler caught me staring at the well-worn copy.

"What's your take on nature versus nurture?" he asked.

I thought about it for a moment, "Well, I know I was raised in a loving family; had an above normal childhood. No sexual, mental, or physical abuse. I wasn't bullied at home or at school."

Tyler nodded, stepping closer.

"My father was an officer when I was young. And then later, a detective. So I may have had an abnormal amount of fear… worrying about whether or not he would come home. But some kids are worriers despite having less to worry about."

He stared at me, "How did you handle that…the worrying?"

I shrugged, "I guess I prayed and hoped for the best. Really, what else is there to do?"

"But then you married…"

I nodded.

"And even though you had a normal childhood, knew right from wrong, were raised by someone whose whole purpose in life was to enforce the law, you still became a hunter."

I slowly began to nod. I couldn't take his observation as judgment; we were the same animal. By this logic, I assumed he was attributing it, what I became, to a change of nurture; my husband's adultery.

"What about you?" I asked, "Nature or nurture?"

He pondered how to answer this, "I guess I'd have to go with nature."

"Really?" my brows lifted.

"I believe mine, was always there. And even though I didn't display the common outbursts of anger, rage, or abuse of animals, that are thought to be associated with serial killers, I think there was always something I couldn't define, just under the surface, waiting to be released.

"So, you don't think losing your mother at such a young age had anything to do with it?" I asked seriously.

Tyler slowly shook his head, "I wish I could blame it on that, but no. I think it was there long before."

My brow furrowed a bit, knowing that his mother had died when he was five or six. He was aware of these thoughts, these feelings, before then? But…he only killed adulterers? Maybe that was just where his moral compass landed? I knew that mine was geared this way; what I saw as justifiable. Then there was the slew of cheating stepmothers. They may have helped form the direction of his nature.

"Can I get you something to drink?" Tyler quickly changed the subject.

"What do you have?"

Handing me a Coke, he gave the short and sweet tour. The bedroom was a decent size and he did indeed have a four poster bed with a heavy quilt of cream and green stripes and an abundance of pillows.

The bathroom was immaculate with the older style white subway tiling throughout the whole space. The sink and fixtures looked like they were right out of the 40's, when I assumed this house may have been built.

The kitchen was a u-shaped room, not big, but then, what does one man need?

"It's a lot different from the way you grew up, your father's house. You don't miss the space?" I questioned.

"There's space outside," he gave me a palms-up.

I had to laugh. I had always felt the same way.

"So you're comfortable here?" I looked at him sidelong.

"For now," he nodded looking around at his space. "You ready to head home?" he asked me.

"What else did you have in mind?" I asked with a grin as he drew closer, reaching out for me.

"Well…this space has no memories. At least…not any of my own," he grinned.

I laughed, "And you'd like to remedy that?"

"I would," he grabbed at the sides of my skirt, pulling them up to reveal my hips before dropping to his knees in front of me.

I don't know what it is about having a man pull your panties to the side instead of taking them off. But as he did, his tongue searching for that spot that made me catch my breath, it made me feel like a dirty girl in the most delightful way. If he only knew how much of a turn-on this was for me. Maybe one day, I'll explain it. But the thought disappeared as my attention was pulled to my favorite of all distractions: him.

The warmth of his mouth, the talent of his tongue working, made my eyes fall closed and heart beat harder. My fingers thrust and curled into his hair, holding him close. Seeing his head between my legs was such a lovely view. I felt myself being pulled to that place where his tickle became my passion. Driving me on, I felt the familiar and welcome burn of an inevitable explosion. Knowing I was close, he grabbed my ass, holding me tight as I began to shake. My skirt dropped around his nose and I quickly reached for it so I wouldn't miss seeing him as I came. His eyes looked up, watching me as I nodded to him. His fingertips curled, grasping harder as his own excitement grew.

Watching me, ecstasy transforming my face, he moaned with me, into me, as my whole body shook with the release that left me more than satisfied.

Smiling down into his face, our eyes met. "Your turn," I bit into my bottom lip, waiting for him to take me. Pulling me to the floor with him, our lips locked. I loved the taste of me in his mouth, on his tongue.

"How do you want me," he asked, pushing his erection

against my stomach.

My head gave a small shake, "How do YOU want me?" I grinned, sliding my hand up and down, from the tip to base. He watched as my hand tightened around him. Watching the head pop out the top of my working fist, his breathing coming faster.

He moved behind me, bending me over. His hands grabbed a hold of my ass cheeks, spreading them apart. Running a warm hand from my low back up my spine, he moved me into the downward dog. In he pushed the head, making my breath catch. "You're always so wet." He sounded intoxicated by the thought, the feeling.

I knew he had been brought close just seeing, feeling, what he had done to me; I knew that he worked this way. My excitement drove him, could start his *burning*, a new. I could feel him holding back, his breathing slowed as he gifted me long, deep, slow strokes; just tipping me now, in and out.

Looking back over my shoulder, I could see him watching how my pussy sucked him, begged for him.

He flashed that devilish grin before his hands tightened around my hips. Pulling me back into him, I felt every inch of him push its way inside in one long, mind blowing stroke. Immediately my spine, pelvis, began to rock. My jaw, lifted to the heavens. I could hear him trying to keep himself there; in that moment that was all warm, wet ecstasy. She tightened, squeezing him, as he moved from head to base.

"Suck me?" he asked.

Have sweeter words ever been spoken? My tongue traced my lips, in preparation. Slowly he pulled himself, inch by exquisite inch, from my toy box. I turned on my knees to face him, watching intently as he stroked himself. I bowed down. Swirling my tongue around the tip of him, the taste of us mingling, had my mouth watering. I couldn't tease him the way he had teased me. I needed him, now. I slid my hungry mouth down his engorged shaft, I heard him ask, "Do you want it?"

My muffled sound of excitement was nothing more than a whimper. My lips were begging him, as they tightened, and pulled their way back up to his magnificent head.

"I love the way you suck me," he said, drawing closer with his every breath…with my every down stroke.

The word didn't bother me this time; the L word.

"I'm gonna come, baby," his fervor peaked, as I devoured him. "Oh, God I love fucking your mouth." His once ridged body, slowly, began to relax. He lay back patting his heart.

"*Mmm*," I licked my lips and kissed him, before laying my head on his chest. "And I like that you're not grossed out about kissing me afterward."

"Why would I be," he looked truly perplexed.

"From everything I've ever heard or read, a lot of men have a problem with even the thought of kissing afterward," I told him.

"That never made sense to me. I mean if I'm grossed out by my body, shouldn't you be, as well? Plus, you don't seem to mind kissing me afterward."

"I agree, but that's because I taste incredible," I pushed my middle finger into my honey pot then pulled its creaminess lightly across his lips, before kissing him."

Tyler licked his lips, grinning, "That, you do!"

But honestly," I told him, "on this subject, you're a single diamond in a mountain of coal,"

"I think your favorite, is the taste of us mixed together," he wrapped his arm around me, pulling me against him.

"It is," I admitted.

"Just one more reason I enjoy the hell out of you."

We sat for a while in the rosy afterglow of shared pleasure, before he asked, "Did you want to go home?"

Seeing as I had no intention of staying at his house, I said yes. Part of me wondered if he was tired of me, needed some alone time. And the other part of me wondered if I did, too. I had spent the whole day with him. As amazing as it was, this was abnormal for me. Actually, this was the most time I had spent with any one person, since before my husband died.

As we headed back down the boardwalk, passing in front of Dango's, he pulled me inside.

"I don't know about you," he said, "but all of our expelled energy has left me hungry. How about we grab a couple of sandwiches to go?"

Funny, but that was exactly what I had been thinking since I saw the sign, earlier. I nodded, "Best pulled pork in town," I offered.

I grabbed two paper plates. The pulled pork came wrapped in foil, but was still so messy wet, that it dribbled everywhere when you took a bite. Sitting at my living room table, we enjoyed the sandwiches and chips that came with them.

"Damn," Tyler said. "You're right. That is the best pulled pork I've ever had."

I nodded with a full mouth.

"I'm guessing you probably want some alone time, now," his head cocked, trying to examine my expression.

Did I? I wasn't sure what I was feeling? Worried about the impact my answer may have, I said, "Yeah…probably. I mean, it couldn't hurt to get a full night of sleep," I grinned.

As Tyler stood to leave, he turned to me, "I left my phone number next to the bed."

I stared at him quizzically, "You did?"

"I left it this morning, before I went to get everything ready for today. I want to make sure you have it, if you need me," he leaned in and kissed me, deep.

"About today," I wrapped my arms around his neck and looked into his eyes, "thank you. It was a wonderful day."

"Anytime," he pushed the hair back from my eyes. "And again, if you need ANYTHING...," that devilish look returned as he left the statement just dangling in the air. He leaned in giving me a quick kiss before heading out the door.

Closing the door behind him, I went and collapsed on my couch. Today had been great, I smiled at the thought. But one thing still bothered me a little. When Tyler asked me about nature versus nurture, his answer was nature. It's not that I didn't believe him. It was that he had aimed his kills at adulterers that confused me.

I knew he had never been married, so what pushed him in this direction? Had he had a longtime girlfriend, or even a fiancé who had cheated on him? He had already said that he didn't consider anything actual adultery until vows were exchanged, so that didn't really compute in my mind.

All his stepmothers were accused of, and divorced due to cheating, I reminded myself. Having this inside of him, this particular beast, may have been influenced by these women. They could have been the catalyst for his *decompression* being geared this way; toward this type of person. Rolling everything around in my head left me exhausted. Why did I feel the need to try and analyze him? I was lucky to have found him, to have stumbled across him, and lucky to be alive, I laughed at the memory.

Taking myself to bed to sleep alone, now gave me mixed emotions. Was I really missing him?

11

I tossed and turned well into the wee hours of the morning. When I finally decided that it was no longer worth trying to find Mr. Sandman, I went to press brew on my coffee maker.

Grabbing the morning paper from the front porch, I stared at last night's news. Still no person of interest in Mitzi's case. I wasn't sure why her death preoccupied me so. The thought that it could have been a stranger, just wasn't logical to me. As Tyler had pointed out, there were security patrols, cameras, and the upper-crust community, was gated. I shook my head at the thought, it wasn't likely.

When my phone began to ring, I knew it had to be him. I could count on my fingers how many incoming calls I had received in the last year. Although there were a few about my car's extended warranty.

"Hello," I said.

"Good morning," his voice rang. "How did you sleep?"

Should I be honest, say that sleep was hard found and even harder to hold onto? "Not too bad," I answered. "You?"

"Horribly! It was almost impossible to sleep," he admitted.

I couldn't help but grin.

"Without the sound of you snoring on my chest, how could I?" he continued.

My jaw dropped, "I don't snore!"

Tyler laughed, "How do you know you don't snore?"

"I've never been told I snore!" I reasoned.

"Maybe once upon a time, you didn't, but I guarantee you, you do," he laughed.

"Well…maybe I was just exhausted, did you think of that?" I pretended to sound more offended than I really was. "Maybe I shouldn't let you wear me out so much?"

"Hey, hey, hey, I did say it was hard to sleep without hearing it, didn't I? Don't go crazy with this needing to be less worn out, stuff," he laughed. "I missed you," he added in a serious tone that made me smile from ear to ear.

Glowing, I said "I missed you, too." Even admitting this little bit of myself, was both frightening, and freeing.

"Did you have plans today?" he asked.

A huge smile pushed up my cheeks. "I do not. What did you have in mind?" I asked seductively.

"Well, that, of course…but today is Mitzi's funeral," he said with just a hint of apprehension.

Normally the thought of going back to Naples and being surrounded by those people, would be an out and out *No*. But I was so intrigued by her murder.

There had been such a long silence that Tyler felt the need to explain further. "She was a friend of the family. Her parents and my father, are very close. It would be disrespectful if I didn't attend."

"Wouldn't it be disrespectful…to bring a date?" I wondered out loud.

"Not at all. Plenty of business associates will be there with their family members and spouses, who had never met her personally," he assured me.

Reluctantly, I remembered Derrick's funeral. It was true. There were several people there I had never met, never seen before.

"Plus, you're not a date. You are my support system through this very trying time."

He said this so deadpan, I didn't know if he was being serious or not. "I won't have to wear one of those sashes like a support animal, will I?"

"Truthfully, I feel more emotionally supported when you wear nothing…but…" he left his answer dangling in the air.

I smirked, "What time should I be ready?"

"10am? Will that work for you? It's a long drive."

Yeah, that'll work," I told him.

"Good, I'll be over in ten minutes."

"Huh? You said 10am. It's 7:45," I pointed out.

"Yeah, but I'm feeling a need for emotional support," he hung up.

Stripping down to nothing I answered the door buck naked. "Your emotional support human is ready for detail," I grinned.

Running at me, he picked me up over his shoulder and carried me off to the bedroom. Throwing me on the bed, he grabbed me under my knees, pulling me closer to the edge. "This bed really is the perfect height," he grinned.

had never seen so many limousines and hats in all my life as when we pulled up to the church where Mitzi would be memorialized.

Helping me out of the limo, Tyler whispered in my ear, "I really wish you would have worn the black wraparound dress."

My nose crinkled at the thought. "Why?"

A grin pulled across his face.

Shaking my head, I tried not to laugh at this very inappropriate time. "It's too short to wear to a funeral," I pointed out.

Turning his palms up, "Doesn't that only confirm why I would wish you would have worn it?"

The huge church was surrounded by grass with a round driveway. Apparently, the rich didn't do the *park and walk* thing that others did, being dropped off out front leaving their drivers to go find parking and wait for them.

If it hadn't been for the stained glass windows, the church would have looked like a small castle. There were no visible signs of denomination that I noticed. Looking around for any telltale symbol, I was stymied: No crosses, no statues dedicated to a savior, no bibles sitting in the back of the pews.

"What religion is this church?"

Tyler looked around, "I don't think it has a religion, per say."

This seemed rather odd to me, and it showed by the look on my face.

"This church is open to all," Tyler said.

But looking around, I thought, all that are from old money, maybe.

Just as we sat in a pew, eight rows back from where the casket sat with an open lid, Tyler's father walked in. As Tyler and I stood, his father embraced him and said something in his ear. Extending his hand to me, Mr. Whitmore thanked me for my attendance then quickly excused himself.

Sitting back down, I watched as Mr. Whitmore took what I knew to be a pulpit. At the moment, I had no idea what his roll was in this church, or in Mitzi's life.

Tyler saw the confused look on my face and said, "He was Mitzi's…well kind of like a godfather."

I slowly nodded wondering if he had been asked to eulogize her.

I felt a chill run through me. It started at the base of my spine and ran its way up to the base of my skull. Before I ever knew from *where* I was receiving the frozen stare, my whole body shuddered hard.

On the other side of the church, in the third row pew, sat Daniel. His jaw was set hard, a sneer on his face as he stared daggers into me. The way he looked at me; it was like something collided inside him. His projected combination of hate and yearning caused my own eyes to go cold. I could feel ice moving through my veins.

Tyler turned his head, catching the look on my face, "Are you okay?"

I'm fine," I smiled up into his concerned eyes.

Looking around to find just where my polar gaze had been a moment before, Tyler spied Daniel's stare.

Smiling widely for Tyler, Daniel gave him a small wave of his hand.

I pretended not to notice their interaction as Tyler gave him one curt nod, then squeezed my hand.

When the church was packed to capacity, Mr. Whitmore stepped to the microphone that would be needed for a gathering of this size.

"I first want to thank everyone for being here this day," Mr. Whitmore looked around at the crowd. "It is a solemn day for all gathered. Death…," his voice rang out, "…it is always hard to accept for those left behind. But it is even more so to lose a loved one, so young…and in such a way," his eyes fell closed. Wiping a trailing tear from his check, he took a moment before he continued.

As I sat through Mr. Whitmore's beautiful eulogy, a few words from her father, and her best friend, I felt the shiver from Daniel's stare, several times. Knowing now where he sat, the looks he sent my way, I refused to acknowledge him. But just because I refused to see him, didn't mean no one had. I felt Tyler's hand squeeze mine again. Out of the corner of my eye, I knew he had caught Daniel's head swiveling away from where we sat. Possibly more than once.

I did find it odd that there was no mention of God, an afterlife and no one asked us to bow our heads for prayer. At the end of the service, if you could call it that, Tyler asked if I would attend the wake, held at his father's home.

"I'd like to check on my dad, give him some support. He's really shaken by Mitzi's..." he swallowed hard.

I nodded, not needing him to try and figure out just how to phrase the ending of her life; death, murder. Neither had a good ring, and both were horribly accurate.

"Thank you, Simon," I said as he opened the limo door for me.

"You're welcome, ma'am," he nodded.

Leaning in close to him, I said, "I'd like it if you would call me Audra."

Simon nodded and tipped his hat, "As you wish, ma'am. Audra," he corrected himself.

Tyler grinned, "And I'd like you to refer to me as *Hottie Mc Naughty*," he told Simon.

"Get in...asshole," Simon said.

My eyes rounded as I stifled a laugh.

"Are you saying I'm not hot, Simon?" Tyler asked feigning offense.

"No, I'm not saying that," Simon's head shook. "But I am saying you *ARE* an asshole," he smiled.

Tyler clapped him on the shoulder and laughed good-naturedly.

Back at the Whitmore Chateau, we once again waited in a line of limos to be dropped off at the door.

"These people aren't fond of walking, are they?" I asked.

"It's not socially acceptable," Tyler was only half-joking.

As I exited the limo, Tyler escorted me inside. It seemed as if today most the people were far too preoccupied to give me the stares and looks I had received on my first visit here.

Tyler escorted me to the backyard which was acres of green

grass adorned with statues, walkways, gardens, and a long rectangular pool.

On the grass, a gigantic white tent had been erected. Round, eight seat tables filled the huge space. Two bars, with six bartenders each, sat at both ends of the tent. But I noticed no one was walking up to the bar to order a drink. Instead, there was waitstaff for each table. Back-up wait-staff stood at the ready to help dispense large orders of food or drink, in a prompt manner.

"I take it they don't like to wait in line for anything, either?" I asked in a hushed tone as we took our seats.

"They do not," Tyler confirmed as he scooted in my chair, and placed a kiss on my cheek.

Within a short time, the room was buzzing with conversation. Slowly our table began to fill. I was introduced to the Walther's, Mr., and Mrs. The Bowler's, an elderly couple who appeared to have sight and hearing-impairments. When Daniel and his wife approached the table, Tyler greeted them politely.

Leaning in to kiss Daniel's wife's cheek, he introduced her to me as Tiffany.

As Daniel began to pull out the seat next to him, Tyler apologized but said that he was to hold that seat for his father.

"So I guess…there's no room for me, here?" Daniel asked, his eyes quickly scanning me.

"No, I'm afraid there isn't," Tyler smiled, putting his arm around me.

The smirk that graced Daniel's face was turned to Tyler. "Well, that is a shame, Tyler," he said, and escorted his wife away.

I wasn't sure I was reading this right. Had Tyler given Daniel his left-over's, as Daniel had once implied? The thought seemed out of place to me. After all, Daniel was married. And with Tyler's code? I couldn't see him thinking it wasn't right for a married women to cheat, was a murder-able offense, but it was acceptable for a man, friend, or no. That just wasn't adding up, for me.

Tyler saw the clouds in my eyes and said, "Daniel was my brother Joel's, only friend. Besides me, that is."

"So, you two are close?" I asked, hoping his answer would stop this gnawing that had started in my stomach.

Tyler shook his head, no. "We hung out a bit when we were younger, but we grew apart a long time before Joel passed."

It wasn't exactly the answer I was hoping for. But the thought that they weren't thick as thieves anymore, was something, I told myself.

Mr. Whitmore arrived after most of the gathered had been seated. Making his way through the crowd, handshakes and hugs were exchanged. His puffy, red-rimmed eyes were a telltale sign of his deep despair. In that moment, I was so sorry for the loss he felt. I knew full well that he had lost the great love of his life. Simon had said that Mr. Whitmore had never loved another, the way he had loved the mother of his sons. And now, in just over a year's time, he had lost his eldest son and his Goddaughter.

When Mr. Whitmore approached our table, he had the look of someone who was emotionally exhausted. I had seen that look on my own father's face after my mother was killed.

Mr. Whitmore ordered a double of Glenmorangie, letting out a deep sigh after his first long swallow. Turning his eyes to me, he said, "Thank you again, for being here," and raised his glass to me.

"Of course," I said. "I'm very sorry for your loss, sir."

Mr. Whitmore nodded, "Thank you. She was a lovely girl,"

he stared off. "She learned how to swim right there, in my pool," he pointed. "Gangly, little thing…scared to death," he chuckled a little at a memory brought to mind.

Tyler too, grinned and squeezed my hand.

A moment of silence passed before Mr. Whitmore's face contorted. Slamming his fist on the table, he growled, "What kind of animal…can do that to another human being? Just choke the life out of another human being? Soulless bastard!"

I felt myself swallow hard. I didn't know all the details behind Mitzi's death, but seeing his anguish, a horrible thought came to mind; *I am that kind of animal.* Suddenly, I felt a wave of nausea wash over me. Blinking back tears from the thought, the reality of what I was; I was suddenly sickened. Tyler noticed my reaction and squeezed my hand. When I wouldn't raise my eyes to his, he squeezed again.

What was I feeling? Was this guilt? My heart began to race, threatening to pound out of my chest.

When I looked up, Mr. Whitmore was looking from me to Tyler, then back to me again, with a look of distress on his face.

"I'm sorry," he extended an apology to me. "I shouldn't speak so brazenly of these things." Mr. Whitmore stood and excused himself.

Was he worried that his blatant expression of feeling was too much for polite conversation? I was still trying to control my breathing and stomach spins when Tyler suggested a walk.

"Give me a moment alone," I asked, still shaken by this pooling of emotion. Standing, I kissed Tyler's cheek before walking off toward the house to find a restroom.

Splashing cold water on my face and trying to steady my nerves, I heard a knock on the door. "One moment, please," I informed the knocker. A few more deep breaths then I would be ready to face the crowd of mourners.

When I pulled open the door, Daniel was standing there. I let out a sigh and tried to move past him. Putting his arm across the doorframe to bar my way, I took a step backward into the restroom.

"Aren't you happy to see me, Audra?" he grinned.

"Not especially.."

"That's not what I wanted to hear," his head shook slowly. "Especially after having seen the show you put on for me."

"You weren't even a thought. And I mean that, Daniel." Everything I had felt moments before the guilt, the fear, the self-loathing, they were all being washed away. *HE* was exactly the reason I hunted, killed.

"Why are you fighting this so hard? You and I know it's just a matter of time before Tyler casts you aside for someone more…" his hand reached out to graze my collar bone, "accept-able," he sighed. "Do you want me to fuck you on Mr. Whit-more's desk…like he did?'

"Remove your hand," I hissed, almost grateful that I hadn't packed my gun into my clutch bag.

"Or what? This is a big house, Audra," one cheek pulled up, giving him a cockeyed grin. "No one would ever know…and no one will ever hear you," he whispered.

"This is the boast of your prowess?" I asked with my own amused grin.

Huffing, Daniel took a step toward me, "I *CAN* make you scream," his jaw so tight, the muscles in his neck protruded. "And I promise you, when I do get what I want from you, I'm going to make you hurt."

"If you don't back away from me right now…*you're* going to hear me scream," I warned him.

His face was immediately transformed by rage, "I don't enjoy playing the cat and mouse game, Audra!" his hand moved up, cupping the side of my neck.

"I'm not playing anything with you," my slit eyes, never blinked.

"I will NOT be denied!" his grip tightened on my throat. Through gnashed teeth, he said, "Especially by some little…" suddenly his words were cut short by the sound of approaching footfalls. Quickly removing his hand and taking a step back into the hallway, he tried to control his visible rage.

I heard Simon's voice coming closer, "Sir, is there a problem?" he asked Daniel.

As I ducked under Daniel's outstretched arm to exit the restroom, Simon turned his concerned gaze to me. Cocking his head, he asked, "Everything alright, Audra?"

Looping my arm through Simon's, I told him, "Just a little overwrought by the emotions of the day."

"And you, sir…," Simon turned suspicious eyes to Daniel, "is there something I can help you with?"

"Daniel looked smug as he spat, "No, I don't need any help…from the help."

"Simon," I drew his attention back to me, "would you be so kind as to escort me back to the yard?"

Turning his stare back to Daniel, Simon answered, "I'd be happy to."

When we got out of earshot, Simon asked, "*DID* I interrupt something?"

Slowly, I began to nod, "Yes…and I thank you."

Simon nodded, "I've never liked that guy."

I turned my head to him and forced a smile, "That makes two of us," I confirmed.

Tyler looked concerned when he saw me returning on Simon's arm, "Everything okay?" he asked standing quickly.

"Just felt a little woozy. Lucky for me, Simon was nearby and came to my rescue," I put a kiss on Simon's cheek. "Thank you."

Simon nodded, "You're welcome, Audra," he said then excused himself.

I wasn't sure what Simon may tell Tyler later, but as for right now, this was neither the time nor the place.

"I am so sorry. I should have insisted on going with you," Tyler's head shook.

"Next time I won't be so stubborn as to deny your gallantry," I smiled. I knew now that I would never give Daniel another opportunity to corner me, again.

On the drive home, I thought about the momentary rush of guilt I had felt for the families of those I had extinguished. As much as I tried to tap back into that feeling, it was no longer something I could call forth. It was like a wave that had hit me hard then just receded into oblivion. It was just...gone. Daniel had forced the feeling away with his inappropriate behavior. He reminded me that some men didn't deserve to be treated as humans; didn't deserve mercy. Singlehandedly he had reignited a fire in me.

"Are you feeling okay?" Tyler asked, as he reached for my hand.

I nodded and gave his hand a squeeze, "I'm fine."

"You had me worried. For a moment there, you turned a little green. You're sure you're okay?"

I sighed and brought his hand to my lips for a quick kiss, "Just a momentary rush of emotion."

"You want to talk about it?"

No, I'm good now."

And I was. In my mind, I was busy picturing the life leaving Daniel's body. No remorse, no guilt, just a feeling of utter satisfaction washing over me. Pulling up to my house, I felt almost renewed, alive again. I knew that today probably hadn't had the same effect on Tyler. Seeing his father so anguished (not to mention his own feelings about Mitzi's death), may have been weighing heavily on his mind.

Before he exited the Jeep I caught his arm, "Are you alright? I mean, I know how difficult today must have been for you."

Tyler thought for a moment, "It was," he admitted. "But more so for my father. I got to talk to him alone for a moment while you were in the house. They still don't have any leads. They know she had intercourse, but ruled out rape. There was no DNA found, and her fiancé has an airtight alibi…thank God," his head shook.

"I didn't know how close your family was to Mitzi, until today," I patted his hand. "I'm very sorry."

"She was something," his head swiveled back and forth. "She had a big crush on my brother growing up," he smiled.

"Really?" I grinned.

"Oh yeah. Joel was a handsome man. I mean, he was a severe introvert, but kind and gentle with the people he let into his life. Mitzi was one of those people," Tyler recalled.

I remembered seeing pictures of Joel when I had been spying on Tyler and the Whitmore family. He was handsome. I could see a woman not only being attracted to his looks, but also the fact that he wasn't quite like everyone else in the circles they ran in.

Tyler grinned, "She was his first."

My eyes popped out a little, "Mitzi?"

Nodding, Tyler added, "Actually, I think she was his only."

"But, they didn't date?" I questioned.

"Joel wasn't built that way," Tyler's head shook a little. "I don't think he understood the dynamics of a relationship. He couldn't quite figure out what dating entailed, what was expected of him."

I rolled this thought around in my head.

"I mean, Mitzi wanted someone who would bring her flowers and take her places, but that wasn't Joel. He didn't think about people *needing* these things, because…he didn't."

"Ah," I nodded, realizing that Joel was more introverted than I had even imagined. "But he still had…drive…sexual desire?"

Tyler pondered how to answer this question. "I think… Mitzi seduced him when he was nineteen. Well, he was nineteen, she was seventeen. From what Joel told me, they were in the pool one night, swimming, when Mitzi cornered him and asked if he wanted to see her."

My brows rose.

"When Joel said he did see her, confused by what she meant, she took off her bikini.

My brows rose.

"I guess Joel didn't move. He just sat there on the stairs. So she swam over to where he was sitting, and asked him if he wanted to touch her. When he asked, "Why," her next move was to ask if she could touch him."

"Oh," I bit into my lower lip. I could picture this in my head: Joel's confusion, Mitzi's lust.

Tyler continued, "When Mitzi reached down and started rubbing him, I guess his body reacted…possibly for the first time in his life." Tyler gave a palm-up, "I'm not sure, I mean I don't think he had ever even touched himself, from the way he explained it."

"That must have been quite the surprise for him," I thought out loud.

"I imagine it was. He wasn't like a young boy trying to get his rocks off. It was more like he didn't have any idea what his rocks were for, what they were capable of."

"So…was he okay with…the ending?"

"I guess he got close and pulled away; it scared him a little. But Mitzi was determined. When he stood to move away from her, she grabbed his shorts, pulled them down and went down on him until he finished."

My eyes rounded, "Wow! I mean, how did he handle that?"

"He said that he loved the beginning, but didn't like the finish," Tyler's head shook a little.

For every man I had ever met, the finish was the whole point. "Did he say why? I mean was it painful, or just grossed him out or…" I couldn't come up with anything else off the top of my head.

Tyler's head shook again, "No, he said it felt good, but he felt like he lost control, like his mind wasn't properly focused during that time. He didn't enjoy losing control."

Now I nodded, "I think I can understand that. Not that I have ever felt that way about orgasm. But considering how he was, who you told me he was, I think I can understand how it must have felt from his point of view. So he never," my head shook, "did the actual deed?"

"Oh, he did. And it was with Mitzi. He just wouldn't allow himself to finish."

My eyes rounded with the implication of what *never finishing* meant. A flash of Tyler and me…him refusing to finish;

how I would interpret that as a woman. I knew from personal experience how this would make me feel: insecure and unwanted were the first feelings that hit me. Sure, the first couple of times, it would be mind-blowing, to just go and go and go. But then it would become like a challenge to take him where he had taken me.

"So did they just…stop, one day?" my eyes turned to Tyler.

"Well, he broke up with her, for lack of a better term. Considering the fact that he didn't really understand that they were an item," Tyler made air-quotes with his fingers. "He just told her that they couldn't have sex anymore. That was pretty much the end of it."

"And he was never with anyone else?" my brow furrowed.

"No. I think he would have told me, if he had," Tyler nodded.

We both sat there quietly for a few minutes. Thoughts were rolling around in my head and warming me. Finally I said, "I think something is really wrong with me."

Tyler looked concerned, "What do you mean? What's wrong?"

"I mean, I can't help it."

"Help what?"

"I keep thinking of you, at nineteen years old. I know you weren't an *innocent* by any means. But if I picture you as a nervous young man, and me as a slightly younger, but more experienced woman…bending you to my will…making you want things you never knew you wanted…"

Tyler began to grin, "Oh yeah? Would you have been willing to teach me a thing or two?"

I nodded, my hand reaching across the center console to rub

his quickly growing bulge. "Do you like it when I touch you here?" I asked, leaning over to lick his ear.

"*Mmm,*" I do.

"What else do you like?" I whispered.

"I don't really know what I like," he played with me. "Maybe you can show me?"

Hurrying into my house, we ran for the couch, like a couple of teenagers. For the next two hours we played, *Do you like this,* and *Can I touch you here,* until we were thoroughly exhausted. I was determined that he *finish* as many times as he could. It may not be everyone's form of therapy, but in my mind, you give people what they need during times of great tragedy, not what society considers *normal.* And normal? Neither of us could boast this flaw.

13

I awoke to the feeling of being *close*. I was already making soft sounds of pleasure when I came out of a great dream. "Mmm," what are you doing?" I asked lazily as Tyler's head lifted from between my thighs.

"Time to worship," he grinned sucking on his lower lip.

"Oh yeah?" I asked tucking my arm behind my head, enjoying the view I had of him.

"Just lay back and close your eyes."

When I did, a small shock of pleasure shot through me, leaving me purring like a kitten.

After I worshiped him in return, I made coffee. "Ya know," I said over my shoulder, "today would be a lovely day for a hike. It's supposed to be a little overcast," I added. "You game?"

"Oh, so I give you a few pieces of information about me and you try to use them against me?"

Setting his coffee on the table I leaned down to brush his lips with a kiss. "I prefer to think you told me a few pieces of information about yourself, and I'm using them to accommodate you."

Pulling me down on his lap, Tyler nuzzled into my neck, "I do love how well you have accommodated me."

"Mmm, if you keep doing that, I'll have to accommodate you again." I turned his jaw to kiss him long and deep. Leaning back I asked, "Do you have a favorite place?"

His grin was naughty, as he brought his fingertips to my lips.

"A favorite place to hike?" I corrected the question.

"There aren't many in South Florida, but I do have a favorite of the few that exist."

We drove for a while. I was just enjoying the view, and being outside. I hadn't realized before just how much time I spent not only alone, but indoors, since moving to Florida.

"This is the only true hiking path in Biscayne National Park," he said as I spied the Spite Highway Trail sign. Handing me a can of Super Pest Be Gone, he informed me, "The mosquitoes are kind of bad here."

Covering myself head to toe in insect repellant, I coughed my way out of the plume of aerosol surrounding me.

Tyler laughed, "I think that's probably enough."

"I got it in my mouth," my face squished up.

Handing me a water bottle," he was still laughing and shaking his head.

I swished the water around, and around, before spitting it out on the ground. Tyler stood there staring at me, as I repeated this act two more times. "Why are you staring at me like that?" I asked.

"It's just…I've just never seen you spit before," he joked.

"Would you prefer it?" I asked, my brow rising.

"No," he said quickly, his head shaking like mad.

Wrapping his arm around me, we started down the path. Hardwood trees shaded the trail. It was so green. I had almost forgotten that we were basically hiking in a swamp. Tall grass made me wonder what kind of well-hidden animals we were coming into contact with, unknowingly.

"So…alligators?" I asked.

"Possibly," Tyler nodded.

"Crocodiles?"

"Also a possibility."

"Snakes?" I asked looking around at the tall grass we were passing.

"Yep," Tyler tried to keep from smiling, amused by my rising paranoia.

"Poisonous?" I moved closer against his body.

"Mmm," his brow furrowed playfully like he was trying to remember, "A couple," he nodded again.

"Fantastic," I said under my breath.

"I thought you liked hiking," he looked sidelong at me.

"I do!" I nodded, my eyes still drawn to every heard, but unseen movement in the grass and trees. "I just haven't had to worry too much about being eaten on the hikes I've been on."

"You hiked in Big Bear, right?"

"I did," I confirmed.

"Don't they have bears and big cats in those mountains?"

I thought about the elusive, and tree-dwelling Mountain Lions. I slowly nodded wondering how many times I may have just been *lucky*, to not have run across one.

"So…?" he left the question hanging.

"I guess I'd rather be cat-scat than croc-crap?" I said seriously.

Tyler stared down at me for a moment then began laughing. Pulling me closer against him to kiss the top of my head, he said, "I'm not going to let you become crap or scat of any kind."

Wild flowers were in bloom and flies of all varieties, including butter and dragon, hovered, zipped, and zoomed in every direction. Tyler pointed out several different species of birds. Spying a Brown Pelican, as he called it, he told me that these huge, strange looking birds were in fact endangered .

"There are quite a few endangered species that live here in the park," he said staring at the Pelican.

I couldn't help but smile at him, "So you study them? Birds, I mean?"

"No. But Joel did. He studied every bird, mammal, amphibian, reptile, insect, and fish you could think of."

"I bet he was a great person to have around when you had a science report due," I smiled.

Laughing, Tyler said, "That, he was. But the truth is he never talked about mundane things. So when he did talk, I listened intently and absorbed as much as I could from those conversations. I really enjoyed the things he was passionate about: Nature, animals, science."

I nodded, "A brilliant mind."

"Indeed. He was very logical, analytical. But he did have trouble reading people; their emotions, intentions."

I watched a cloud fall over Tyler's eyes. In that one moment, his normal jovial self, seemed haunted and sad. Maybe he just missed his brother. Maybe talking about him in the past tense was too much to bear. I knew that I never spoke of my parents, even though I missed them, dearly. It was just too painful. Not the memories. Those were wonderful. But the reminder that I had to miss them, the feeling of *missing* those wonderful moments, was horrible.

"You okay?" I asked.

Slowly Tyler began to nod, "Yeah. A part of him will always

be with me," he stopped and turned to take me in an embrace, squeezing me close.

As we headed back down the path, a snake slithered across on his way to who knows where. My arms wrapped around Tyler's neck before I swung myself up into his arms.

"Shit, shit, shit!" I yelled.

Tyler cradled me, laughing loudly, "It's an Eastern Indigo Snake. He's not poisonous and he's probably more afraid of you, than you are of him."

"Oh yeah, I didn't see him jumping into your arms!" I pointed out.

This snake was by far the longest I had ever seen in real life. When it passed in front of us, it stopped and raised its head like it was acknowledging us. I shivered in Tyler's arms.

Tyler continued to carry me onward, kissing my cheek, "Who would have thought a hunter such as you, would have such a great sense of humor, or a fear of animals?"

"What I hunt…I can read. Probably because it's usually only *the one thought* that's preoccupying their brain."

"Speaking of that…hunting," Tyler clarified raising his brow, "have you had any desire to do so?"

I thought about the question. Then I thought about the thought that I hadn't thought about it. "Huh. No, I haven't," I answered. "You?" I asked, my confusion clearly showing on my face.

Tyler's head shook as he answered seriously, "No."

I stared up into his eyes, neither of us expanding on our thoughts. I had no reason to doubt him, considering how I hadn't had the desire, either. Now I had a new question added to my list of things I would most likely make myself crazy overanalyzing: Why not? On the drive home, Tyler had his hand resting comfortably on my thigh. I was anything but. I couldn't stop wondering, *why*. Where had the thought, the desire, gone?

Even though I hadn't ever hunted on a regular basis, I did think of hunting on a regular basis. Every time I saw the creepy checkout-guy sporting his wedding ring, but still visibly staring slimily at the tits of the woman in front of me in the checkout line, I thought of hunting. I wanted to hunt. Every time I saw a rich, old married man parading around a young thing that was a bit too skanky to be the other person on his joint account; I wanted to hunt. I didn't always do it, but it was something I always thought about…until now. Even Daniel, I knew I wanted to end him. But before, my mind would have been preoccupied with not only how I wanted to end him, but the method that would be used, and where, when he should take his last breath. It made me uncomfortable to think…was I changing…again.

After a while, I noticed that Tyler had been stealing glances of me, "You okay?" he asked.

I nodded, "Yeah, I'm fine."

When we pulled up in front of my house, I said, "Would you mind if I took some alone time, tonight?"

A look of concern flashed across his face again, "You sure you're okay?"

My head nodded, "I'm fine. Just have a bit of a headache. I think I need to go lie down."

"You sure you don't want me to take care of you?"

"No, I'll be fine," I exited the Jeep.

"Hey," Tyler searched my face when I turned back to him, "can I get a kiss?"

Leaning in across the passenger seat, I gave him a quick peck before I hurried up to my doorstep.

Shutting my door, it hit me just like that; I was uncomfortable with him now. I wasn't sure why, or how, but it felt like I was changing and he was the reason. As much as I fought the thought, I mean, he's a hunter, too. So why all of the sudden did I feel like it was *him* that was changing me? We could be changing together, I pondered the idea. Why does change have to be a bad thing? I questioned myself and moved in every possible thought direction for hours until I heard knocking at my door.

14

I knew who it had to be. Opening the door, he stood there, gorgeous as ever. Him; in his white button up long sleeved shirt, and a pair of well-worn jeans. His delicious-ness almost made me forget everything I had been thinking and over-thinking. As my gaze worked its happy way up to his eyes, my head shot back. He looked angry. Not pissed exactly, but angry.

Worried, I asked, "What's up?"

His voice was low, "Why didn't you tell me?"

At this point I was baffled. Was I supposed to say I was uncomfortable but now I wasn't sure if I should be? Even scarier, how did he know?

"What are you talking about?"

"Why didn't you tell me about Daniel?"

I threw my hands up in the air, "Because I didn't know what to say."

Simon told me that he walked up on you and Daniel in the restroom. He said Daniel had you barred inside."

I turned and took a few steps back so Tyler could step inside.

"Simon said that Daniel sounded pissed when he approached. And when he saw you, you looked relieved that he happened upon the two of you." To my turned back, he asked, "Is that right?"

I nodded and spun to face him, "Yes." I was trying to figure out why his anger was aimed at me.

Walking up to stare down into my confused and irritated face, he asked, "What did he say to you?"

I gave him a palms-up, "Which time?"

"He's cornered you before?" Tyler's jaw tightened.

"Yeah, the first time we met. Well, not cornered," I clarified. "But in my personal space. It was out on the patio at your father's house."

"What did he say to you?" His already visible anger, rising to another level.

I let out a deep sigh, "He implied that you give him your leftovers," I answered as unemotionally as possible. "That you're absolutely fine with sharing and basically, my days with you were numbered. I'm not speaking verbatim, of course, but that was the gist of the conversation in a nutshell."

Tyler's face changed from one of anger to one of fear, "And the second time?"

I stuck my tongue in my cheek, "He reminded me that it was just a matter of time until you sent me on my way. He said that your father's house was big, and no one would ever hear me, or ever know. Then he said he could make me scream. Of course, that was after I said something derogatory about his lack of prowess."

Tyler looked sickened, shaking his head.

"Also, you should probably know that he watched us fuck in your dad's study. I didn't know he was there until the end. For that matter, I don't know how long he had been there. But he WAS there, and I should have told you."

Tyler took a step forward and grabbed my hands, "Why didn't you?"

"I didn't really see him as a threat, then. I figured him having seen us together, would make him back off. I made it clear, even if you did dump me, I wouldn't turn to him," my head shook.

Tyler's head shook, too, "So this whole time, you've been taking me at my word, instead of believing him? Even with your trust issues?"

"I'm not about to lie and say that his words didn't have any effect, raise any fears or issues, but yes, I trust you. As much as I *CAN* trust another human being, I trust you."

Tyler grabbed me in his arms, lifting me off the ground as he laid a huge kiss on me.

When he set me down, I had to ask, "Is there anything I should, or rather, need to know?"

Tyler let out a long breath and nodded.

"Am I going to need wine?" .

His brow rose, "It couldn't hurt."

Sitting on the couch with the biggest wine glass I owned, I said, "Okay, spill it!"

He took a deep breath and began, "When I was younger, early twenties, I was a dog, for lack of a better term."

I nodded, not exactly shocked.

"I ran with a few of the *Heir-Boys*, as we affectionately named ourselves. We were spoiled, drugged out on the best coke you could buy, and dodged trouble with the help of our family name, and expensive lawyers. Daniel was one of the pack."

He wasn't exactly painting a picture of someone to whom I

would have given a second glance. But, I was quite sure he wouldn't have looked at me twice then either.

"Never-ending money, and coke, entertains a certain type of relationship. And, I indulged in them every chance I could," his eyes dropped to the floor. "I wasn't about relationships. And with a particular type of woman, I never had to worry about them thinking there was more to our interaction than the completion of the agreed upon transaction. It was just a financial arrangement, with blow as a perk."

I nodded blankly, taking a huge swallow of my Cabernet. Tyler watched my facial expression change when he described his old self. I'm sure it wasn't a good change in his eyes, but still, he continued.

"Daniel's family lost most of their fortune. A combination of the 2008 stock market crash and an expensive, very risky financial venture left his family bankrupt. In our circle, some, if not most, will shun you once you become one of the have-nots. We, my family, continued to support him and his family. And I personally, supported his habits. "

"Women?" I said.

"Women, booze, coke, you name it. I felt like I owed him," Tyler shrugged. "He had been such a good friend to Joel. I myself, once considered him to be like another brother. It was a year or so after his family lost most of their fortune and were about to lose their home, that I bought a large amount of coke; so he could go out with a bang," Tyler's brow rose as he let out another soul crushed sigh.

I noted Tyler's breathing changed…whatever was coming… it was bad. I could feel it in my bones.

"I rented out the penthouse of one of Miami's finest hotels. I had locked myself in one of the bedrooms with three high-priced call girls, booze, and enough coke to kill us all, twice. I was high as a kite, when I thought I heard a scream," he swallowed hard, reliving a horrible memory.

I reached out my hand to his knee, "It's okay, you don't have to tell me," my head shook. But I wasn't sure if I said this for his benefit, or my own.

"No," his head nodded, "I do," his eyes finally looking into mine. "Joel didn't usually come with us, but every once in a while, he craved a change of pace. He knew he was in a safe place, with me, Daniel, and the boys. Tonight though, it was only Joel, Daniel, four call girls and me. I was really fucked-up when I thought I heard a scream. Fortunately, the girls in my room were more fucked up than I was. They didn't hear a thing over the music. A couple minutes later, Daniel banged on the door. When I opened the door, he was standing there, covered in blood. He stepped out of the eye-line of the women and said we had a situation. I left the girls there in the room with the booze and dope, and walked into the bedroom at the other end of the penthouse."

Tyler looked like he was going to be sick. He took a few deep breaths before continuing.

"There was so much blood; on every wall," he ran his fingers through his hair. "The blood drenched body of a woman, the forth call girl, was lying on the floor."

I watched as the memory made Tyler's face turn green.

"Standing in the middle of the room with a knife in his hand, was Joel. I thought I was going to throw up, but I was more worried about my brother. It was like he had gone catatonic. He just stared forward at the wall, lost inside himself. I didn't know what to do, so I called for help."

"You called the police," I asked baffled that Joel had ever seen the light of day, again.

Tyler's head began to shake, "No." He took a deep breath, "I called my father. I didn't say what had happened, just that we needed him. Joel needed him, right now. When dad showed up, Simon was in tow. The first thing Simon did was give the women in my room a shit ton of money and sent them on their way. They were so fucked up, I don't know if they even realized that woman number four was missing.

I admit this wasn't at all what I was expecting. I took a long pull off of my wine glass and handed it to Tyler hoping it would help calm his nerves. After taking a large gulp, he continued.

"My dad wanted the story, and of course I didn't know what the fuck happened. One minute I was having a foursome, and the next, I was staring at this gruesome sight and the void in my brother's eyes. Daniel said it started in the living room. He offered the other woman money to *take care* of Joel. When she started rubbing on Joel, he got embarrassed and ran off into the other bedroom. Daniel said the woman grabbed the soda can out of his hand and took it into Joel's room, closing the door behind her. Twenty minutes later, there was a scream and then she was dead."

"What was in that soda?" I asked.

"Cocaine…and a lot of it…it was Daniel's." Tyler's head shook. "Dad tried to talk to Joel, but he was just…gone. The next thing I knew, someone was knocking on the front door of the penthouse. Simon said he'd get it. Four guys I had never seen before, or since," his head shook, "walked into the bedroom carrying duffle bags. At that point, Simon whispered something to my father and told us to leave. Dad, Joel, Daniel, and I, got in the limo and headed home."

"I'm guessing that's when your father became more overpro-tective?"

"Yes. Who can blame him, right? I had let him down, let Joel down and was the reason an innocent woman was..." Tyler let his chin fall to his chest.

"Did Joel ever tell you what happened?" I asked.

"He said the last thing he remembered, was taking the soda from the woman. The rest was a three day blackout. When he did *come back,* he didn't remember anything, so we never told him about the woman; what he had done to her," Tyler's eyes fell closed.

"That's when you and Daniel had your falling out?"

"Actually, it was the blackmail that separated Daniel and me," Tyler looked sidelong at me.

"Blackmail?" I questioned.

Tyler nodded, "Daniel knew Joel didn't remember anything. And to make sure it stayed that way, or wasn't brought to the attention of the police, he wanted money. A lot of money," Tyler's eyes shot to mine. "I guess I should have expected it. His family was damn near broke, he was losing the life he had grown accustomed to. Then his father committed suicide."

"Because of the money?" I questioned.

"The money he lost on the Market, as well as the money he had been embezzling from those who had supposedly bought stock for the medical venture which went belly up before the product was ever approved. He lost hundreds of millions. Daniel's father was looking at serious jail time."

"Oh," my eyes rounded.

But even before his dad took his life, Daniel didn't seem to feel anything: not about the woman who was murdered or the moral dilemma of just discarding her. He even said, if she hadn't lived as a whore, she wouldn't have died like one. I thought of him as a brother and it turned out that I had been buying the company of someone who would sell out my brother, hurt my brother, his best friend."

"How much?" I asked.

"Ten."

"Million?" my eyes rounded.

"Yes," Tyler sat back, finishing my wine.

I was trying to wrap my head around the whole story. "He's still invited to family functions at your dad's house?"

"That was part of the agreement. He would be treated exactly as he had always been. That included access to Joel. And that's how *I* became so overprotective. I didn't trust Daniel not to tell Joel. What if he said something that, I don't know, tapped into a hidden memory?"

I nodded. I could see how this possibility, added to all Joel's other…quirks, could be a frightening thought for someone who really loved him. The more silent Tyler was, the more I pondered.

"With your pastime being what it was, couldn't you just, ya know, alter your code…just this once?" I gave him a palms-up.

"Oh, believe me, I've thought about it, pictured it, even planned it out in my head."

"But?" I asked.

"Daniel isn't stupid. After seeing how one phone call to the right person made something this heinous, disappear, he found a sure fire way to protect himself before he extorted my father.

I cocked my head, "How?"

"He wrote down the whole story, implicating everyone and put it in a safety deposit box. Then he told us that if anything unnatural happened to him, if he went missing, in his will, he had left *someone* a key to the security box, the whole story, names, dates and details inside, with specific instructions to reveal my family for their sins. He even showed us a copy of the will with the name of said person, blacked out."

"But, it's just Daniel's word against your family."

"I checked-in with cash under an alias. I was never even questioned," his head shook. "A rich boy paying cash to party in a hotel room wasn't really unheard of in Miami. The cleaners, as I refer to them, had scrubbed the room until not a trace of blood could be found. All of the security tapes from that night had disappeared, and I'm pretty sure I know how, or rather, who, made that happen. Since there was never any video proving that the women had been there, or what room they had been in if they had been there, they had nothing to go on but the other women's statements. And none of them ever came forward. Pretty sure I know why that is, too. But the police *DO* know from two eyewitness accounts: a doorman and another call-girl who was visiting another room, that the missing call-girl, had been there. She was last seen entering the hotel. But of course, no body was ever found, so she's still thought of as just another missing person. And not to sound crass, but a dead hooker, call-girl, or prostitute…they aren't a high priority for the police department in Miami."

I had to give Simon credit. He tied loose ends, very well.

Even though it's a cold case and Joel has passed on, it could still ruin my father and Simon, if what happened was ever revealed."

I nodded slowly.

"He told us about the Will, and safety deposit box; sent us screenshots. But who knows if there ever was one. And if there is, is it just one person he's left this information to?"

All of this was hard for me to hear. But it was so much harder to see the anguish he had been, and still was, living with.

His eyes were trying to well up, "I feel horrible about that poor woman. I really do. I even sent her family money anonymously, not that it could ever make up for their loss…or my guilt."

I moved closer to him, reaching out to squeeze his hand in mine. "You have to know this wasn't your fault," I tried to get him to look at me.

"But it was," he turned his eyes to mine.

I saw so much pain and self-loathing, in them.

"I knew his quirks. I knew that he wasn't…like…us! I should have kept him safe from the world," his eyes squeezed closed. "I was supposed to."

"But you never had any indication that you needed to keep anyone safe from him, did you?"

Tyler was silently staring at the floor. Finally he said, "No, never."

"Then how could you have ever imagined that something like…*this,* would happen." My head shook, "No one can prevent something they could never imagine happening."

He wanted to believe my words. I could see the inner battle he was fighting. But the rush of guilt from reliving that moment, that memory, was a worthy opponent. "I just wish that I had never brought Joel with us. I wish I hadn't been such a self-indulgent piece of entitled shit."

"Is that when *you* changed? The way you thought…the way you acted, or treat others. That's when you pulled away from the life in which you were raised, isn't it?"

Tyler nodded. "I didn't *hang out* with the crew, anymore. I still made public appearances as necessary: weddings, balls, birthday parties and fund raisers. But I didn't do the after-parties, rub elbows, or partake in the drugs that flow in that circle."

I took a moment to think of the way his world had crashed down. And how Joel's had crashed, too. Even if he never had to relive the memory and guilt the way Tyler would for the rest of his life.

I stood and went to the kitchen. I needed another glass of wine, and Tyler needed one of his own. Tyler walked up behind me as I poured.

He asked in almost a whisper, "Does this change the way you feel about me?"

Turning quickly to face him, I looked at him like this was the craziest thing I had heard all night. "No. I hate that you have this memory inside you. But, no! I think it makes me appreciate you, who you turned out to be, even more."

Tyler looked like this was the last thing he expected to hear. "I don't see how it could," his head shook.

"Look, the way I see it, yes, you were a spoiled, maybe even horrible person, I don't know," I shrugged. "And even though you had someone there to clean up your mess, Joel's mess," I broke off, "you could have adopted the mindset that you were invincible…untouchable. You could have continued to be that person. You could have had no remorse, no guilt," my head shook wildly. "Guilt is an emotion we *choose* to keep. You do know this, right? And only someone with a conscience, someone who acknowledges their *wrongs,* will ever allow themselves to feel guilt. And in my mind, only those people…" I took his hands in mine, "…only those people will ever change their ways, try to rectify mistakes. Even if they never really can, they'll try! They work to change the way they think, act, and treat others."

Tyler's eyes began to water again, his breathing deep.

"They work to become the kind of person they want to see looking back at them from the mirror. You did this, Tyler," I wrapped my arms around his neck and let him burry his face in mine.

We just held each other for a while before he pulled his head back so he could look at me. "I don't want you to think I'm a good guy for telling you about this horrible part of my past."

My head cocked at him, "What do you mean?"

"My intentions…I never intended to tell you any of this," his head shook. "I would have taken this to my grave, left you in the dark, if it hadn't been for Daniel's interest in you."

I was having trouble understanding why he said this. "Are you under the impression that I want to know all of your secrets?"

"Well shouldn't I be? Isn't that what couples are supposed to do?"

"I believe that some secrets…are meant to protect the ones you love."

He searched my face, "You believe this?"

I thought about my wording, "Some secrets are kept protecting the secret keeper, alone. The true word for this is lying. But some secrets, *ARE* kept solely to protect the people involved, or those who would only be damaged by hearing them. If there's no personal agenda attached to them, they are only being kept to protect and not to deceive, then I don't always need to know. You told me something, a dark secret, so I would understand and know that I needed to protect myself from Daniel. Even though you didn't know if it would change how I thought of you. You didn't have to tell me, but you did…for my safety."

"I can't help but think this has to have changed your opinion of me," he looked down at the floor.

"It did," I raised his chin so he would look at me. "I love you more, now. And I love the extent you would go to, to protect me."

Tyler slept with his head on my chest. I felt horrible that some part of me, wanted him. It had to be the furthest thing from his mind. So instead, I did the other thing I was good at when I needed preoccupation: I overanalyzed.

Most of the story he told me, made sense. I wasn't positive, but I assumed the other women (the ones who made it out alive that night), didn't live long afterward. I didn't know this, but it was where my mind instinctively went, or wouldn't they have also tried their hand at blackmailing? This was how my mind worked. It threw out all kinds of possibilities, before dwindling down the list to the most probable scenario. Being this way, another question I had dismissed while listening to Tyler's confession, was rearing its head.

He was so remorseful, carried so much guilt, yet he became a hunter? I was having trouble making sense of the glaring contradiction of his personality traits. How could he feel so bad for a, well I won't sensor my thoughts, a prostitute who makes her living screwing anyone who will pay her. But he had no problem killing adulteresses? Were any of the women he slept with that night, married? And then he had said, he thought he would throw-up when he saw the room covered in blood; the slashed throat of the woman on the floor. In fact, just retelling the story, I thought he was going to vomit. He had turned green and his mouth was visibly sweating from the memory. Not that I would prefer he be desensitized, but given our…hobby…wouldn't he be, by now?

And if nature, not nurture, was the reason behind his kills, would the dead woman have affected him that way? He had said he knew from the time he was young, that this was who he was.

I thought about all of my own kills. Yes, the first one, I worried that I might throw up. But that was a fear before the act. When I did end him, there was no nausea, no guilt, and no remorse. Something wasn't adding up; not at all. Yet, when the Piano Man had me on my knees, getting ready to do his thing, Tyler had ended him quickly. I didn't see any sign of remorse then. He didn't get nauseous, scared, or worried about that kill. He handled it just like an old pro. Like someone with twelve other kills under his belt, would. Maybe Joel was the reason for the remorse? Maybe him thinking he hadn't protected his brother, stirred what I had perceived as guilt over the woman's death? But if so, why would he have sent her family money? Well into the night, my mind flipped and flopped, finally exhausting itself into sleep.

When Tyler woke, he woke up like his old self; erect. Rubbing himself against my ass, he was ready to go. As much as I wanted to, all the questions that had rolled around in my brain before I fell asleep, came rushing back. But, he had been so broken last night, and he was feeling better now. I did want him to feel better. That's what I told myself as I began to warm up to him.

"I'm so tired," I told him.

"That's okay. You can just stay on your side and I'll do all the work."

I laughed, "Again, a solution for every problem."

"I'm a problem solver," he said, pushing himself between my legs.

Even though he felt fantastic, even though he gave 110%, I was still having trouble getting there.

"You okay?"

"Yeah, I'm just having trouble getting there," I admitted.

Rolling me over to lay his body on top of mine, he said, "It's because of what I told you. Your opinion of me *HAS* changed," he searched my eyes.

"It's not that,' I shook my head.

He sat up, and leaned back on his palms, "If not that, then what is it?"

I knew what I wanted to ask, but I couldn't bring myself to even say it out loud. So I went with door number two. "Did you supply Daniel with women?"

Tyler's head shook, "Not the way it sounds. Not the way he made it sound."

"Okay," I waited.

"Remember I said I wasn't the relationship guy?"

I nodded, "Yeah."

"Well, that didn't change after. A lot of things changed, but that didn't," his head shook. "I still had desires though. I met a lot of women, who wanted to land a rich man from a good family."

I nodded, knowing full well that some women just couldn't resist an incredibly handsome, not to mention rich, man.

"I was always honest about my intentions and needs. I never lied or tried to paint my interactions with these women as anything more than they were. But most of them, even after being told that all I could offer was that, they would still try to make it more."

I knew this to be a truth, too. Some women are so certain of their ability to bend a man to their will, that they just become unrealistic.

"When they would get too clingy, or started to look at me like I was their knight in shining armor, I would introduce them to any number of my friends. Some of them WERE looking for something more than just someone to share a meal with or a roll in the hay. A lot of these women just wanted to marry rich. Some didn't really care which rich boy it was."

I nodded, "So you never pimped out these women to Daniel?"

"No," his head shook. "He was the one who referred to them as my *leftovers*. I would never call any woman, something like that," his head shook wildly. "The fact that I didn't want a relationship, it doesn't make me a douche bag. I was honest with them. Upfront, the whole time. I didn't pawn these women off, either. I asked *THEM* if they wanted to meet some of my friends. I'd bring them to gatherings and they would choose who they wanted to meet. I didn't set them up to meet anyone in particular. After everything that happened, the murder and blackmail, I never invited Daniel to these gatherings. I didn't want to see any woman I knew," his brow rose, "you know, with someone like him."

"But he still showed up?"

"A few times," Tyler nodded. "Joel, like I said, he didn't have the same falling out that I had with Daniel. So sometimes, Joel would invite him thinking that Daniel's lack of an invite was nothing more than an oversight. And of course, Daniel stayed as close to Joel as he could."

I rolled this around in my head. Tyler seemed sincere and I couldn't picture him doing anything to hurt a woman that didn't fit his code. He wasn't a woman hater, per say. It was a specific kind of woman that got his juices flowing.

Tyler watched me staring off at the nothing, as I absorbed and analyzed the information he had given me.

"Audra?"

I turned my attention back to him.

Taking my hand in his, he said, "Audra...I swear to you...I have never, would never. Not one of them. And certainly never you."

I began nodding slowly.

"I'm in love with you," he said matter-of-factly. "My only thoughts, desires, are to protect you and love you," he swallowed hard, hoping that I could see this in his eyes.

Reaching out to cup his cheek, I said, "I do believe this," I whispered "I believe you."

As his relief turned into kisses, and his kisses turned into a need to prove the love behind his words, I willingly took my place beneath him. I had no trouble *getting there* now that I was set aglow by the rosy intentions of his love for me.

Picking up the paper from my front porch, Mitzi was back on the front page. Dropping the paper on the living room table, I went to make myself a cup of coffee. Unfolding the front page, I began to read.

"Detectives are interviewing staff of Cobalt Security, in the ongoing murder investigation of socialite Mitzi Gardner. Several employees have come forward to say that during the presumed time of the murder, the security company in question admitted to having technical difficulties due to a power outage. Due to the type of the security system at the Gardner Estate, Cobalt Security was on dark-mode for more than ten minutes.

Ray Adams of Cobalt Security, who was interviewed yesterday, said that he tried several times to get Miss. Gardner to update the outdated system, to no avail. "I really wish I could have, ya know, convinced her to upgrade. It's tragic. It's just a tragic loss," he told reporters.

"Having this information brought to light, steers the department in yet another possible direction," said Detective Ortega.

"Indeed," I said out loud.

When Tyler walked into the living room, I was staring off into nothingness, thinking.

"You okay?" he asked staring down at my furrowed brow.

I handed him the paper and went to make him a cup of coffee.

"So now they're thinking that someone at the security company was involved? He read on then said, "I guess ten minutes would give someone enough time to get in and turn off the system."

Setting down his coffee in front of him, I shrugged. "I guess if it was collaboration between two employees. You know, one in the office at the time and the other waiting for a signal that the system was down, but…"

"But nothing was missing, so not a robbery."

I nodded. "Whoever was there, was there for either sex, which we know she did have. Or…"

"Was there to kill her, and sex was…" Tyler said.

"Was just a step in the process," I finished his thought.

Tyler nodded slowly.

"Were the cameras at the estate motion activated?" I wondered out loud.

Tyler shook his head, "I really don't know. But just the guy saying he wanted to update the system, leads me to believe it wasn't top of the line."

"It just doesn't make sense to me. I mean it's an Estate. You'd think you'd be a little more worried about theft," I gave him a palms-up.

I think there's a false sense of security in gated communities, though. Armed guards driving around in their patrol cars, a manned gate."

"And none of the guards admitted any odd vehicles or saw anything alarming?"

`"But there are other ways!" Tyler nodded. "Someone could have scaled the wall or…" he eyed me.

"Or it could have been someone on the inside," I nodded to him. "So we're back to square one."

"It really bothers you, doesn't it?" he sounded a little confused.

"It really does. It just seems so unlikely. Things that don't make sense to me, keep my brain occupied, until they do."

"Well, on a not so completely unrelated topic, my father has asked us to lunch today," Tyler said.

My face squished up at the thought. I had been to Naples twice and both times, I hadn't exactly enjoyed my time spent there. "Why didn't you mention this last night?" I asked, like more time to absorb the thought would help, somehow.

"I didn't know last night if you'd still be talking to me today."

This comment made me nod. I could see how our conversation last night could have gone either way.

Tyler gave me the eyes, "You up for it?"

"Is there ANY chance that I will have another run in with Daniel?"

"This is lunch at the club, so the chances are slim, I would say. And even if he is there, he'd have to go through me to get to you. Dad just wants to get to know you a little better."

I couldn't help but grin. "Does this mean…I'm your girl-friend," I joked.

"Yes," he laughed, "The first one since the ninth grade. Say you'll go. I want him to get to know the woman who is so special to me."

Wrapping my arms around his neck, I smiled, "Well then, how can I refuse?"

15

---

*D*riving to Naples, a sudden shower interrupted the day. I've always loved the way the sunlight broke through gray clouds; when you could actually see the silver lining around them. Maybe that was a sign for me? Today I'd find the silver lining around some admittedly dark thoughts. I took a deep sniff of the rain scented air, and smiled from ear to ear.

Tyler noticed my reaction and grinned. "You really are a rain lover, aren't you?"

"I am. It's like it just washes everything clean, ya know?"

I couldn't tell if his grin was humoring, or understanding me. Squeezing my hand in his, he nodded.

By the time we pulled up at the club at 11:45pm, the clouds had all run away, and the rain no longer fell. Looking up, no silver lining graced the sky.

The club itself looked like it was built in the fifties and remodeled to bring it into the 21st century. It was well built with dark wood bones; plush in every way. I couldn't imagine having been raised with a place like this as my home away from home.

Being led to the large outside patio on the second floor, I watched the wait-staff rushing about with towels, drying off the tables and chairs that still wore tiny droplets of rain. The patio was otherwise empty. Tables that sat from two to eight, all with their own dark red umbrella, awaited the members. Being led to Mr. Whitmore's private 4 top table, we were sat and handed menus. Looking out over the golf course below, I had the desire to run barefoot through the well-kept grass.

"Dad said he'd been here at noon," Tyler relaxed, stretching out his legs and locking his fingers behind his head.

"So, I guess you grew up coming here?" I looked side long at him.

"I did," he nodded. "

My eyes surveyed the panoramic view, "It is beautiful."

Tyler let out a heavy sigh, "It is," he nodded. "So much so, you forget about the darkness this place has witnessed."

This comment confused me and it showed on my face, "What do you mean?" I asked.

Tyler's eyes were drawn away from mine, "Oh, there's dad."

Trying to shake off the shiver that had ran its way up my spine, I stood to greet Mr. Whitmore. I had to admit, he was agile for a man who had eighty-something years on him. He wore a gray sport coat over a peach polo shirt, and slacks.

"Lovely to see you, again." Mr. Whitmore took my hand in his and leaned in to put a kiss on my cheek.

"You, as well. Thank you for inviting me," I said as we all sat.

"So," Mr. Whitmore smiled, "Tyler has told me a bit about you, but I wanted a chance to talk to the woman who has stolen my boy's heart."

I smiled, not sure what to say.

"Come on, dad, you're going to run her off with talk like that," Tyler told him.

"Oh, I doubt that," Mr. Whitmore smiled. "From what you've told me, she's your perfect match."

Now I had to force a smile. Tyler and I only had two things in common, I thought. I doubted he told his father we both enjoyed hunting/killing and excessive sex. So…what had he told him about me?

"Actually, what makes her perfect is how different we are," Tyler said.

Mr. Whitmore nodded, "Yes. That to me is perfect," he gave a palms-up. "Your mother was far more adventurous than me," he looked at Tyler. "Oh, the things she wanted to do. She wanted to go skydiving," his head shook wildly at the thought. "Then there was hiking Everest, going on Safari in Africa, sailing around the world on a tiny sailboat, bungee jumping off the Empire State Building. Now that last one, I don't think they allow, but that didn't stop her wanting to."

I had to smile, "She must have had a daring soul."

"Why yes. Yes she did," he beamed. "And to think, that beautiful, wild and carefree woman, settled for being the mother of our children and my wife." His head swiveled. "Well, I didn't think any man could be so blessed."

A waitress approached the table carrying a tray of Bloody Mary's that to my knowledge, no one had ordered.

The visible wonder on my face made Mr. Whitmore offer an explanation.

"Standing order," he smiled.

"Ah!" I nodded. The three of us thanked our waitress before she hurried off.

"So," Mr. Whitmore said after taking his first drink, "I understand you were married."

Derrick was always the last person I wanted to talk about. "Yes, I was."

"He's passed on," Tyler added quickly.

"I am sorry," Mr. Whitmore nodded. "I do know what it's like to lose someone you love," he gave me a weak smile.

I smiled and said, "Thank you," again. I too, knew what it felt like. But of course that was due to the loss of my parents, not Derrick.

We ordered our lunch and then the conversation took a strange turn.

"So, Tyler tells me that you are quite the introvert?" Mr. Whitmore asked.

My eyes shot to Tyler who visibly winced when his father posed the question.

For me, it seemed like an odd thing to ask about; an odd thing to talk about. "Ah, I guess I am," I nodded.

"I'm sorry. I didn't mean to offend you, or pry" his head shook. "My son, Joel, was the most introverted soul. I'm afraid I've never stopped being fascinated by his ability to escape inside of himself; block out the world. I find it fascinating."

I laughed, "It's okay. I'm not offended. It's just…who I am."

"You see, my wife and I were both such extroverts. Her, even more so than me," he laughed. "If you don't mind my asking, were both of your parents, extroverts, too?"

To answer this, I had to mentally go back to a time that I missed with every part of me. "My mom was very social. She was a room mother for my class while I was growing up. She even worked at the high school I attended."

"It didn't cramp your style? Having your mother there?" Tyler joked.

"What style?" I joked back. "No. I didn't have any friends to speak of; no one to care if I was cool or not. Not that I would have cared," I laughed. "It just wasn't something on my list of needs. And then there was dad. Even though he had a highly social job as a detective, when the badge came off, well, he and I were more alike. I guess I would call him a *socially functional introvert*," I smiled remembering just how very alike we were.

Mr. Whitmore nodded, "Huh, that is interesting. May I ask…what were you like as a child?"

The look on his face changed. He cocked his head, like he was studying me. I wasn't really uncomfortable. I mean, I assumed he was trying figure out if Joel had been textbook.

"Um, I read a lot," I nodded and Mr. Whitmore nodded back. "I was okay in social situations and my surroundings, as long as I wasn't the center of attention. I still preferred to avoid them, true enough. But I was okay. I was functional."

Mr. Whitmore raised his brows, "Where were you most comfortable?" he asked.

"I grew up near the ocean in Southern California. So dad would take me to the tidepools. It was never as crowded as it was on the beaches. What with all the sunbathers, surfers and the swarms of people that crowd the sand on a hot Saturday afternoon, it was a bit much. Dad would teach me about animals and water life; things that held our interest and fascination. But my favorite place was Big Bear. I loved the trails and huge trees, animals, quiet spaces."

Mr. Whitmore nodded like he understood. "Tyler told me he took you to Joel's spot. He said you loved it."

"I did," I nodded. "It really is an amazing place." I reached out to Tyler's hand and squeezed an unspoken thank you.

When our food came, the conversation slowed a bit. Mr. Whitmore did tell me a few stories about Tyler and Joel when they were young. Even though they were funny and made me laugh, they also made me appreciate Tyler even more. The way he understood Joel and went against his own over the top personality to make his brother comfortable, even from a young age, was commendable in my book.

At the end of the meal, Mr. Whitmore asked if my parents ever came to visit me in Florida.

My head shook slightly as I tried to force another smile. "No sir. My mother died when I was twenty. A drunk driver took her life. And my father died when I was twenty-three."

Mr. Whitmore looked pained for me. Reaching out to pat my hand, he asked, "Did he pass in the line duty?"

My head shook, again. I was trying to separate my thoughts from my feelings to keep the tears at bay. I was good at this.

"Cirrhosis," I said. "After mom died…he drank himself to death."

"I am so very sorry," Mr. Whitmore's head shook.

I felt Tyler's eyes watching me; my response.

"Thank you," I said like I was totally detached from the memory. Which at the moment, I was.

Another moment passed before he asked, "So, is there anything you'd like to ask me?" Mr. Whitmore sat back in his chair, folding his hands in his lap.

If I looked shocked by the invitation, it's because I was. "Actually," I set down my glass, "I'd love to hear about how you met Mrs. Whitmore."

Tyler stopped his frittata filled fork halfway to his mouth and turned questioning eyes to me, then to his father.

I was put on alert by Tyler's facial expression. Fear grabbed me inside. Was this something about which they didn't talk? Was it something that stirred painful memories? Oh God, had I over-stepped?

Mr. Whitmore had been silent too long with a blank look on his face before he finally let a small smile pull up his cheeks. He sighed; a long sigh, before saying, "It was fate. It had to be," he looked up to the heavens. "She was here, in Florida, on Summer Break," he began. "She was a college student in her second year at U.S.C.," he remembered.

"Oh, a California girl," I smiled.

"Indeed," he smiled back.

"Well, I had been golfing all day but had to meet a potential advertising client for a drink. So, off to this bar I went. I met with my client. We had lunch, drinks, and discussed business. When my client left our meeting, I realized that I didn't have my wallet with me," he laughed. "Back then, I thought my wallet was what was throwing off my golf game. I was wrong," he gave me a shrug. "It was in the limo and I knew I could have Simon bring it to me, but there were no cell phones at that time. The staff knew me well and they weren't the slightest bit worried about being stiffed on the bill. But when I began explaining the situation to the waiter, this beautiful woman sitting behind me, that I hadn't had the pleasure of even seeing until now," his smile stretched across his face, "she offered to pay the bill."

I had to smile at the thought of some beautiful young woman coming to the rescue of a multi-millionaire.

"She had no idea who I was. Or what the total of the bill was, for that matter. She was ready and willing to do something nice, for a perfect stranger. Then, when I tried to explain that my wallet was in the car and it wouldn't take but a moment to retrieve it," she smiled that dazzling smile of hers, and I was smitten. Both with her beauty and her heart. She just had…a glow about her."

I loved seeing him remembering this moment. I could see how he felt at that exact moment.

"At that time," he continued, "I was considered a playboy, not because I had moves, but because I had never been married," he laughed. "And the not having moves was never more apparent than with my next move."

I waited on pins and needles, cocking my head.

"I handed her my business card," he shook his head.

I winced and laughed, "Well, it's not the worst…attempt at a pick-up."

"I handed her my card like I was a mini-blind salesman who wanted to be the provider for all of her mini-blind needs," he shrugged. "This was the big playboy's move!"

"But it worked," I grinned.

"Well, not at first. She looked down at the card and smiled. She politely extended her hand and introduced herself, then told me to "Have a nice day," before turning and just walking away."

I put my fingers to my mouth to cover a toothy grin, "Wow."

"Embarrassed and wishing I were suave, I don't know if they still use that word, but I wasn't, either way, I went to grab my wallet. When Simon saw me fishing for cash, he asked, "Do you want me to run that back in for you?" I was so flustered, I blurted out, "No, I'm trying to work up the courage to ask out my wife!" Mr. Whitmore shook his head.

Tyler laughed, "I do love that part of the story. He knew," Tyler told me, with a quick wink.

Mr. Whitmore nodded to his son, "Oh, most definitely. So, I'm taking a few moments to try and come up with something to say to her. Then I see her walk out of the restaurant, and I know it's now or never. So as I approach her, she smiled and said, "Oh, so you were coming back?" I nodded like an idiot. Then she hands me the paid receipt for my bill."

I was smiling so big now, picturing the scene in my head.

"So now I know, she did think I was just some schmuck who ran out on his bill. And I'm just trying to find a way to ask out the woman of my dreams. Me, being struck mute by embarrassment, watches her turn, and walk away, again."

"What did you do?" I asked, totally enwrapped in his story.

"I blurted out, "Hey, do want to have dinner with me?" She turned around slowly, ya know, cocks her head like she's considering it, then says, "Okay, but someplace inexpensive. Just in case you forget your wallet, again." Then she turned and walked away, he gave me a palms-up. "I was so flummoxed, I didn't even get her phone number. Something Simon brought to my attention as I walked back to the limo feeling like I had redeemed myself, somewhat. But by that time, I had lost her in the crowd. I was sure she'd never call me. And I knew in my heart, if she didn't, I would never see her again. The thought left me panic stricken."

"Now the search attempt," Tyler nudged me. "You'll love this."

"So I take off running down the crowded street, searching madly as I pass by stores, restaurants, bars, trying to look into each as quickly as I can. But I'm not finding her. By this time,

I'm going mad with the thought of losing the love of my life," his head shook.

I did love this story, and the way Mr. Whitmore turned back into a young smitten man while reliving it in his head.

"So, an officer sees me on the verge of full panic and asks, "Sir, can I be of some assistance?" Well, without thinking, I say, "I lost my wife!" Naturally, the officer has no idea that I'm not married, as of yet," he grinned, "and the woman I'm frantically searching for, I've only seen once, only met just now."

My head was shaking, as was Tyler's.

"So as the officer is trying to figure out how to help this poor wreck of a man, when I hear from behind me, "Your wife?" I turned to see her standing there; her hand on her hip. Without thinking, I grabbed her, wrapped her in my arms and told the officer, "Never mind, here she is."

I busted up laughing, "What did she do, then?"

"Well let's just say I had a lot of explaining to do and I was blessed that she was willing to listen to my ranting over a Bloody Mary," he lifted his glass to me.

"Wow, she still had a drink with you?" I was shocked and it showed.

"I know," Mr. Whitmore grabbed my hand and gave it a squeeze. "So she was forced to think either I really WAS married to someone else, or I was a complete whack-a-doo that saw her one time and fell in love," Mr. Whitmore laughed. "Thank God she took the whack-a-doo in me, as quite a compliment."

"What a great meet-cute," I said.

"We were married two weeks later," Mr. Whitmore beamed. "And I wasn't wrong...she was the great love of my life," he blew a kiss to the sky.

Tyler grabbed my hand and gave it a squeeze when pools started collecting in my eyes.

When we were leaving the Club, Mr. Whitmore took me in an embrace. In my ear he said, "I know he told you. And I know we can trust you."

For a moment, I stood mute in his embrace. He told his father I knew? When our eyes met, I confirmed this for him, "Yes, you can."

On the drive home, I kept thinking about the story Mr. Whitmore told about his beloved; how he knew. To me, that was a magic all its own. But when he said, "I know he told you," I couldn't help but wonder what Tyler told him about me that had made him trust me. Mr. Whitmore had cleaned up after Joel, refusing to allow his *not-quite-like-everyone-else* son, to be sent to prison. But I saw this as a desperate attempt to keep his unwell child, protected. Having never been a mother, I had no idea the extent I would go to, to do the same. It was a horrible and tragic event. Yet, also an isolated snap of his psyche. Had Joel not accidentally ingested the drugs, this tragedy would never have occurred. Did he know that Tyler told me everything? He may have thought that I just knew what happened as far as the murder; Joel's part. But did he also know I knew about his part; the clean-up and blackmail, as well?

"You're stuck in your head again," Tyler's voice broke my chain of thought.

"Your father told me, he knew you told me, and knew I could be trusted.."

Tyler was staring out the window and began nodding.

"Does he know that you told me...everything?" I asked.

Tyler's brow lifted, "He does."

"Did you tell him about Daniel and me?"

"I did. That's why he understood that you needed to know. He knows Daniel's a snake." He went silent for a moment. "He's asking for more money to keep the family secret hidden."

My eyes rounded, "Isn't he implicated in this as well? For keeping the secret, as well as the blackmail?"

"Of course, but any good lawyer would argue that he was too frightened to turn in someone who already made one prob-lem...*disappear*. And the blackmail? He can say it was a payoff to keep silent and continue breathing."

"Why now?" I wondered aloud.

"What do you mean?" he asked, looking sidelong at me.

"Well, this happened," I added it up, "like, ten years ago, right?"

Tyler nodded.

"And the blackmail...what, nine years ago," I questioned.

"That's about right,"

"So, why now? I mean, if at any time he thought he could ask for more money, which he obviously does, why did he wait so long? Is he back in financial straits?"

Tyler's head shook, "Not that I can imagine. When he married Tiffany, he became a very rich man. Rich enough to make the ten million he got from dad, look like chump change."

"You suppose maybe there's a divorce on the horizon. Don't most women like Tiffany have a prenup?"

"Not Tiffany," Tyler said. "She was in love with him for so long. But she had to wait in the line of his debauchery to finally land him. I remember Daniel bragging about this at his bachelor party. He said Tiffany had waived the prenup against her father's wishes."

"So what's changed in the recent past that would make Daniel request another payoff?"

We both thought about what it could be.

"Joel died a little over a year ago," Tyler finally said. "Then of course, Mitzi's death."

"What's the connection between Mitzi and Daniel?"

"Well, when she and Joel were spending time together, Daniel was around a lot. They were friends."

I did the slow nod; it made sense. If Daniel was Joel's only other friend, for lack of a better term, I guess Mitzi and Daniel would have spent some time together. It was a while before I asked, "What did you tell your father…about me?" I cocked my head.

Tyler's eyes shot to mine, "Just the basics. He tried to remember exactly what he had said to his father: "Your husband passed away. You grew up in Southern California. You're an introvert. Not as bad as Joel, but still more comfortable alone," he gave his head a small shake.

"Does he know what you are? What I am?" I added.

Quickly Tyler's head began to swivel, "No. And he can never find out." The look he gave me was one of fear. A shadow moved across his eyes at even the possibility of his father hearing his truth.

I began to nod, "Understood," I patted his leg.

We were quiet most of the way back home, while I did what I do best; overanalyze.

What did Tyler mean when he said, "So much so, you forget about the darkness this place has witnessed," when I said how beautiful the Club grounds were? How deep was the connection between Mitzi and Daniel? Why would Daniel wait nine years to ask for more money, when he clearly didn't need it? Why didn't Tyler ever tell me that his mother was also from Southern California, just like me? Thoughts were bouncing around inside my head. As much as I hated the way they preoccupied me, that was exactly what they did best.

As we pulled up in front of my house, Tyler turned his eyes to mine. "Would you like some company?" he asked with a grin.

"Hmm, that grin," I pointed, "I take it you're not hoping for a cup of coffee?"

"We could start there," he smiled and moved his lips to mine for a soft kiss.

"And where were you hoping it would end?"

"I was hoping it wouldn't."

He cupped my face and brought my lips back to his. Hunger rising, I could feel his needing escalating with my own. Oh, what one of his kisses could do to me. No man had ever awakened my desire the way he could with just one kiss. I was lost in my own world when I heard my elderly next door neighbor fighting with his garden hose.

A little startled, I pulled away from Tyler, back to the real world where people with eyes could see us making out like randy teenagers. Laughing a little, I said, "Maybe we should go inside?"

Stepping out of the Jeep, I called to Mr. Draper who was still fighting with his knotted hose. Not hearing me, I moved into his peripheral view so I wouldn't scare the wits out of him. When he lifted his head and saw me there, I asked, "May I be of assistance?"

"Darned thing," he said. "The wife just piles it up instead of winding it. Drives me crazy!"

I smiled and tried to help.

Mr. Draper threw his hands in the air, "After fifty years of this, I don't even ask her to do it my way, anymore."

Turning, he caught Tyler in his view. "Saw your Jeep here a few times," he reached out his hand to shake Tyler's, and introduce himself. "You did say he would find you," Mr. Draper winked at me.

"That he did," I laughed.

"She's a good girl," Mr. Draper told Tyler, as I finished the unraveling.

"Yes," Tyler beamed, "that she is."

Walking back into the bungalow, Tyler said, "I think that man is a little protective of you."

"He's a kind man," I smiled and hit brew on the coffee machine.

I felt his arms wrap around my waist, pulling me into him. Letting out a long sigh of contentment, he nuzzled into my neck. "I have a question," he whispered.

"Hmm," I hummed, enjoying the feeling of my flesh raising. "What would that be?"

His breath was warm, causing a chill to run over my body, "Are you a good girl?"

A cupped palm moved its way up the side of my body to my breast. His hand began kneading as the kisses on my neck became tiny bites. Fingertips rolled and squeezed my nipple between them as his other hand moved south toward my honey-pot. I loved the way he could derail my thoughts. Never did he force his will on me. But he had the ability to change mine. Three minutes ago, all I wanted was a cup of steaming hot dark roast, and now that *want* disappeared completely. Visions of what he had done to me, like pushing replay of my favorite hits, ran through my mind.

His hand reached further down to grab the fabric at my thigh. Scrunching my skirt up inch by inch, his hand slid underneath to slowly pet my mound. Every part of his body was always so welcome against mine…in mine.

"You know what's wrong with this picture," his voice low and deep.

My head rolled back and forth as his petting turned into rubbing.

"These need to come off," he gave my panties a little tug.

"Mmm, I kind of like it when they stay on."

Turning my body to face him, he grinned, "Oh yeah? Why's that?"

Wrapping my arms around his neck and looking deep into those dark blues, I felt a blush rise to my cheeks. How did he make me feel like a bashful girl, and a sultry goddess, at the same time?

"Because…it makes me feel…" I was little apprehensive to admit just how *much* it turned me on.

"Like a naughty girl?" he moved in to kiss the tender spot just above my collar bone.

"Yes," I admitted.

"Like, back when you had to be careful about your interludes? Far too careful to get caught completely naked," he whispered. "When your parents might walk in on you, at any moment?" he offered me a devilish grin.

I nodded, biting my lower lip.

"Like when you still had to steal your moments…when… and where you could? Knowing that you wanted to feel the body of the person you craved…desired…more than you could bear? You felt that driving force…to have them touch you…be inside you, didn't you?" his hand slid my panties to the side, barely grazing my skin as it moved.

My eyes burned into his. He understood where this thought took me, changed the game for me.

"When the thing you wanted most in the world…was his

tongue between your milky white thighs, slowly lapping at your tender little pearl? Did you fantasized about it, as you sat on the couch together watching movies?"

His questioning was searching for the horns holding up my halo.

"Did you sit there, hands folded in your lap, fantasizing? Were you brave enough to attempt the forbidden? And if you were, would you get away with it?"

I licked my lips, remembering.

"Were you naughty, Audra?" his fingers worked in a V, massaging my hooded pearl between them.

I took in a deep breath from the sensation and the visions he was giving me. "Maybe once...or twice," I added, bringing my hand to clutch his hardened member.

"Did you get fingered on the couch, Audra?" he licked his lips. "Under a blanket, did you wrap your hand around his cock...sliding it up and down?" he asked as one finger circled my opening.

Rubbing his cock, I nodded.

"Did he lie down on top of you, to rub his cock against this sweet spot between your thighs?"

Mmmhmmm," I kissed his neck, my grip tightened around him through his slacks.

His finger pushed inside of me, "Did it make you wet...like you are now?"

I took in a small gasp as he worked. "Yes," I whispered, as his finger slid in deep.

"Were you afraid to make a noise?"

My desire was building, "Yes," I moaned, quietly, burying my head in his neck. My fingers worked at his zipper. I wanted to release him; feel his excitement, real warm and so hard.

"Not yet," his head shook, "still too dangerous," he grinned. His other hand pulled my tank-top bra away from my breast. My nipple readily popped up to greet him. He smiled before his lips wrapped themselves around my hard, pink morsel, with the warm, wet of his tongue, circling.

It felt so good. He felt so good. The warmth, the sensation of his tongue, swirling, and sucking, was driving me mad. Deep inside, his finger still vibrated as it curled to tap the spot he knew would make me gush. I was pulsing with the expectation of being fully sated.

"Did you come, Audra? When he laid himself, swollen and hard, rubbing himself against your clit, did you cum?" he asked again before pushing his mouth to mine. Tongues writhed together as I felt that familiar swelling; my body's natural response to him.

His thumb still rubbing my lovely pearl, he kept me so close, and he knew it.

Tyler's brow lifted, "Did he sneak out of his jeans? Did he pull your panties aside, so he could sneak inside you? Did he dare put the tip...right here?" he pushed his finger as deep as it would go and just held it there.

My head shook, slightly.

His eyes rounded, "No?"

"No," I said, breathlessly.

Raising his brow, "Because you were a good girl?"

I nodded slowly, "I was a good girl," I whispered with bated breath.

Leaning in close, he whispered in my ear, "With naughty thoughts." The warm kisses he placed on my neck were punctuated by more tiny bites. "Did you want him to bring his warn mouth to your breasts? Did you picture his lips puckering around them? Gentle at first, the licking, lapping. Just loving the thought, the feeling, of his mouth touching your breast for the first time. Did your reaction, the way your breathing changed, make him suck them as his erection began to throb? Did your excitement push him on? Did he suck harder and harder until you begged for more?"

"Ahhh," I nodded. So close, he had me so close then he backed off a bit, slowing.

"Did you wonder how his tongue would feel, licking that delicious pussy, of yours?"

I panted hard at the thought, "Yes."

"But most of all…did you want his cock inside you? Did you want him to push you open? You knew there would be pain, didn't you? Oh, but the pain of letting him pop that delicate little cherry of yours," he moaned. "The feeling of your inner walls…so tight but giving ever so slightly…barely enough room for the tip, did you want it, the pain for pleasure?

I remembered the feeling of my first time. The way it felt, being broken into, forced open. "Ahhh," I moaned.

Did you want him to fuck you, Audra? More than anything you had ever wanted, did you want to feel his dick pushing deep inside you?"

I was dripping wet and kept right on the edge. He had brought me to that point. My body begged for him, "Please," I murmured.

"What do you want, Audra? More than anything, at this moment," he licked his lips, his own mouth, watering.

A wicked smile danced across my face, "If you had been that boy on the couch…" I grinned devilishly, while rocking my pussy with his finger work. "If you knew that only two feet away, my body ached. My pussy gushed wet with the thought of you. What would you have done," I hissed."

I felt myself being lifted onto the counter. His pants dropped exposing my need; what I wanted most. Wrapping his hand around his engorged shaft, I watched as he worked his grip, from balls to tip. This view made me want to suck him until his sweet seed exploded into my hungry mouth. I wanted him anywhere, everywhere. Moving his body closer, I felt the head of his dick searching out my tiny box.

Pulling my ass forward on the counter by my hips, his fingers searched out and pulled my little pink panties to the side. My legs opened like a lotus flower. Craning to see his every delicious move, I watched him circle my pearl with the head of his cock.

"Just a little," he said as he slid his dick between my folds. Nestling at the entrance of my creamy little opening, his engorged tip sought passage.

My body cried out, *please,* as he pushed the head of his *love* inside me. I felt her try to resist him at first, "Please," I whispered.

"Oh, but just the tip feels so good, doesn't it?"

I nodded.

"Tell me," his eyes flashed. "Do you want to feel all of me?" He looked down, watching the head working, in and out. "Do you want more?"

"I want…" he pushed deeper before I could finish my thought, my request. Exhaling, the pain mingled with my ecstasy.

"Lean back…and I'll give you all of me…every inch," he smiled.

Pushed back against the cupboards, he pulled my ass so far

forward that no part of it touched the cold tile counter. Kissing each of my ankles, one at a time, he lifted them to circle his neck.

I knew that grin; knew what was coming. Knew I should brace myself.

"Now, baby?" he gave a slow push, gaining entry.

"Now," I panted, "Now!" I was on the verge of begging as he pushed his way even deeper inside, forcing my eyes to roll back in my head.

"Shhh," he put his fingertip to my lips, "they're going to hear us," he said biting into his lip. His grin turned playful when I began sucking on his finger.

Keeping his body close, he rubbed himself against my swollen clit. Just rocking himself deep inside. I was there. The excitement he had manifested in me was bubbling over. I felt the familiar tickle, the pressure, the pleasure, coming quickly.

"Come with me?" I whispered breathlessly. "Come with me!"

"Kiss me...and I will."

He leaned forward; rolling me into a ball, his eyes burning hot.

Holding me as our moans were stifled by a deep passionate kiss, I could feel just how fast this brought him here, too. I could feel it in his thrust, in his breathing. Our arms circled each other; holding each other just where we needed to be. As the moments between our rising pleasures came in faster, and faster intervals, it was too much, I pulled my mouth from his and howled. Unbridled and unashamed, I begged him to fuck me; "Harder, harder," I cried out until we both burst. I felt like my head would explode. My toes curled, my body shook as the warmth of his *gushing* mixed with mine.

My legs slid down his shoulders, as I unfolded forward into

him. Both of us, holding on for dear life, we caught our breath.

It had never been this way with anyone else. I felt as though I could be exactly who I was with him; no hiding, no pretending. At that moment of total realization, without any fear, I cupped his face in my hands. "I'm in love with you, Tyler." I had said it before, but I never allowed myself to be so certain. Never had I allowed the thought, the feeling, without some reservation. And now, despite myself; even with all my hang up's, issues, and fears, I knew.

His eyes searched mine as his smile began to grow, "You are, aren't you? I can see it," he marveled. "But more importantly, I feel it," he whispered pressing his lips to mine. When he pulled back, he said, "I'm in love with you, Audra. Like I said, I have been...since the day I first laid eyes on you."

I felt the burning sensation of tears working their way to the surface. This is what it's supposed to feel like, I told myself. Like your heart may explode from an overload of joy. For the first time in my life, I felt what real love felt like when it was returned to you. How had I settled for less than this all those years? I had never felt truly loved as a woman should be.

My watering eyes, dropped, still worried about the embarrassment tears had always brought me.

Lifting my chin to gently wipe away the single tear that I fought so hard to hold back, Tyler kissed where the trial had been. "It's okay," he said and pulled me close, holding me against him. "Everything is going to be okay."

That night as I lay my head on his chest, just listening to his heartbeat. I slept in total contentment. Somewhere between asleep and awake, I felt connected to him in a totally unusual way. I saw us from behind closed eyes, as I drifted somewhere above, just watching.

16

I hit brew on the coffee machine as Tyler snoozed quietly in my bed. Retrieving the morning paper, I almost refused to take off the rubber band. I was in such a wonderful mood and couldn't help but wonder if I wanted to be riddled with the news that was so seldom good these days. I was surprised by a tiny column on page six, far away from the breaking news.

Today will be the reading of the last Will and Testament of Mitzi Gardner.

The article went on to sum up both her life and death. I felt my heart sink. I couldn't help but think, this is how it ends. Just a few words about who we were: the things we had done, how we ended, and what we left behind. Less than a paragraph to sum up a whole life. Well, not a whole life, I reminded myself.

Walking out of the bedroom in a pair of black brief boxers, Tyler emitted a low growling sigh as he stretched. I had to grin; he was a gorgeous man to watch waking. His hair tousled. The five o'clock shadow across his jaw added to his unquestionable sexiness.

"Coffee?" I asked as I headed to the kitchen.

"Yes please," he grinned as he followed along behind me, giving my ass a playful slap. Wrapping his arms around me, he nuzzled into my neck, as I loaded another French Roast single into the machine. "I slept *SOOO* well," he whispered in my ear.

A smile pulled up my cheeks. "Me too," I admitted.

Heading back to the couch, Tyler asked, "What's going on today?"

"I have no plans, as you well know," I grinned. "But the reading of Mitzi's Will, is today," I sighed.

Tyler's eyes rounded, "That's today?" Jumping up he took off like lightening to the bedroom. A moment later, he returned with his cell phone stuck to the side of his head.

There was no hello when whoever was on the other end, answered.

"I know," were the first words out of Tyler's mouth. "I know," he said again. "I'll be on time," he hung up.

I wore a concerned expression, "Everything okay?"

"Yeah, Dad and I were both asked to attend the reading of Mitzi's Will. I guess she left us something," Tyler's head shook.

"Oh," was all I could say at the moment. I knew how Mitzi's passing had affected Mr. Whitmore. His loss and grief was painful to witness.

Tyler darted back into the bedroom and appeared a moment later, buttoning his pants. "I'm sorry, luv. I have to go," he leaned in and kissed me.

"Of course," I told him. "Please drive safely," I said as he headed for the door.

He turned and smiled, "I will. I love you."

I love you, too," I said and smiled back before he closed the door behind him.

I immediately felt bad for both Tyler and his father. It was going to be a hard day for them. I had no doubt of that. I hadn't been alone, really alone, in a while. Oddly enough, I didn't know what to do. But I felt like I should be doing something. It was a strange feeling. I wanted to do something nice for Tyler, show him that I was thinking of him, would be there for him. Maybe I could make him dinner? I knew he loved Mexican food and I was no slouch in the kitchen. I decided I'd make him something special. And if he was too upset to eat tonight, it would be there when he was ready.

Heading to the grocery store, I couldn't stop thinking about him. I tried very hard not to think about yesterday. This was a solemn day for him. I shouldn't be walking around in a state of heat, I chastised myself. But the memories we created would *play* in my mind even when uninvited.

After picking up all the ingredients to make Tamale Pie (something I knew would only taste better after a night in the fridge), I headed home to spend my day cooking and cleaning.

As day faded into night, I still hadn't heard from Tyler. I was worried, but I wasn't sure what had me worried. Had he been in an accident? Were he and his father licking their reopened wounds over a bottle of good Scotch? Did he just need some space? I would understand if he did. Mitzi's murder brought up more than just childhood memories of her. They brought with them memories of Joel, as well.

I let out a deep sigh as I put the fully cooled Tamale Pie in the fridge, and headed to bed. Sleep didn't come easily or stay long, as I tossed and turned until daybreak. I wanted to hear his voice; know he was okay. But my mind kept saying, if he needs space, give it to him.

I had been up for an hour when I heard the morning paper

hit my porch. Reading that there had been no accidents reported, no deaths fitting his description, I could breathe a little easier. Since my husband's death, I was more than aware that accidents did happen. I knew there was always the unexpected you had to consider. It just didn't seem like him, not to at least let me know he was alright. He had to know I'd be worried.

3pm came and went, and now I was on the brink of madness. Dialing his number, I listened to the ringing until I received his voice message.

At 5pm, I took a walk (or so I would call it when I ended up at his apartment a few blocks away). Knocking on the door, I heard no movement, nothing. Heading back home, I played out every scenario in my head. Maybe he went to Joel's spot? There wasn't reception out there. Maybe he was just sleeping off a hard-drunk night? But my gut had been churning for hours, and I could no longer pretend it wasn't.

At 7pm, I tried to call one more time and again got only his voice message.

At 9pm, with three glasses of Cabernet under my belt, there was a knock at my door.

Letting out a relieved sigh, I answered.

There he stood, the man of my dreams. But he wasn't smiling, or moving toward me as I opened the door wide for him to enter. He just stood there, blank-faced.

"Are you okay?" I asked. Something I had wanted to ask for over twenty-four hours.

He stood like stone, cold and dead. Finally he said, "We need to talk."

From his demeanor (not to mention those horrible four words that never meant anything good was coming), I felt my stomach churn again.

I stepped aside and waved him in.

"No," his head shook. "I'll be quick. I won't be able to see you for a while, Audra."

My head stared to shake slightly, "What do you mean?"

"I have work to do for my father, and I won't have time to see you."

He was being so cold, detached. I was trying to gather my thoughts. What was happening?

"You won't be able to see me…for a while…or you won't be able to see me, again?" I asked.

"I don't see the point of dragging this out, Audra. I can't see you anymore, and you need to move on."

"Move on," I repeated like I didn't understand the concept. Finally as his words sunk in, my eyes rounded, "Are you serious?" This was beyond surreal for me. "The other night…you told me…"

Tyler cut me off, "I'm sorry if I led you to believe that there was something more between us. I'm sorry," he repeated. His dark blue eyes, iced over.

A moment passed before I said, "You're sorry *IF* you led me to believe…" I let my words drop, just like my heart had dropped into my stomach.

Tyler seemed unfazed by the damage he was causing. "Audra, you're a great woman. Maybe you should start over… somewhere new?"

With his last comment, I was dragged back to the reality of the situation. "Are you evicting me…as well as breaking up with me?"

"I just think maybe we both need a fresh start," he said without an ounce of emotion. Everything I had seen in his eyes just days ago, was gone. No concern, no desire, no love.

It felt as though he had punched me in the gaping hole he left in my chest. I hurt in a way that I didn't think was even possible. He had awakened in me all the things I had feared, and was ripping them to shreds just when I had allowed them to *exist*.

I wanted to stare deeply into his eyes, see if there was anyway anything remained between us. But when I tried, he looked away. In that moment it became crystal clear. He didn't love me, didn't want me. Never did.

"I'll be out by the end of the month," I said in the most informal detached way that my now altered defense mechanisms could muster.

As he turned to go, he said, "Let me know where to send your deposit once you get settled," then turned and walked away.

As I closed the door, my heart began to pound again, hard. Had it stopped for a moment there, I wondered. I felt as though my chest was caving in as the sobs began to force themselves from my body. Tears flowed. Tears I could never cry for my husband. Tears I couldn't release after the loss of my parents. Now, there was no stopping them. My vision blurred as they rolled down my cheeks, one right after the other. Breathing hurt; like my lungs had given up the desire to work. I was breaking inside. I could feel it. The pain was shattering into smaller shards that sliced and tore me open from the inside.

17

Sliding back down onto my couch, I searched for an answer. Why did he do this to me? Daniel's words came uninvited to ring in my ears, "You're nothing more than a game to him, Audra." Was I? Is that all this, I, was?

It seemed like I would never stop crying. But maybe that was the way it felt when you couldn't for so many years. So many heartbreaks I had faced, numb. At some point though, the tears did stop, and I needed another glass of wine.

I sat and picked apart everything in my head. He was doing everything he said he wouldn't. He wasn't pushing me away. He was throwing me away. I knew I wasn't the kind of woman that would fight to keep someone, who wasn't fighting to keep me. At that moment, I wished I had never met him. I wished that our paths had never crossed. That I had never looked into those dark blue eyes and felt all my buried and forgotten desires, awaken.

By the time I finished glass number four, I was looking for a house to rent. I knew what was happening. My defenses were rallying. I was, for lack of a better term, emotionally shutting down. This was necessary so the survivor in me could take control. I wondered about that therapist I had gone to see before I moved to Florida. If the logic I had already shared with her on the *healing process* bent her mind, she should see what was coming now. What I knew was coming.

Wasting no time, I began packing. 1 am, and I was pulling out the boxes I had saved from my tiny storage shed in the back-yard. I knew this part of me, well. I was manic. I had always believed that wallowing was counter-productive. When life knocked you down you didn't stay down, screaming to the heavens, "Why me." You figured out the next step in your process, what *needed* to be done.

At 6am, I had all my knickknacks packed (not that there were many of those. I had never been a *knickknack* woman), most of my kitchen and book collection. Everything I didn't use on a daily basis, was boxed up.

Finding an old photo box, I sat down to take a breather. I wondered if I even wanted to stay in Florida. I remembered what had piqued my interest in Florida in the first place. It wasn't just the abundance of married cheating men, but my father.

When I was young, he talked about wanting to take me to Florida. He had worked in Miami on a fishing boat one summer in his early twenties and loved it. The way he described the beaches, sunsets, and the overall feeling of the lifestyle intrigued me.

Searching through the old photos, I found the picture of him I loved; him holding his catch for the day. I never knew why it wasn't framed and hanging in our living room. There he stood, proudly holding the huge tuna. The smile on his face, was pure bliss. This was six years before he joined the police force, met my mother, and settled down. I was just a twinkle in his eye, I thought. Well, a far-off twinkle at that point. My parents enjoyed a few years alone, building a life before I made my debut. Dad had taken another fishing trip to Florida when I was eight. I remembered how I pouted about not being invited to go with him. But the trip was only for the guys on the police force. He didn't bring home any pictures from that trip, though. Tucking the photo back into the box, I let out a sigh and went to make myself a cup of coffee.

Where should I go, I wondered? I had more money than I needed to live comfortably for the rest of my life. It wasn't like anywhere was home to me. Southern California was where I had lost everything I once loved. I knew without question I had no desire to be there, again. Florida wasn't exactly what I hoped it would be. Being honest, it was so much more. But now it was time to move on. I could throw a dart at the map and go wherever the *flight* led me.

By 10:30am, I was exhausted but starving. I knew that I wouldn't touch the tamale pie and it would need to be thrown out along with a file of stored memories.

Walking into Dango's, I made my way to the deserted corner of the bar. With the morning paper in hand, I ordered a pulled pork sandwich and a beer from the waitress as I took a stool. An article caught my attention:

The ten best small towns in America: As I read about each one, a strange realization began to dawn on me. It wasn't as though I hadn't thought about it before, but the desire to hunt, to kill, was gone. I knew it had slowly (or quickly, depending personal opinion), faded from my persona. The overwhelming need had just…disappeared. My brain hadn't dove into the thought of hunting like it had previously; not even really skimmed the water as of late. The more I thought about this, the more confused I became. It wasn't like I had run a normal cycle. I mean, killing wasn't like going through puberty, where everyone would eventually have to face it head on. Yet, it felt like I was just done; the cycle, complete.

After I ate, I took my boggled brain back home where I hoped to nap before continuing with my packing.

As I went through the clothes in my closet, set on clearing out my hunting attire, there was a knock at my door. Without warning, my heart lurched forward in my ribcage. Was it him? I sat quietly wondering if I even wanted to answer the door. Looking out through my bedroom window, I knew I couldn't see my porch, but I could see if his Jeep was at the curb.

A black Lexus: Not him. Not the police, either. Maybe it was his lawyer hand delivering my eviction notice?

Again the knock echoed through the bungalow. Walking to the door, I looked out the peep hole.

There Daniel stood. "I know you're in there," he said. "I just want to extend my apologies."

I let out a long sigh. Tyler told me to beware of Daniel. But then again…Tyler also told me he was in love with me, and then dumped me less than 48 hours later with no explanation. From Tyler's description of Daniel's persona, he was a snake. Unfortunately, I was having trouble not thinking they both belonged in the same den. What if everything Tyler told me, was a lie? I wasn't prepared to go that far, though. Daniel had shown me who he was first hand; as a man, as well as a husband and a human being.

Meanwhile as my thoughts came back from their walkabout, Daniel kept talking, "Please just give me a chance to explain."

Explain what? I wondered. That he was an asshole, a womanizer, soulless parasite that suckled from the teat of misfortune?

"Look, you don't have to let me in, just open the door so I can talk to you without disrupting your neighbors."

I shook my head. This was against my better judgment on every level. Opening the door, I stepped out quickly so he wouldn't try to step inside. He wore slacks and a sport coat, giving the visual impression of a well-bred man. I couldn't speak as to what his parents had tried to instill in him. Manners? Respect? If they had, I had to assume they would be quite disap-pointed.

"What do you want, Daniel?" I asked folding my arms across my chest.

"First…," he stepped closer. "I wanted to apologize for treating you like…"

"A whore?" I asked. "Or am I just a slut, if you didn't intend on paying me?"

"Look," he put his hands up submissively, "I was out of line."

"Okay, thank you," I turned.

"And I also wanted to extend my condolences."

I turned back to see the shit-eating grin, which was more *him,* on every level. "And what would that be for?"

The way his eyes scanned me now; he licked his lips as his focus hovered over the V-line in my tiny cotton booty shorts.

"I hear you and Tyler, are no more," he took another step toward me. "I hear he let you down easy though. That was nice of him, right?"

One of my cheeks pulled up, working its way into a cock-eyed grin. "You hear a lot of things, don't you?"

"I do," his smile became sinister. "I've heard secrets."

I stared at him, "Pray tell."

"Well, from what I saw," he grinned, "you're the fuck of the century." He moved closer, "I also know you suck cock...as if your life depended on it," he laughed.

Now I was on guard, but I held my poker face. I knew Daniel had seen Tyler and me, in his dad's office, but there had been no oral during that interlude. Had he been watching us, spying on us? I laughed, "Ya know, I've heard secrets, too," my eyes rounded. "Nothing that interests me, though," I grinned as we stared daggers into each other.

"It's funny you should say that," he bit into his lower lip. "See, I know a secret about you...that you don't know."

"Is it that I'll take it in the ass? Because that may have been grossly misinterpreted."

Daniel smiled and licked his lips again, "No...but what a wonderful image you've given me for my spank-bank. Believe me," he nodded, "I'll be fucking some twenty dollar whore later, and I'll be thinking of you," he whispered. "But let me get back to the subject at hand. Tell me, Audra, how do you suppose you stumbled upon Tyler Whitmore? Did you think it was fate?"

I had to assume now that it hadn't been.

"Tyler Whitmore, one of the richest heirs, to one of the richest thrones in all of the world. What...did you really think he went slumming at some dive bar and met the fuck-girl of his dreams? Is that what you thought, Audra?"

"Well, I don't have to worry about what I *was* to Tyler Whitmore, anymore, now, do I?" I reached for the doorknob.

"Oh, but you should. You see, Tyler's known of you...about

you, for quite a while…long before you ever laid eyes on him. You were kind of a project for him."

Something in the way he spoke, the look on his face; he was far too smug to not be taken seriously.

"I asked him once why he was following some nobody, to bar, after bar, and just watching her from afar. It bordered on stalking," Daniel laughed. "He gave me some bullshit answer about how he was intrigued by you."

I could feel all the hairs on my arms, the back of my neck, rise.

"But, I knew the truth. Joel had already told me the dirty little secret."

Something in my stomach churned again. I was wrestling hard with my poker face, but I'd be damned if I let him see anything else.

"And why would any of this concern me now?" I asked as though totally disinterested. "Even if what you say is true, I think it's safe to assume he's *over* being intrigued by me."

His smile pulled across his face, "Or is there something…*MORE?*" The posed question lit him up, like a child on Christmas morning. "Just tell Tyler, if he wants to tell secrets, I'll be telling you, his." Daniel turned to walk away.

"Once again, Tyler and I, are done. I won't be telling him *anything* for you," I offered him the same smile he had given me.

"Oh, now see, I don't believe that for a second. You do know," he grabbed his sunglasses from his coat pocket, "curiosity killed the cat."

"Wouldn't that be reason enough, not to let curiosity get the best of the cat?"

Throwing his head back, he laughed, "Good luck with that, Audra. Oh, and thanks for the visual you gave me. In my mind, you won't be able to say *no*." he got into the black Lexus and drove away.

"Fuck," I said to no one. My curiosity was more than piqued and I knew packing wouldn't slow it down. I needed to scrub something.

hile scrubbing the tub, I tried to kill the flash I had of Tyler on his knees. Then me on my knees bent over the tub wall with him behind me, holding my hips tight as he slammed deep inside me.

He knew about me before we met? That meant we didn't meet by chance. I wasn't stalking him that night. But he was stalking me. He already knew what I was? My head shook at the thought. Before he said hello, before he rented the room, before we…ugh, my stomach turned again. He was there…for me. *Why*? What if I had just shot him when he came out of the bathroom that night? By then, he had to know it was a possibility. I had played right into his hands. And he in turn…played in my…*everything*. I was going to be sick. Turning quickly to hang my head over the toilet bowl, I tried to still my watering mouth.

Why? The word echoed in my head again; like a loud scream that only I could hear. It was deafening every other thought. He had planned this *meeting*. He had planned our joining…but why?"

I went over everything in my head; our meeting, following

me home, buying my house, doing everything he could to accommodate me. Why? Professing his love for me; in front of his whole social circle, his father. Was this just a sick game for him?

My body, my mind, running on, with no sleep at all, was staring to bend as I chased my thoughts in circles. Pouring myself three fingers of whiskey, I sat and tried to calm the demon inside. She was antsy, angry…almost murderous. Unlike the *me* who existed in my daily life, she, my demon, had no time to feel brokenhearted or dejected. Those thoughts didn't exist in her. I poured her another healthy shot, trying to ply her into submission. What she offered was rage. What she demanded was respect. She carried the scales of judgment that called for balance.

Sleep finally took me in a drunken embrace. When I woke, I had the tiny headache behind my eyes that toying with my demon will bring. Walking out of my front door to retrieve the morning paper, I saw a huge stack of unassembled boxes sitting on my porch. Looking at the pile, I let out a long sigh. Three houses down, Tyler's jeep was parked at the curb.

As I started down my stairs, the engine revved and away he went. Back inside the bungalow, I grabbed my cell phone and dialed his number.

I was surprised he answered. At this point, I had to assume that he didn't want to speak to me.

"Thanks for the boxes," I said.

"Just wanted to make sure everything was going according to plan," Tyler said.

"Well, I couldn't tell you that. See, none of this, was part of my plan. Why don't you tell me the plan, so I can make sure it unfolds correctly?"

"I sent you a link. It's a place in Colorado. I thought you might be interested," he said.

"Much appreciated, Tyler," I tried to match his detachment. "But I think I can find my own place."

The next thing I heard was the phone disconnecting. I grabbed a stack of boxes off the porch and went to work right after I washed down three Ibuprofens.

I kept fighting the thoughts; Tyler had stalked me. Scarier yet, he knew what I was, when he did. And yet, I had been so careful. There were so many questions that rose inside of me; so many questions I wanted him to answer. But some part of me knew, I was safer gone. Gone from him, gone from Daniel, gone from Florida.

Opening the link Tyler had sent me, there was a beautiful log cabin. 2000 square feet and a fully finished basement. It sat on top of a mountain, staring down over the small, sleepy town below. I hated the fact that he knew me well enough to know this was a place I would love.

Late in the afternoon, having packed damn near everything I owned, I walked down to Dango's for a bite. I enjoyed my pulled pork as much as I could, knowing it would likely be my last. Sending the owner of the cabin an e-mail offering full price, I released a heavy sigh. Wasn't I supposed to feel the weight of all this, remove itself from my shoulders?

As I stepped off the boardwalk, I saw Tyler's Jeep roll by again. Was this a game to him? What was he expecting me to do next? I was starting to become paranoid of his intentions. But if I was paranoid of him, what I saw next elevated my fears. Daniel was sitting in his car watching me. From behind dark glasses, I tried to pretend I hadn't noticed him. I wasn't part of their little game anymore, was I? Why were both men circling me like buzzards over a dying corpse? What was I missing?

Walking up to the bungalow, I stole a glance over my shoulder. Tyler's Jeep had just pulled up at one end of the block. Slowly turning my head in the other direction while reaching for my mail, I spied Daniel's at the other end.

Shutting the door behind me, it became clear; it was time to play defense.

I changed my clothes, threw on a long blonde wig, and grabbed a few things before heading out my back gate down the long alleyway behind my house. I pulled my cell from my purse and called for a cab.

At *Zoomer's* car rentals, I pulled out my California driver's license and a credit card in my married name. I had kept them both just in case I ever needed a little time before someone could find my paper trail. It wouldn't be hard to do, to track me down; I knew this. But I was hoping I wouldn't need much time to do what needed to be done. On my way back, I stopped at a florist and picked up a beautifully boxed bouquet of lilies.

Pulling up to the curb on the block before mine, one car and the cross street separated me from Tyler's Jeep. I couldn't see him from where I was parked. But I knew he was in there, just watching. All the cards I held depended on him answering my call. Would he, I wondered.

When he answered his phone, I was met with silence. My head shook. Letting out a long sigh, I said, "I have questions… and I've left to go get them answered. I have a twenty minute head start on you," then I hung up.

Now I sat and waited for him to make a move. A few minutes passed when there was no stirring. But then I saw Tyler exit the Jeep and cross the street to my house. Up the stairs he went, knocking on the door. Skirting the house, I saw him looking into my bedroom window. I had purposely left the curtains open. And when he walked down the long driveway to my backyard, he'd find the open backdoor and the gate to the alleyway, standing wide.

I waited patiently for him to search the house before I watched him dart for his Jeep. Off his Jeep sped, passing Daniel's Lexus before taking a left. Daniel wasted no time. Turning the car around, he gave chase.

Pulling my rented Camry out of its hiding spot, I followed Daniel, who followed Tyler.

I figured Tyler knew where I was going to get my questions answered. As he pulled onto the freeway headed for Naples, I knew my assumption had been correct.

I kept a safe distance, wondering the whole time. I posed the question to myself, now what?

My cell phone rang, breaking me from my thoughts. I looked down to see Rudolpho flashing across the screen.

"Mr. Whitmore," I said, indifferently. "You may want to ask your father to open the gates for me."

"Audra, you need to turn around. You're not safe," Tyler added.

"From?" I let the question hang in the air.

"You need to turn around," he repeated.

"Am I not safe…because of the secrets you've been keeping from me? Is that it?" I asked. I waited for an answer as silence echoed through my phone. "I'm afraid you've forced my hand," I pushed END.

Again, and again my phone rang, flashing his alias name, but I was on a mission now. When Tyler took the off ramp that led to his father's house, I continued on for another mile, taking the next off ramp. I needed Tyler to get to his father's house before me.

I hated to use Mitzi's name to gain entry to the beautiful gated community, and still wasn't sure it would work, given the circumstances of her death. I told the guard at the security post that I was there to deliver flowers to the family. I hate to admit it, but being a woman, I really was seen as less of a threat. If they only knew, I thought. The maid who had answered the phone must have had quite a few deliveries for the same reason. I gave my married name, the name of the florist I worked for, and in a minute or two, the gates opened. So much for their top-notch security, I thought.

When I pulled up across the tiny lane from the gates to the Whitmore Chateau, I could spy Tyler's Jeep. He was still trying to call me frantically, but to no avail. What I didn't see. was Daniel's Lexus. For this to play out correctly, I needed him in tow.

As I waited, the sun beginning to set, I wondered if I had misplayed my hand. Just then, I saw headlights coming up the lane. He'd know it was me. A Camry parked alongside all of these million dollar homes? I prepared for him to accost me.

19

As my driver's side door was pulled open, I was face to face with a Sig P220 45 caliber.

"Out!" Daniel said looking around to see if we were causing a commotion. My initial take of his eyes, of his body movements, was that he was high as a kite. This hadn't been part of the plan I had worked out in my head. The crazy demon-woman inside of me said *improvise, strategize.*

Daniel dialed a number on his phone, "If there are any surprises, she's dead," he said to whoever had answered his call.

"Should I put my hands up," I asked when he put his phone back in his pocket. "Or should we go for the more incognito approach?"

"You just do what you're told and you may get out of this with your pretty little head. I like you as a blonde, by the way," he said as he shoved me toward the opening gates. At the front door, I was placed in front of Daniel, just in case we were met with a quick ending.

Simon answered the door. Stepping back from the entry, Simon lifted both arms over his head, then raised both pant legs.

Turning in a circle, he lifted the hem of his shirt to clearly show his empty waistband. I spied a scar on his right side abdomen. Clearly, it was a gunshot wound. My eyes traveled to his. There was no hint of what he was thinking, just a cold dead stare, that he quickly turned on Daniel.

"Move," Daniel ordered both of us ahead of him.

I couldn't help but notice just how many times Daniel swung his gun in directions where he imagined sound or movement.

Simon led us to the office where Tyler and Mr. Whitmore were awaiting our arrival.

"Well, this room should bring back some memories, huh, Audra?" Daniel asked.

Tyler didn't look surprised to see me, why would he? But the way he looked at me; anger filled his eyes.

"You sit," he aimed the gun at Simon and pointed to a wingchair. "You two, he said to Tyler and Mr. Whitmore, "stand up." Moving in on them, he patted each of them down from behind then ordered them to sit.

Mr. Whitmore looked frail. I knew he was elderly, but it was only now that his age showed. He looked as though he had been up for days. He must have been expecting this outcome.

Pulling one pair of handcuffs from his back pocket, Daniel handed them to me. "Cuff him," he pointed to Simon with the barrel of the gun.

"You don't want the honor?" I asked sarcastically. "I guess you didn't have enough cuffs for all of us," I questioned. "You could have borrowed some of mine," I offered.

"Do it," he yelled as he watched over my shoulder. Each cuff *clicked,* one at a time, behind Simon's back. I stared down into

Simon's eyes for a moment. I was met once again with that dead stare. He was a hard read.

Forced back into a wingchair, I sat and waited for something to happen.

"I see you both have drinks," Daniel said to Tyler and his father. "Kind of low class to not offer Audra a drink, don't you think?"

"I'm fine," I said, hitting him with eye grenades.

Daniel laughed at my open disdain, "I do love the way hate just pours from your eyes when you look at me. But, soon, all that hate, that seething, you'll be sending it elsewhere. And I do believe you'll be in need a cocktail," he grinned.

I stared at him; was he right? I wasn't sure what was coming. But it may be in my best interest. If I was about to catch a bullet, I may prefer a little mind-numbing. "Double whisky, no rocks."

Watching me take the drink Tyler offered me, Daniel then turned his attention to Mr. Whitmore, "I want the journals. Hers and his," he said. "I know she left them both to you."

For the most part, I was out of the loop, but it wasn't hard to conclude that *her,* meant Mitzi.

"They won't do you any good, now," Mr. Whitmore's head gave a slow shake.

Daniel's rage exploded, "Give them to me!"

"I can't. They're in a safe place, that even I can no longer reach," Mr. Whitmore told him.

Daniel's head shook, "Oh you're going to make this so much harder than it needs to be. Just the money, the journals and use of your jet," he paced around the four wingchairs we sat in, all facing each other in a tiny circle of hell. "Maybe If I was to take the girl…your last connection to Joel? Maybe then you'd be more forthcoming with my request?"

Mr. Whitmore's eyes dropped, as mine shot to his, and then to Tyler's.

Tyler's eyes clenched closed.

"Oh, so many secrets," Daniel laughed psychotically. "This shit is so good, you couldn't write it!"

I was still searching for answers, but neither Whitmore, would make eye contact with me.

"So, who's going to tell her?" Daniel asked. "Mr. Whitmore? Tyler?" he aimed the gun at him.

When Tyler's eyes opened, I could see the anguish in them.

"Fine, I guess I'll play the villain. After all, I am holding the gun," Daniel chuckled. "Audra," he spun to face me, "when do you think Mr. Whitmore and his son Tyler first laid eyes on you?"

I had that creepy sensation that left gooseflesh in its wake. I stared at Daniel, like a deer in the headlights.

"You're not going to play my game?" he pouted, pushing his bottom lip out. "Fine, I'll forgo the suspense." His eyes went wide and wild, "It was your seventeenth birthday. I know because Joel showed me a picture of you. You," he laughed, "in that poofy-armed pink formal dress. It was hideous, by the way, truly. But you've come into your own over the years."

I was having trouble breathing. The air had been sucked from my lungs. I had to keep control over my emotions, over the situation. Seventeen? My memory wandered back in time. I remembered the birthday as well as the hideous dress.

Daniel waited for my reaction, "Audra?"

Determined not to appease him, I said, "It was in style, then."

But Daniel wasn't done, "Personally, I liked your wedding photo the best," his head nodded. "A sweetheart neckline compliments your assets, well."

Tyler's eyes fell to the floor.

"You sure know a lot about women's fashion, Daniel," I grinned, hoping to make him think I wasn't ruffled in any way.

"I bet right now, Audra, you're wondering…WHY? Why was Mr. Whitmore keeping such a close eye on a girl he didn't even know? Seems odd, doesn't it? But Joel, oh, he was so fond of you. He would say how beautiful you were, how smart, a chip off the old block…just like him. Even if his darling little sister's existence, was only to be acknowledged as the family's dirty little secret."

My narrowed eyes shot to Mr. Whitmore, as my demon quickly began to add up this information. What was Daniel saying? It only took a second for my stomach to churn at the unbelievable thought. Was he saying Mr. Whitmore, was my father? Was he saying…that Tyler and I…were brother, and sister? I felt the nausea rising inside me.

aniel's head cocked, You're looking a little green Audra. You might want to take a drink. That's why I was kind enough to offer it to you. You see," he continued, "Joel found out when he was young that Mr. Whitmore here, couldn't have been his father. He was a genius, you know. Joel always said, "Some things you have no reason to question…until you do."

My heart was pounding furiously in my chest. I could hear the blood rushing in my head.

"It was an everyday science project on blood typing, which spelled it all out for him," Daniel paced behind Mr. Whitmore. "Joel had a lot of questions, then, didn't he? His mother having died the year before; he couldn't ask her about playing the whore, could he?"

Tyler sat, jaw clenched. I knew that look. I had seen it before when the Piano Man threatened to take my life.

My attention was drawn back to Daniel, "He wanted to meet his real father, know where he came from…who he was.

He wasn't much like you, Mr. Whitmore, or his mother, was he?"

"His mother was pregnant with him when we met. It didn't change the way I felt about her...or him. He was my son, regardless of whose DNA he carried." Mr. Whitmore's eyes turned to meet mine, "When Joel found out, he wanted to... needed to meet his father. It was important to him. So it was important to me, as well."

Daniel broke our stare, "Yes, I know it was. And when Audra's dad, Mr. Murphy, came out for Joel's eighteenth birthday, they had their moment, didn't they?" Daniel grinned at my shocked face. "Joel found out he had a sister. But unfortunately, this huge shock was a bit too much for Audra's mother, wasn't it? She wanted no part of the family Mr. Murphy had unknowingly spawned before they were wed."

I wasn't sure what I was feeling. There were a jumble of emotions and thoughts running mad in my head. "Tyler?" I called to him. His eyes closed at the sound of my voice. "Damn it, look at me!" I yelled.

Tyler's eyes slowly lifted to meet mine. It was there. I could see it, but still I had to ask, "Is this true?"

Tyler took a deep breath, "Yes," he whispered.

"And that's why you...stalked me? Because I was Joel's sister...his blood?"

Tyler's eyes locked on mine, he began to nod.

Daniel laughed, "Oh what a tangled web."

I felt sick to my stomach. All this attention, all his understanding and accommodating, it was because I shared an affliction, a defect with his brother. My brother, I heard my mind clarify. Just saying that in my head, my brother, set my whole world to spinning.

"I want the journals!" Daniel yelled out into the quiet that had crept across the room.

Mr. Whitmore just stared at Daniel for a moment, "Let everyone else go, and I'll give you everything you asked for; the journals, money, the jet, everything."

"No, no, no," Daniel's crazed face swung back and forth. "I've trusted you before to make things right. I won't trust you again."

"What's in the journals? Why do you want them?" I trained my focus on him. I had always seen a hint of craziness behind Daniel's eyes, but nothing like this.

Daniel's laughter filled the space completely as he threw back his head and let his inner psycho free. "Because…they exonerate Joel…and implicate me. In fact, implicates might be too soft a word," his grin was pulled up like the joker in the old Batman series. "I think the word *incriminates* is more accurate."

Daniel spun with the gun in his hand at another imagined sound.

"How?" I asked boldly, trying to draw his attention back to the reality of the situation.

"Oh, it's a long story," Daniel circled the chair to stand in front of me. Putting the muzzle of the gun to my chest, he slowly rubbed it against the curve of my breast.

Tyler instinctively stood, and was quickly met with the barrel of Daniel's gun. "I don't want to have to tell you again, Tyler," Daniel warned.

"You see, dear Audra, once upon a time," Daniel laughed manically, "my family and the Whitmore's, were best friends. Wealthy, content. No, we were elated. We were overjoyed being two of wealthiest families in Florida. We were seen, referred to, as the upper crust of the upper crust. Of course the Whitmore's more so than us," he gave a small shrug. "But the one percent, is still the one percent, am I right?" he winked. "Why, the world was at our fingertips," he made the crazy eyes again. Rounded with just a hint of psychosis.

It seemed to me, that minute by minute, Daniel was diving deeper into a hole inside of himself. Watching him slowly unravel, I again questioned the possible faux pas in coming here.

"But then, my father's pharmaceutical company, hit on something so huge, it would have revolutionized a whole sub-group of people. It was to be the savior for all of those who were functionally-dysfunctional."

My eyes narrowed. Turning my head to study the look on Mr. Whitmore's face, Tyler's; what the hell did Daniel mean, *Functionally-Dysfunctional?*

"You see, your brother," he grinned at me, "Joel, had all kinds of needs and quirks that made him…special. That was WHY he was asked to be part of the study that would eventually lead to our company becoming the richest in the world. Step aside, anti-depressants. Move over, Adderall! This one drug would straighten out all the blurred lines: from depression, to A.D.D., A.D.H.D. Mania, Bi-polar and any other variation of anti-social behavior. It would bring out all the very best qualities in a person, while silencing all their fears, insecurities, making the way their brain fired, better than normal."

"Watching you praise this drug," Mr. Whitmore's jaw tightened, "proves that you're just as crazy as your father! You know this isn't what it did! You saw first-hand what it did do! It ruined people's lives. It ruined families!" he shouted.

"And that's why you made sure that the drug would never be approved by the FDA, didn't you, Mr. Whitmore? It was you! You and your friends in high places. The ones who owed you a favor, made sure my father would be bankrupted, lose everything!"

"That drug, ruined lives!" Mr. Whitmore yelled again. "It ruined Joel's life, you twisted son-of-a-bitch! You and that drug are why…" Mr. Whitmore fell silent, reliving something that caused him to grab his chest. I could see the agony in his eyes.

"You mean why Joel killed all those people, or himself?" Daniel smiled and retrained the gun when Tyler yelled, "You piece of shit!"

"Well, I guess since you've seen the journals, the cats out of the bag," Daniel laughed at their pain. Turning his attention to me, Daniel asked, "Are you feeling left out, sugar tits? Would you like to know what's in the journals?"

From the pain I saw in the Whitmore's faces, I was positive that knowing, was necessary.

Daniel laughed, "You see, Joel was used as a guinea pig, by his own father, no less."

"I was trying to save him!" Mr. Whitmore's voice deepened as his jaw clenched. "Your father said they had already studied the drug, had seen the drug, work."

"Right," Daniel nodded then addressed me again. "I'm sure that part of the story, you were never told. Of course, it wasn't until the journals, that the Whitmore's found out that it wasn't just Coke Joel had unknowingly ingested that night with the dead hooker. After my father's drug had been tested on Joel, well let's just say, it didn't work for him the way it should have. Isn't that right Mr. Whitmore?"

Mr. Whitmore sat like stone, his eyes squeezed closed. The hand that still clutched his chest, clenched the fabric.

"No," Daniel's crazy face shook as small balls of foam gathered at the corners of his mouth. "Unfortunately, Joel had a psychotic break," he sighed. "He had to be detained from his own madness. In fact, he became more locked in his thoughts. But now…they had been altered by a growing detachment, one that could be inserted into his mind."

Tyler looked sickened. This must have been what he and his father had been doing the night Tyler never returned to me; reading the journals.

"You see, Mr. Whitmore hadn't been allowed to watch the medical trial. But Joel told him that he couldn't remember anything, for three whole days. He didn't know if he had eaten, slept. He had no memory of his reaction to the drug, either. What was he thinking, doing, was he functional?" Daniel let out a heavy sigh. "For someone like Joel, who never ran on auto-pilot, it was disturbing, and frightening. I guess it fright-ened Mr. Whitmore, too, didn't it?" he asked. "To have your genius introvert, lose three days of conscious thoughts. Why, given the right message, like a subliminal thought pushed into his vacant mind…" Daniel's face contorted, "you could have yourself a mental slave." Unable to rationalize, or question morality, much less mortality." Daniel's voice fell to a whisper, "Why, given the right message, you could have a real killing machine."

I watched a tear roll down Mr. Whitmore's cheek.

"What they didn't know," Daniel leaned close to my ear, "was that my father had taken several samples before the drug was supposedly erased from existence. And even better, they didn't know that I had been the one planting those messages in Joel's blanked out little head. Fueling a homicidal rage to erupt in him after the drug was administered, without his knowledge."

Tyler's chest heaved and fell. The pulse of his neck, gave away his rapid heartbeat. I could see it there in his eyes. He would kill Daniel with his bare hands if it wouldn't put anyone else at risk.

My eyes narrowed, "I don't understand: if Joel couldn't remember anything, what was in the Journals that could implicate you?"

"His losing time, of course! You see, I had him believing that it wasn't the drug that had caused the missing time, the blank spaces during the drug trial. It was him. Just the way his broken brain worked. And since I started drugging him after the trial ended, he believed it. And I think I could have kept it going, used him as my pawn, if it hadn't been for Mitzi."

"Mitzi?" I questioned.

"Ah, yes, the great love of Joel's life. When I convinced him to stop seeing her for her safety, well, she wasn't one to give up easily on his love. But I knew, the way she followed him, stalked him, she was going to be a fly in the ointment. And so she was. You see, I recorded Joel's kills."

My eyes rounded as they shot to Tyler. His chin dropped to his chest. "Joel's kills?" I let the question hang in the air as truth began to dawn on me. Tyler's last kill, excluding of course the Piano Man, was just over a year ago. Right before Joel died.

"Yes," Daniel laughed. "Your sweet brother, was a killing machine…when properly motivated, that is."

"The drug?" I said.

"You're following along nicely," Daniel said condescendingly. "Why, maybe there is some of him in you. Admittedly, until now, all I saw in you, was a great pair of tits, and a warm place, to play hide the cock."

Tyler's jaw tightened, "Don't speak to her that way."

"Oh, you're worried about how I speak to her, but you didn't mind dragging her into all of this shit," Daniel asked. "Parading her in front of everyone, practically baiting me? What's say I bend her over, right now, and fuck her until her eyes go crossed! Right here, right over the top this chair, while you watch."

Horrified by the thought, I knew I needed to drag Daniel back from where his mind was taking him, "So you drugged him, gave him a subliminal message, and then recorded him killing?"

"I did!" Daniel smiled the smile that was taking on more of a psychotic appearance every moment.

"Why?" I asked.

"Why, you ask?" his eyes bulged from his head. "Well, I'll tell you, why, Audra!" he spun his body to face mine. "Mr. Whitmore was the reason my father took his life. My father sank everything he had into that drug. His money, as well as others, who were convinced of its success. But Mr. Whitmore contacted the FDA and chirped in the right ears; powerful ears. Why he even threatened to use his vast fortune to sue if the drug was ever approved. My father lost *EVERYTHING*," he yelled turning to raise the gun at Mr. Whitmore." *WE* lost *EVERYTHING!*"

My body tensed, thinking that Daniel was definitely worked up enough, not to mention high enough, to pull the trigger.

"But the drug," I said loudly to pull his focus back to me. "The drug would have failed anyway; would have caused so many lawsuits. Your father would still have been ruined if it had been approved."

Daniel swung the barrel back to me, and nodded, "True. It wouldn't have ended well, either way. And my father was weak. Too weak to do a few years in a white collar jail for falsely taking money from his unwitting backers. Too weak to be broke. So when they found my father, dangling from a noose in the men's locker room of the club, well, right then I decided to take something from Mr. Whitmore."

I thought back to a comment Tyler had made at the club, "You almost forget the darkness this place has witnessed." A shiver ran up my spine, "So you drugged Joel, and commanded him...to kill?"

"The first kill, was an accident," Daniel admitted. "You see, I drugged the soda, that's true enough. But when the whore screamed, obviously she was very much alive. She screamed because Joel freaked her out when he went catatonic. She thought he was in medical danger I guess," he shrugged. "Not like I ever took the time to ask her," he laughed. "If she had called the police, like the phone in her hand suggested she planned on doing, they would have tested Joel for drugs. And with the state he was in?" His head swiveled, "There's no doubt there would have been tests ran; a thorough investigation. And as an unknown drug, well I couldn't take the chance that it could have been linked back to me or my father's work. And it would have been," his teeth gnashed. "I knew there was no way Mr. Whitmore wouldn't have spent his vast fortune finding out everything he could about the drug that turned his precious boy into a lump of clay. Not to mention the origin of the drug. Since my father was the only person who would have had access to the drug, and it was presumed that all samples had been destroyed, they would have been led directly to me. I wanted Whitmore to think the drug never caused the catatonia. That the drug did work and always had. I wanted him to believe that his son was just broken. That my father committed suicide because of his demands to have the drug extinguished. I wanted him to know what he had done! He made a sad face before grinning from ear to ear.

I could see the crazy bouncing off his face; taking over his mind.

"So, after I calmed the woman down with some ridiculous excuse for his demeanor, throwing out some neurological nonsense, I took the phone from her hand. She seemed relieved that she wouldn't end up in the middle of police questioning and have to be bailed out on prostitution charges. But I was left curious about Joel's state of being. I snapped my fingers in his face, called his name. Nothing, no response. In that moment, I couldn't help but wonder: Was he open to the power of suggestion in that state of mind?"

I felt ice run through my veins. Mr. Whitmore's eyes shut tight. Tyler looked like he had gone numb. Only Simon stared at Daniel with a hatred that burned. "I had to know," Daniel whispered. The devil smile on his face, made my stomach knot. "So, I handed Joel my buck knife, and gave the command: Kill her," his eyes sparkled. "I really didn't expect it to work," Daniel laughed. "But a moment later, he walked over to me and grabbed the buck knife from my hand. He was totally detached from the act. He stomped up to her like Frankenstein. She was about to scream again when he just…slit her throat. One long, deep cut," Daniel said slowly. "When he was done, he returned to the position I had first found him in. Just starring at the wall in front of him, with the bloody knife in his hand."

"What about the blood on the walls?" Tyler asked. "What I saw when I walked in?"

"Oh, that was me…just playing in her life-source," he shrugged. "I smeared her around a bit."

I didn't want the horror of this to be present on my face. And I was surprised that somehow, it did horrify me. I needed to detach from the thoughts. "How does Mitzi play into all of this?"

"Ah, her," Daniel nodded. "She knew something was wrong with Joel. He was complaining of losing time. I wish she had been a dumb woman. You should all be kept as dumb as possible," he said to me, then sighed. "But she wasn't. She soon made the realization that Joel only lost time when he and I spent time together. You'd think that Joel would have figured it out. But that brotherly love he had for me?" He shook his head, "I guess it just wouldn't let him even consider the thought that I could ever hurt him, ruin him, his family." Daniel sighed dramatically, then laughed. Mr. Whitmore turned green. I couldn't imagine what reliving this was doing to him. Daniel smiled at the Whitmore's pain, then turned his focus back to me. "For a while, Mitzi wouldn't let us be alone. I needed to rid him of her. I thought I had been successful in doing so, but I was wrong. And how did I know, you might ask? Well, she was following him… and me. I should have known she would," Daniel's teeth gnashed together, again. "Fly in the ointment," he huffed. "She saw the last kill firsthand," he sighed. "She also convinced Joel that he wasn't in his own mind. And why you ask would she say this?" His head shook, "She was hiding in the closet the last night I drugged him. She filmed the drugging, as well as the horrific murder," he sighed. "She had proof of all of my wrongdoings."

Suddenly, I couldn't help but wonder, did the police have her phone? Of course they must. Would there be proof there, besides the drugging? I tried to push the thoughts away, as Daniel continued on.

"All of the sudden my plans were wrecked. I wanted to set him up for all these kills. To have Mr. Whitmore's pride and joy, his poor defenseless, broken boy of a man, sitting in a cell while he awaited a lethal injection. But NO! That bitch ruined the plans I had worked on for years to bring to fruition. And she had a second form of proof! After we headed out of the house looking for a kill, she grabbed the glass I had used to drug him, taking with her the trace contents left in the bottom. Usually, I was smarter than that. I should have taken the glass. But I had become so certain of my plan, my vengeance, I got sloppy."

I nodded, "So, that's why you killed Mitzi?"

"By that time, Joel had twelve kills for his rap sheet, and I was just about ready to pull the trigger," he laughed at the gun in his hand. "That's when Joel confronted me. He knew everything! I had already sent a video of Joel killing some poor defenseless woman to Mr. Whitmore in hopes of getting more extortion money out of him. Not that I needed it, I married well," he smiled. "I just wanted to know he suffered from seeing what was on the tape, as well as having more money stolen from him. But I now knew the evidence Mitzi had would have landed my ass in the cell next to Joel. Or even worse, exonerated him completely. When the three of us met, Joel, Mitzi, and I, we decided that it was best for all concerned if we kept our sins under wraps. Joel knew Mitzi would be in trouble for not turning us in. And he couldn't handle the thought of putting her at risk. He of course banished me from his life."

I noted the venom in his words.

"And really," he shrugged, "who could blame him. But Joel *WAS* a tender soul. Drugged, or not drugged, Joel couldn't deal with what he had done. Even if it was done drugged and on my command. He still had to pay for his sins."

I shuddered, I knew what was coming. It was no accident.

"So then Joel, another fly in the ointment of my attempt at

the Whitmore wreckage I worked so hard to cause," his head shook, "mailed his journal, his last will and testament, and a suicide letter to Mitzi. I was sure of it! It made sense. She was the love of his life. His only love, and Mr. Whitmore's goddaughter. He did this right before taking the solo flight that he then nose-dived into the Atlantic Ocean."

Mr. Whitmore looked like he had been hit in the stomach, a tear rolled down his cheek.

"How did you kill Mitzi? How did you get to her? She had to be wary of you in every sense of the word." I reasoned.

Daniel laughed, "That wasn't hard at all," he smirked. "Joel had snuck into her house a hundred times, and I with him, on more than one occasion. Her security code as well as the password on his computer, it was the date she took his virginity. Not exactly hard for me to get! I knew all the places that the camera's couldn't catch; all the dark zones. Not to mention, Mitzi had given Joel the code to turn off the cameras, to keep daddy's little girl from looking like the whore she was," he shrugged. "You know, if you think about it, he really did love her. If he had only known..." he sighed deeply, "...that I was going to break into her house, sneak up the stairs into her bedroom and fuck her while I strangled the life out of her, I bet he would have stayed around for one more kill," Daniel's head nodded.

My stomach turned as the men in the room held their eyes closed.

A moment passed while I fought my revulsion enough to speak. "I'm still a little confused," I admitted.

"What part of this has your little head rattled?" Daniel smirked.

I didn't appreciate the assault to my intelligence, but I posed the question anyway. "The paper said that there were signs of consensual sex? Did she consent…to you?" my face squished up.

"Ahahaha," Daniel howled laughter. "That woman was so loose, I could have fucked her with a traffic cone, and never touched the sides."

My jaw dropped.

"You son of a bitch!" Tyler went to jump up but was quickly hit with the butt of the gun. When he started up again, despite the blood running down his temple, Daniel turned and brought the barrel of the gun to my face.

"Tyler," Mr. Whitmore yelled and shook his head, as Simon fought his cuffed wrists to no avail.

"You Whitmore men and your chivalrous hearts," Daniel gave a shake of his head. "What is it with your family?"

Mr. Whitmore stood, "Take me! Take me and my money. Just leave them alone! I'm the one you want," he yelled.

Daniel was still breathing hard from his ten seconds of action. "See what I'm saying," he gave me the palms-up, then addressed Mr. Whitmore. "Look, that would be easier on you, wouldn't it? But I'm not trying to make this easy. I want this to hurt." Daniel laughed. "So, no! What I am going to do is, I'm going to take your last connection to Joel…as well as the money he left her."

21

My eyes rounded, "What? What money?"

"You don't know? Well of course you don't." Daniel's eyes popped from his head. "That is hilarious. Were you ever going tell her?" Daniel looked from Mr. Whitmore to Tyler.

I looked to both of them, too. Tyler's eyes were begging me to try and understand, but which part? The part where he wasn't like me; it was actually this brother I never knew I had…his brother. Was it the fact that he had been secretly searching me out, long before we ever met?

"You see, like I said, Joel knew about you," Daniel nodded. "He flew to Los Angeles with Tyler in tow on more than one occasion. I guess Tyler went the first time to keep an eye on Joel. Your mother didn't want him to disrupt your life. Or at least that was the excuse she used for keeping you in the dark. But truthfully, I think she was just jealous of your father having another child." He gave a shrug, "Pretty pathetic considering Mrs. Whitmore had been nothing but worm food for years," he laughed. "But according to Joel, Tyler had taken a liking to you. He was at your high school graduation, weren't you Tyler?"

My head turned.

Tyler let out a shaky breath then nodded his head. "Joel wanted to tell you, but he couldn't, wouldn't, disrespect your mother's wishes. And after your mother passed, he knew how much pain you were in. Your father sent letters and pictures on a regular basis. And after your father died?" Daniel shrugged, "He figured you had had enough trauma and shock. He was afraid to disrupt your life, the way having a sister and not being a part of her life, had disrupted his." Turning to Tyler he said, "You were at her wedding as well, weren't you?" Daniel rolled the gun around in his hand.

Tyler swallowed hard, "Yes. I was."

A memory returned to me. Me, mounted on top of Tyler, staring down into his eyes after I told him I thought I was falling in love with him. "I've been falling for you…since the first moment I laid eyes on you." The words echoed in my head. The beating of my heart began to pound harder in my chest. He loved me. Years ago…he loved me. Looking up into his eyes, I saw it there.

"Now I'd say you had a little crush," he grinned at Tyler. "But if that was true, why would you be following her around like you did? Watching her from afar?" Daniel smirked. "Why wouldn't you, the legendary Tyler Whitmore, just go up and introduce yourself? I mean any normal woman would be dumbstruck to have your attentions turned to them. Or were you just curious about where your brother's trust fund would go if something happened to him?"

Tyler's jaw lifted, his eyes burned hot, "You know damn well I didn't care where his money went. Better to her," he nodded to me, "than anyone else. He loved her. He loved you," Tyler said, turning his attention to me, making sure I understood. "He wanted to be your brother, he wanted you to know!"

I had never tried so hard to fight back tears in all my life. I had a brother: Someone who could have made me feel normal. Someone who could have been my friend. Someone who may have understood me.

"So, my taking her, and the money...would probably cause you great pain. The kind that breaks you from inside, and leaves you unable to repair?"

Tyler stared daggers into Daniel before answering, "Yes." He turned a pleading look to me.

"Funny, Audra doesn't look as love bitten by you and your sweet words as she once did. Did he break you too, dear?" he asked me.

I looked at Tyler and set my jaw, "Yes."

"So you do understand that you've been dragged around by the nose, don't you? You've been stalked, lied to, and then just sent away, disregarded," he gave me a palms-up with the gun in his hand.

"I did what I did to protect her," Tyler growled.

Daniel pointed to Tyler, "You shut your mouth, I should have kept a closer eye on you and what you were doing with her. I should have known the only real interest you had in her was protecting the money. And those lips," he smiled at me, "they were just a bonus, right? Now Audra, you know. These men just want to steal from you," he said slowly as if I wasn't following the conversation. "Tyler has used you, and that sweet ass of yours for his amusement, while he tried to mind fuck you into leaving Florida. He was trying to push you away from anyone who knew the truth about the missing parts of your life." In a condescending tone he asked, "Do you understand now?"

My eyes narrowed, letting the anger swell inside me. "He did everything you said he would…and so much worse," my voice quivered with emotion.

"Didn't I tell you this would happen?" he nodded to me. "Didn't I try and save you from all of this? I tried to give you a way out before you were wrecked by their sick games, didn't I?"

"You did," my expression showed the embarrassment I felt for what I had allowed to happen to me. I could feel tears pooling in my eyes.

"But you didn't want to hear any of it, did you?"

I shook my head and let a tear fall. "I'm so sorry I didn't believe you. I thought I was in love. I thought he loved me," I whispered. "Can you ever forgive me?" I asked hopelessly.

"But I do…Tyler started to say.

"Oh will you shut the fuck up," Daniel turned the gun on him. "You don't get to speak to her!"

"I really am so sorry…" I drew his attention back to me, "that I didn't believe you. I'll do anything to prove it to you."

Daniel watched intently as I bit into my lower lip.

"Oh," his head bobbed up and down, "I bet I can find a way for you to give your penance."

Reaching out to run his finger over my lips, they parted slightly. I let him stroke my full bottom lip. His stare warmed, watching intently as his fingertip slid across the silky pink skin. I let my mouth open slightly, giving him access to my warm tongue. Playfully, my teeth grazed the tip of his finger while I stared up into his crazed eyes. Rolling my tongue around it, I began to lightly suck.

"So I guess the question is," Daniel extended his hand to me, smiling with his last bit of sanity, "will you come willingly? Knowing what the Whitmore family tried, and did do to you," he shot Tyler a hateful grin. "With all the secrets, all the lies," he smiled that rabid squirrel smile he was boasting. "So, will you come with me?"

I looked around at the faces staring back at me, and let my expression turn into one full of hateful loathing. "I'll come willingly," I reached for his hand and let him help me stand. Turning to Tyler, I said, "I hate you! You, and your whole family of liars!"

"Audra!" Tyler said, the pain of my words, cutting deep.

"Don't bother, Tyler," Daniel pushed the gun back in his face. "She's made her choice and now, you'll have to live with it, won't you?"

"I can't believe I let myself be so manipulated," I said staring dreamily into Daniel's eyes.

"This place, them, it will all be just a memory soon," he said putting his hand to my cheek.

I leaned in close to his ear, "I can't wait to give penance," I whispered.

He smiled smugly, but then saw the hunger in my eyes as I licked my lips. "What, now?" he grinned, looking around the room.

I nodded slowly, "I like the thought of him watching me… you know…on you," I moved closer so my breast was rubbing against his arm. "I want him to see my lips wrapped around you. I want him to see me offer you my penance." I could see the pulse in his throat pound faster as I spoke. "I want to take you there. Drive you over the edge, and suck you dry," I panted. "I want to swallow Every. Last. Drop."

I watched his mouth water as he watched my lips pronouncing the words slowly, making him begin to swell. A smile pulled up his cheeks, "Would that make you happy, my sweet?" he whispered.

I gave him a small nod of my head. "I want him to see what he lost," dragging my tongue slowly up his neck. "And I want him to watch as he loses me…to you." My hand slid down his quickly growing erection to cup his sack.

Daniel rolled this thought around, "Hmm…that would probably be pretty damaging, right? I mean, knowing the girl of your dreams is sucking another man's dick? Well, that's one thing. I'm sure it would suck," he grinned. "But actually seeing your dream girl sucking another man's cock?" His eyes rounded, "That's going to be way more fucked up for the little golden-boy to behold!"

I purred, "I want this to be his last memory of me. I want what you do to my mouth to haunt him until his dying day." Turning my hate filled eyes back to Tyler, "I want it hurt," I said with absolute distain.

Tyler looked like he was going to be sick from the thought alone. His eyes squeezed closed.

I smiled coyly, "You said you wanted to hurt him. Let's hurt him together." Dropping down to my knees, with my back to Tyler, I unzipped Daniel's pants and let them drop to the floor.

From my view, I could see Mr. Whitmore's head turn away, not wanting to see any of this. I could only hope that Tyler wouldn't turn his.

"I can't wait to feel your lips around my cock," he said.

"I promise, no one will ever make you feel the way I do," Grasping his manhood in my hand, I smiled a wicked little grin.

He turned his nose to the ceiling, waiting to feel my warm mouth mimicking a swollen, juicy cunt.

I kissed around the area, dragging my tongue around his

well manscaped hairline. I traced around the base. Sitting back on my knees, I bent myself forward, the back of my shirt rising.

Just as I was about to go all in, from the back of my waistband, Tyler pulled my 40 cal. Why no one ever searches the woman these days, is beyond me. But this little flaw in equality, had served me well. And there's always the very true fact: I'm not like other women.

Tyler took aim quickly. His arm fully extended even before Daniel's head dropped forward to see where my lips had disappeared to.

When Daniel's attention was finally drawn back to reality, the last thing he saw was the barrel of my gun in Tyler's hand.

Daniel, realizing he had been duped, attempted to aim the barrel of his gun down at me. Before he could even get his finger on the trigger, Tyler shot him once in the center of his chest. It was instantaneous.

Daniel's body fell backward, into Simon's lap. Simon squirmed and yelled, "Someone get this piece of shit off of me?

I stood quickly, throwing myself into Tyler's arms.

"Oh God, for a minute there, I really thought you were going to do…that…to him," he pointed at Daniel's dead body. "I thought I'd rather die, than see you with another man."

All I could do was laugh and shake my head, "Do I have to tell you again?" I cupped his face in my hands, "I don't suck other men's dicks," I laughed and kissed him over, and over, again.

Mr. Whitmore stood, "Forgive me my dear, but it may be a short while until I can look you in the eyes again."

I blushed, "Mr. Whitmore, I am so sorry…"

Putting up his hand to stop the conversation, he said, "No, no, your method was more effective than any of us could have hoped for. We are grateful, Audra. And you, you're a very lucky man," he patted his sons shoulder before stepping around us to retrieve the handcuff key from the pocket of Daniel's corpse.

I put my hands on my hips and cocked my head, questioningly. "What are we gonna do with him?"

"I have a suggestion," Simon's thick New York accent drew the words out slowly.

THE FINAL CHAPTER

In the end, it wasn't like we could have ever let Daniel go. He did have information on Mr. Whitmore and Simon that still held the possibility of ruining them. It wasn't a chance we were willing to take.

Turns out, Daniel had sent all the dirty little secrets about the Whitmore's, to Mitzi. He wanted to make sure that if anything ever happened to him, she would know the horrible truth about Joel, and his family. When he finally realized that she already knew more than she should have, and that she could bury him with what she had learned while spying, she had to be eliminated.

Unfortunately for Mitzi, she already held the truth of that horrible secret and died to continue protecting Joel's memory, and the family. And the rest...the Whitmore's involvement, Simon's, it could now be denied if it was ever brought to light. Especially since they had found evidence in Mitzi's journal that pointed to Daniel being her likely killer; her distrust of him, her fear of him. There were a few pages ripped from the journal before it was turned over to the police. But no one could pin the missing pages on anyone but Mitzi. After all, don't we all have chapters we'd rather not remember? For a few months, we held our breaths wondering what would be found after Daniel disappeared. But day, after wonderful day, the possibility of this happening, faded.

Although Tyler and I decided to keep my previous extracurricular activities a secret from Mr. Whitmore, Simon was privy to my curious lack of conscience when it came to Daniel. I received a raised brow from Simon when I asked excitedly over the whir of my new toy, "So, do I cut at the joint or just above?"

Turns out, the elderly man who owned the air boat, the father of the man I had met, had been doing favors for Simon, for years. Simon and I were taken out on the boat by the nice old man to a place heavily populated by crocodiles. Daniel's body had been dismantled (the word I used to soften the fact that we went to work on him with saws). The old man assured us that come sundown, nothing would be left of him.

Yes, Daniel became a missing person in the eyes of the law. But, considering the fact that he had been embezzling large sums of cash from his father-in law, most assumed he ran away to a country with no extradition to start a new life, rather than face life in prison. Or there was also the possibility that he chose another way out, just as his father had done before him.

On the day Tyler and I wed, we had a private conversation in my dressing room. I know many fear the superstition of seeing the bride before the wedding. But in our eyes, we had both tempted fate on several levels, several times, and were now comfortable letting her guide the way.

Me, standing in my Vera Wang dress, with my hair and make-up just so, I made a promise to him that my hunting days were over. It's a strange gift to give your betrothed, I'll admit. But it meant more than just me not sneaking out of the house to find victims to hunt. It meant I had healed, in the best way. I did add the addendum that this verbal contract would only be upheld as long as his dick wasn't holing-up in someone else. He agreed to my terms without hesitation.

There was another little secret that Tyler had kept from me, but wished to confess before I took his name: Obviously, I knew about the Piano Man, and Daniel; saw them both extinguished with my own eyes. But they weren't the *only ones,* like the revelation in the Study that night would have left me to believe. Turns out, he did have one other kill under his belt. In fact, two more, to be exact.

Tyler had flown to Los Angeles to inform me: not only about the fact that I had an unknown half-brother, and that he had passed away, but also about the money left to me by Joel. Thinking that the *blow to* my mind may have been easier to handle coming from my husband, he set up an appointment to meet Derrick and explain.

Patiently sitting in the waiting room for twenty minutes without another soul to acknowledge him, he began to hear muffled sounds from Derrick's office. Walking in on Derrick, with his head between his secretary's legs, it sent a jolt to Tyler's heart. According to him, he was already in love with me at that time. He couldn't handle the thought of me being stuck for the rest of my life with such a devious, not to mention cheating bastard. So, Derrick's break line had been snipped, to save me from such a horrible fate.

Tyler, decked out in an Armani Tuxedo, his dark blue eyes tried to read my reaction. Patiently, he waited to see how I would take this news. Would I walk away from him, leave him standing there in his tuxedo; just walk out of the chapel...just walk out of his life? Would I scream at the top of my lungs about how much I hated him for wrecking my earlier life?

Would I kill him? Given my past, I couldn't really blame him for this being a concern.

Staring blankly at him, I asked, "Do you remember me saying that in a relationship, secrets only turn into lies, if they are kept solely protect you, and not the one you love?"

"I do," he nodded, swallowing hard from the *cold as ice* look I was wearing.

Rushing into his arms, I threw a lip lock on him that could have curled his hair.

You see, part of the anger I had felt over Derrick's death, was that he never stood in judgment for what he had done to me. Never did he have to feel the wrath of the heart he had broken. Turns out, that wasn't true at all, or not completely. A heart that loved me far more, far better, than Derrick's ever could: One, that Derrick's heart didn't deserve the right to stand in the way of, made sure he paid.

In the gazebo in the Whitmore's back yard, I stood facing him. His hand in mine, was the most beautifully normal, I had ever felt. It was a small ceremony: Just a minister, Mr. Whitmore, Simon, and the two of us, as I became the next great love of a Whitmore man's life. And with a ring, I vowed to love, honor and respect Tyler, until my last breath.

THE END

Don't miss FALLEN GRACEFULLY
Available Now

After a messy and humiliating divorce, massage therapist, Grace Fully, just wants time to regroup, lick her wounds, and heal.

FBI Special Agent Fall Linn has been investigating Russian syndicate boss Dimitri Knushka and tracking the packages that will take Knushka down and finally bring him to justice. But after the package is intercepted by Grace, she is cast into an even worse role than divorcee—she's become a loose end. Now, Linn will stop at nothing to protect Grace from a fate worse than death... and try not to fall for her in the process.

Turn the page for an excerpt from *Fallen Gracefully*.

1

FALLEN GRACEFULLY

No one wakes up and says, "I'm going to die today!" Let me reiterate: aside from suicide victims, no one wakes up and says that.

I did my morning routine: Coffee, workout for an hour (which is actually just dancing like a mad woman), shower, dress and off to work I go. It's been this way since I moved to Clackamas, Oregon a year ago.

I'm a massage therapist, so my days are filled with pulled hamstrings, pinched nerves, piriformis syndrome and sciatic issues. For seven hours a day, five days a week, I do my best to relieve other people's pain and help them relax.

Then, I head home in a car that just barely made it into the 21st century, to change into jammies, crack a beer, and sit outside on my third-story balcony. The sounds of the city are muted here as I enjoy a cold one and look at the stars.

If I'm hungry I grab something which usually consists of cheese and multigrain crackers, since I live alone. A few beers later I head to bed to start the day over again with the next sunrise. In all truthfulness I lead a boring life; not that I mind much.

Tomorrow I would wake up, make coffee, dance, shower, dress and head to work like always. But tomorrow would be a little different. At the end of tomorrow, I would be on vacation for a whole week. I could go home for a few days?

Just an hour from here is the small country town that claims me as one of their own. Mom, Dad, my sister and her family still live there. So does my lifelong best friend, Kris, short for Kristina. But if you were a friend you knew better than to call her by her Christian name. She would sooner respond to "Bitch." Not in a good way, but she would respond at least.

Truth was I missed everyone. I missed home. Now all I had to do was decide if I missed being home more than I wanted to avoid my ex-husband and the woman he had been screwing during our five year marriage. Hard choices required another beer.

I hadn't dated, not even once since the divorce. In all honesty, this one had done some damage. Aside from the wreck it made of my self esteem, it also gave me some trust issues. Even if those weren't in the forefront of my brain, I just couldn't even handle the thought of all that *getting to know you*, stuff. But in my case, heartbreak was always good for the waistline. I had dropped the ten pounds I had wanted to lose for the last two years. Twelve to be exact. Maybe it wasn't heartbreak that trimmed my waistline, I thought, patting my nonexistent stomach. Maybe it was not having mom constantly stuffing me with meat and potatoes. I smiled to no one. The woman was a great cook and I missed her.

Just then, the phone rang. "Hi mom," I answered.

"Hi my girl," rang back through the receiver. "How are you?"

"I'm good. How's you?" (Family talk)

"Not too bad. Made a few batches of chocolate chip cookies...just in case."

"Ah sweet bribery," I laughed.

"Is it gonna work this time?" she questioned.

I let out a sigh.

"So that's a no?" she asked.

"I'm still not sure," I admitted.

"Honey, I know it's hard for you, but it's been a year."

"I know mama. It's just so weird facing everyone. Knowing they all knew. Damn near everyone...but me, that is," I laughed.

"You couldn't have expected them to tell you?"

"I didn't. Really, I didn't. It wouldn't have been their place. It's just so...humiliating. I mean, I had her redecorate our house. The one she's now living in with my ex-husband. I just don't think I'm ready yet."

"I understand. Either way, I'll be coming to your place next month to get my Gracie fill."

I smiled, "I can't wait. I made us pedicure appointments at *Touche.*"

"Oh I love Portland. Speaking of Portland..."

I took a draw of my beer, here it comes, I thought.

"Have you met anyone?" mom asked.

"Since I talked to you three days ago? No."

"It's just...someone out there...deserves someone like you," mom said.

"Well then, he's gonna have to find me," I laughed again.

"Well, that's what I pray for at night."

"Well, with you praying it's bound to happen, mama."

"I better go wake your father from his easy chair and coax him to bed. I love you, Gracie girl."

"I love you too, mama." I hung up the phone and let out a deep sigh.

The moon was starting to dip when I finished my beer and headed to bed.

I woke from a dreamless sleep, pulled my long blond hair into a ponytail and did my morning ritual. While I brushed my teeth, I noticed that my right shoulder was a little stiff. I mentally went over which L.M.T. I would have work on me. I decided on Greg for arm and shoulder work. But that would have to wait, seeing as how all of our therapists were booked out weeks in advance.

When I opened my front door, a small box was staring at me from my doorstep. Leaning down, I realized it was for the man on the second floor. This happened often enough that I wasn't surprised. He spent a great deal of time out of the country on business. He had asked if I would mind babysitting the packages until he returned home.

I carried the package down one flight to his apartment, and gave his door a rap. I waited a moment with no answer, so I carried it back up to my apartment and placed it safely inside under my claw footed couch. Out of sight, out of mind, I thought to myself. I would catch him later when he returned home from God knows where.

He was a nice man, in his late fifty's, I imagined. Russian, I think. His accent was beautiful, even if it did make me think of Boris and Natasha from the Rocky and Bullwinkle cartoons. His hair showed no sign of thinning, although the salt and pepper *do* had more salt than pepper. He was about my height, 5'9" I'd guess. Impeccably dressed, he always wore slacks and a button down shirt topped off with a blazer, a very expensive looking watch and wing tips. I wasn't sure what he did for a living, but he dressed far above the standards of what our rent would indicate. But not everyone who made good money needed to live in a mansion.

I drove two miles away and pulled into my usual spot. I waited for our desk girl, Emily, to arrive and unlock the doors.

In my private room; I lit my candles, made sure I had enough lotion in my bottle and turned on the towel warmer. I was ready for the day.

I had three one hour appointments before lunch and was ready for a rest. Sitting in the break room, I ate the cheese, crackers and grapes I had brought from home.

Annie came in for her lunch break as well. She was a little shorter than me, with a smile that transformed her and made her green eyes sparkle in her caramel face.

"Hey, I forgot you worked today," she smiled at me. "I thought you were on vacation?"

"Starts tonight," I smiled back.

"So, are you going home for your vacation?" her brows arched.

I shook my head, "Not really sure yet."

She gave me the sad eyes, "You should do something with your time off. Do you have any plans?"

"No. I think I may just stay home. Do some spring-cleaning. Relax."

"It's winter, Gracie. You need to get out. Would you like to come with me and the girls tonight? There's a bar in downtown we're all dying to check out. We're going to have expensive cocktails and sing karaoke."

Laughing, I shook my head again, "Not really my thing. But

thank you for the invite."

"You're always invited!" her eyes rounded at me. "Just once, it would be nice if you accepted."

"It's not you guys, it's me."

"Are you really giving me the, *it's not you it's me*, speech?" she laughed.

I laughed back and threw a towel at her, "Well, it is me."

I had two more appointments to go; each of them an hour and a half. After the first, I was informed that my last appointment had cancelled. Looking at my schedule, I nodded. It was Ms. Spicer. She was an eccentric, to say the least. Chances were that the stars weren't properly aligned for a visit today. Secretly, I was thrilled. I was ready to just go home, crack a beer, and put my feet up...possibly for a whole week.

I said my goodbyes, after I put my name down on Greg's book for the week after next. In my car I remembered that I was not only short on beer but toilet paper. Two things I didn't want to run out of...ever.

I drove passed my apartment complex to the grocery store a mile away. This was one of the few stores in the Portland area that hadn't been remodeled. It was now 70's chic.

My beer was on sale, a case for the price of a twelve pack. I decided that this was a good buy, considering it had no chance of going bad in my fridge. Next, I noticed that toilet paper was also on sale. But it was one ply. I wasn't even sure why they sold that, much less tried to pass it off as a great buy. I would pay the extra money for a little comfort. My big splurge.

Back at my apartment, I put the case under one arm, and grabbed the T.P. with the other. Up the two flights I went. I knocked on my downstairs neighbor's door and waited. Still no answer.

Picking up my case of beer, I climbed another flight and fought a little with my keys before finding the lock. I walked through my tiny living room and clicked on the kitchen light with my elbow as I passed. Putting the beer in my fridge, I noticed how devoid of food it looked and decided to order a pizza. Grabbing a beer, I twisted the top off and took a long much needed and wanted pull off the bottle.

When I set my beer down...a hand cupped my mouth. Another arm wrapped around my waist. I grabbed for the beer to use as a weapon but it was just out of reach. I tried to throw my head back in an attempt to break the nose of whoever had me but I hit his chest. I tried to kick his legs, stomp his foot and bite the hand covering my mouth, all to no avail. I was being dragged backward down my hallway to my bedroom.

I'd love to say that I remained calm. But that wasn't really on my agenda as the picture in my head was me raped then killed on my bed. Police would come to examine my apartment, take my beer and use my toilet paper. My legs flailed as I tried to break something, make enough noise to concern my neighbors. It also popped into my head that my Russian neighbor wasn't home apparently. And the woman on the first floor was practically deaf. I kicked my dresser hard and felt immediate pain in my heel.

"You're gonna hurt yourself!" said the deep voice from behind me. "Stop!"

I stopped for a moment to wonder; why would a thief, rapist, murderer, care if I hurt myself? I pondered this then returned to trying to bite his hand while flailing my body as best I could. I refused to give up easily. If I was going out, I was going to make it the worst experience of his life, too. And maybe leave some telltale sign of who it was that did whatever this freak planned on doing to me. I got my body turned just enough that I got one arm free. That hand balled into a fist and punched him square in the ball-sack. I heard him squeak, as he quickly re-pinned my arm to my side.

"Oh...my..." he breathed, resting his head on my shoulder. I lifted my good heel and stomped down hard on his foot with my Doc Marten Mary Jane's. This had the less desired effect of him falling on me. To the bed we went face down, with him on top of me. The tables not well in my favor to begin with, had taken a turn for the *even worse.*

He was heavy on me and I was already having trouble breathing, considering how frightened I was. I got my other arm unpinned and threw an elbow backward, which hit him in the ribs. This forced the air from his lungs. Then I felt my other wrist being pulled up. I heard click, as one hand was cuffed to my headboard.

Handcuffs? Really? Do most rapists bring cuffs? What kind of kinky murderous freak was he?

He was still lying across me, holding my mouth with his other hand.

"Don't fight. Don't yell. I don't want to have to gag you."

Those words...scared the hell out of me. I was already having trouble breathing. Gagged would not make this feat any easier.

"I'm not gonna hurt you!" said the deep, out of breath voice.

This brought no comfort as I assumed anyone who thought breaking into your home and raping you, wasn't considered hurtful. He was undoubtedly certifiable. Maybe he wasn't going to rape me? Maybe he was a thief? The more I rolled this thought around in my head, the more I felt kind of sorry for a would-be thief that would try robbing me. I had just short of nothing: An old TV? An old wedding ring I hadn't had the heart to sell. Not because I was sentimental about the damned thing, but because I thought it contained bad juju and I was reluctant to pass it on to someone else. I had a laptop that held the same ranking as my car; Old, beat up and the drive barely worked. And again, what thief brought handcuffs?

"Tell me you won't scream!" he said, pulling me from my thoughts.

How the hell could I tell him...anything? Finally, I just nodded in agreement.

"Are you nodding that you will be quiet, or not?"

I stopped and tried to look back at him with a much furrowed brow. Was he kidding me? I huffed through his hand as he rephrased the question.

"Will you be quiet?"

I nodded. He wasn't asking me for a promise or a *pinky swear*? Not a very smart would-be thief, rapist, murderer, if you ask me. Everyone knows an agreement isn't promised until a pinky is involved.

He removed his hand cautiously and I took a few much needed deep breaths. Slowly, I felt his body remove its weight from mine. My lungs felt like they might once again fill with air. Now I had a new problem. I was panic breathing. I was getting dizzy. What little light from the kitchen that made its way into my room was being shrunk by blackness. I was going to pass out...and did.

* * *

Want more?
FALLEN GRACEFULLY is now available!

ABOUT THE AUTHOR

Edith Scheffer is a SoCal native, now blissfully transplanted to the Pacific Northwest. A gypsy at heart with the soul of a witch, Edith has wandered but never been lost. She loves sleeping under the stars and moon, walking in her bare feet, dancing to an eclectic playlist of favorite songs, and proudly parenting her exceptionally fierce and fabulous daughter, Brenna. Edith can mix the perfect drink (bartender by trade), massage your aches away (licensed massage therapist), and entertain you with her many novels (yes, she writes, too!). Her works include The Janie Chronicles, *Winged*, and *Fallen Gracefully*. You can discover more at edithscheffer.net.

facebook.com/AuthorEdithScheffer

goodreads.com/edithscheffer